In *First Impressions* Sarah Price has crafted a lovely setting with memorable characters and a fascinating plot—all specialties for this talented author. The conflict is realistic, and the ending will leave you satisfied but wanting more. I can't wait for the next one!

—KATHI MACIAS
MULTI-AWARD-WINNING AUTHOR OF MORE THAN FORTY
BOOKS, INCLUDING *THE SINGING QUILT*
WWW.BOLDFICTION.COM

Sarah Price's *First Impressions* is a heart-warming story of faith, family, and renewal. It will delight fans of Amish fiction and those who love a tender romance.

—AMY CLIPSTON
BEST-SELLING AUTHOR OF THE KAUFFMAN AMISH BAKERY
SERIES

Author Sarah Price is a devotee of Jane Austen and lover of all things Amish. In *First Impressions* she has mixed two unlikely worlds into a curious blend: a retelling of *Pride and Prejudice*, where much is made of misunderstandings, and an Amish world of clear roles and high expectations. A sweet, engaging story that will satisfy Price's many fans.

—SUZANNE WOODS FISHER
BEST-SELLING, AWARD-WINNING AUTHOR OF THE INN AT
EAGLE HILL SERIES

Readers know that when Sarah Price writes a book, they will be both captivated and fully charmed by her one-of-a-kind characters. *First Impressions* will certainly catapult her to the top spot of the best Amish fiction authors. Fans will be pleasantly surprised and delighted with her adaptation of Jane Austen's

Pride and Prejudice. Sarah Price's *First Impressions* has the makings of a true classic.

—MICHELLE DAWN
DESTINATION AMISH...A PLACE WHERE BOOKS
COME TO LIFE
WWW.DESTINATIONAMISH.COM

Sarah writes so well in so many different genres, it's dazzling. Here her writing is crisp and clean and sweet. There's never a dull moment reading Sarah's work. This book is a real treat.

—MURRAY PURA
AUTHOR OF *AN AMISH FAMILY CHRISTMAS*

Sarah Price continues to explore new territory when it comes to writing Amish Christian fiction. Her ability to forge new paths is a true statement to her talent and skill, not just as writer, but also as a masterful storyteller. Her talents are a true gift to her readers.

—PAMELA JARRELL
WWW.WHOOPIEPIEPLACE.COM

FIRST
IMPRESSIONS

FIRST IMPRESSIONS

AN AMISH TALE OF PRIDE AND PREJUDICE

THE AMISH CLASSICS
BOOK ONE

SARAH PRICE

REALMS

Most CHARISMA HOUSE BOOK GROUP products are available at special quantity discounts for bulk purchase for sales promotions, premiums, fund-raising, and educational needs. For details, write Charisma House Book Group, 600 Rinehart Road, Lake Mary, Florida 32746, or telephone (407) 333-0600.

FIRST IMPRESSIONS by Sarah Price
Published by Realms
Charisma Media/Charisma House Book Group
600 Rinehart Road
Lake Mary, Florida 32746
www.charismahouse.com

All Scripture quotations are from the Holy Bible, New International Version. Copyright © 1973, 1978, 1984, International Bible Society. Used by permission.

Cover design by Bill Johnson

Visit the author's website at sarahpriceauthor.com.

Library of Congress Cataloging-in-Publication Data

Price, Sarah, 1969-
    First impressions / Sarah Price. -- First editon.
        pages cm. -- (The Amish classics ; 1)
    Summary: "Set in Lancaster County, Pennsylvania, book one of The Amish Classics series is a retelling of Pride and Prejudice, covering the same issues of manners, upbringing, morality, education, and marriage within the Amish community. SERIES DESCRIPTION: The Amish Classics Series is a retelling of novels by Jane Austen in a contemporary Amish setting. The main storylines are accurately followed but told within the Amish culture and religion"-- Provided by publisher.
    ISBN 978-1-62136-607-2 (pbk.) -- ISBN 978-1-62136-608-9 (ebook)
    1. Amish--Fiction. 2. Lancaster County (Pa.)--Fiction. 3. Austen, Jane, 1775-1817--Parodies, imitations, etc. I. Austen, Jane, 1775-1817. Pride and prejudice. II. Title.
    PS3616.R5275F57 2014
    813'.6--dc23
                                                                2013050280

14 15 16 17 18 — 9 8 7 6 5 4 3 2
Printed in the United States of America

Dedicated to my husband, Jean Marc Schumacher.
If ever there was a Mr. Darcy and Elizabeth Bennet,
it is definitely the two of us.

❧ *A Note About Vocabulary* ❧

THE AMISH SPEAK Pennsylvania Dutch (also called Amish German or Amish Dutch). This is a verbal language with variations in spelling among the many different Amish and Mennonite communities throughout the USA.

In some region, a grandfather is "grossdaadi," while in other regions he is known as "grossdawdi." The word for mother is "maam" in some communities, "mammi" in another, and still "maem" in yet one more.

In addition, there are words such as "mayhaps" or "reckon," the use of the word "then" and "now" at the end of sentences, and, my favorite, "for sure and certain," which are not necessarily from the Pennsylvania Dutch language/dialect but are unique to the Amish and used frequently. Other phrases such as "oh help," "fiddle faddle," and "oh bother!" are ones that I have heard repeatedly throughout the years.

The use of these words and phrases comes from my personal experience living among the Amish in Lancaster County, Pennsylvania. For readers who are not familiar with such terms, I have italicized the words and included a glossary at the end of the novel.

❧ *Preface* ❧

THE IDEA FOR this book was a long time in coming. I started to read quite early in life, and my taste for books transcended the typical chunky books that preschoolers are made to read. I confess that my first love was Laura Ingalls Wilder's books, which I devoured practically on a daily basis. To say I was a bookworm would be putting it mildly. Children would take bets whether or not I could finish a book a day, a challenge I won easily on most days.

So my transition to classic literature came at an early age, with my favorites being Jane Austen, Charlotte Brontë, Emily Brontë, Charles Dickens, Thomas Hardy, and (a personal favorite) Victor Hugo. Christmas was fairly predictable in my house. Just one leather-bound book always made it the "bestest Christmas ever."

In writing Amish Christian romances, something that I have been doing for twenty-five years, I have always tried to explore new angles to the stories. I base most of my stories on my own experiences, having lived on Amish farms and in Amish homes over the years. I have come to know these amazingly strong and devout people in a way that I am constantly pinching myself as to why I have been able to do so. I must confess that, on more than one occasion, I have heard the same from them: "We aren't quite sure what it is, Sarah, but...there's something deeply special about you."

Besides adoring my Amish friends and "family," I also adore my readers. Many of you know that I spend countless hours using social media to individually connect with as many readers as I can. I found some of my "bestest friends" online, and despite living in Virginia or Hawaii or Nebraska or Australia, they are as dear to me as the ones who live two miles down the road.

Well, something clicked when I combined my love of literature with my adoration of my readers and respect of the Amish. It is my hope that by creating this literary triad, my readers will experience the Amish in a new way. They will experience authentic Amish culture and religion based on my experiences of having lived among them and my exposure to the masterpieces of literary greats from years past.

I thank the good people at Charisma Media for sharing in my enthusiasm, especially Adrienne, who reached out to me and listened with an open mind.

It's amazing to think that a love of God and passion for reading can be combined in such a manner as to touch so many people. I hope that you too are touched, and I truly welcome your e-mails, letters, and postings.

BLESSINGS, SARAH PRICE
Sarahprice.author@gmail.com
http://www.facebook.com/fansofsarahprice
Twitter: @SarahPriceAmish

"For I know the plans I have for you," declares the LORD, *"plans to prosper you and not to harm you, plans to give you hope and a future."*

—*Jeremiah 29:11*

❧ *Chapter One* ❧

THE REDDISH-GOLD RAYS of the setting sun lit up the sky behind the roofline of the large white barn. The double doors to the hayloft were open and two robins sat on them, singing a song of good night to the rest of the farm. The black and white Holstein cows lazily meandered through the back pasture near the stream, a few pausing to dip their heads and drink from the refreshingly cool water in the fading heat of the late spring day. One of them, a fat one with a white chain around her neck, looked up, her soulful brown eyes scanning the barnyard before giving a deep, investigating "moo."

A young woman, wearing a rich blue dress and no shoes upon her feet, walked down the lane. Her head was adorned with a white, heart-shaped prayer *kapp*. A few strands of brown hair had fallen free from the neat bun that was hidden beneath the organdy fabric and clung to the back of her tanned neck. Two white ribbons hung from the *kapp*, casually resting on her back as she walked. Two brown chickens ran in front of her, a rooster close behind.

When the rooster saw the woman, he stopped and puffed his feathers at her, his neck bulging out as if ready to attack. "Scoot!" she admonished, kicking her foot at the brightly col-ored rooster to shoo it away.

As she approached the end of the lane, she paused, glancing around for a moment to ensure that no one was on the road before she stepped off the driveway, shaking the cool dust from her bare feet before stepping onto the warm black asphalt of the road that led to town. It was the mailbox that beckoned her, a dented gray mailbox with a single nameplate resting atop: *Blank*.

From the distance the sound of an approaching horse and buggy could be heard, the familiar clip-clopping of its hooves against the macadam reaching the woman's ears long before the animal actually came into her sight. She paused, one hand on the mailbox and the other covering her eyes from the setting sun that hindered her from seeing who was approaching. Still she waited, listening as the clickety noise of trotting hooves was now joined by the gentle hum of the buggy's wheels. Together the two noises made music, Amish music that was as rich to her ears as was any *Ausbund* hymn that the congregation sang on church Sundays.

The young woman waved to the driver of the buggy as he passed; then, with a slight turn, she opened the mailbox and leaned down to peer inside. It was full of letters surrounded by a folded newspaper, which she promptly pulled out and tucked into the crux of her arm. *Perhaps today the letter will come,* she thought. Her *maem* was eagerly awaiting news of the old Beachey farm, located a short distance from the Blank property. Just a few weeks prior the tenants who had been renting it for years had left. It was just a matter of time before the new occupants arrived, and word on the Amish grapevine was that Jacob Beachey might be returning himself.

Slowly the young woman walked in the direction from which she had come, past the imposing white dairy barn. Although the barn could hold at least sixty cows at any given time, the farm on which it was built was not, by any means, considered a particularly wealthy farm. Indeed, the property was only one hundred acres, most of it used for growing corn, hay, and tobacco. Unfortunately many of the fields lay dormant during the growing seasons, crop rotation affected by demand rather than personal desire.

The lane wrapped around the barn and toward a large, old

white house with four plain white square columns that held its frontal overhangs. The house looked out of place, as if it should belong in the Deep South, way back when. The chipped paint on the columns and on the crooked shutters that flanked the downstairs windows hinted of a house where the owner was too busy working the land to worry about the upkeep of his home. Lounging under a worn ladder-back chair, a gray-striped cat lifted its head, looking at the woman as she approached the steps leading up to the porch.

"Come, come, Lizzie," a voice called from inside the kitchen window. "Stop dawdling and let me have the mail already!"

"Sorry, *Maem*," the young woman said as she opened the screen door and disappeared inside.

Her mother had been waiting for her, standing near the door and watching impatiently as she slowly made her way up the lane with the mail. "Honestly, Lizzie!" *Maem* sighed. "You know I'm expecting that letter now, *ja*?"

Lizzie didn't reply but merely nodded, handing the bundle of mail to her *maem*, who proceeded to snatch it before hurrying into the kitchen. Lizzie followed, her eyes adjusting to the darkness inside the house, for it was still too early to light the kerosene lamp that hung over the kitchen table.

The bench was pushed out from the table, and there was a pile of roughly folded clothing set upon it. The top of the table was crowded with pans and bowls covered in flour, in desperate need of washing from the day's activity of baking bread for church service the following day. Lizzie's older sister, Jane, was busy at the sink, her back to the door, as she washed more plates and cookware that had been sitting upon the counter, left over after both dinner and supper. There had been too many other chores for anyone to have bothered washing them earlier. Jane wore a pale green dress, much the same as Lizzie's, except for its color. Despite her prayer *kapp*, tendrils of blonde curls hung down her back, having escaped from her bun after she spent the afternoon weeding the family garden.

"Is it there, *Maem*?"

Lizzie turned to look at the sitting area conveniently set in a sunny part of the kitchen. Her three younger sisters, Mary, Catherine, and Lydia, were sitting on wooden chairs, their heads bent over pieces of material they were busy cross-stitching. Like her, they were all brunettes and had their hair parted in the middle and pulled back from their faces, a neat bun pinned at the nape of their necks. Only one wore a prayer *kapp*; the two others wore nothing to cover their hair. As she looked at her sisters, watching their expressions, so eager and bright, Lizzie knew that not one of them had really been paying much attention to her task. Indeed, they had been waiting for Lizzie to return from the mailbox.

"Now hush a moment, Lydia!" *Maem* snapped as she flipped through the assortment of envelopes. "My word," she muttered, glancing at her daughter with a look of grave frustration. "When was the last time you fetched the mail, Lizzie?"

"Two days ago," she replied. "I was at market yesterday, remember?"

Her *maem* made a soft noise as if dismissing Lizzie's statement, but it was clear that she had forgotten that Lizzie went to market on Fridays. "Now, let's see," she mumbled, holding the mail and walking toward the sitting area. She set the paper on a plush chair that no one occupied; that was *Daed*'s chair. Surely he would want to read his weekly newspaper, *Die Botschaft*, later that evening. "Here it is!" She tossed the rest of the mail onto the table by the chairs and held up a single small white envelope, her eyes glowing eagerly. "I knew that they would write to us! Oh, how dreadful of them to wait so long!"

The three younger daughters tossed their cross-stitching aside, as eager as their *maem* to hear the contents of the letter.

The two youngest, Catherine and Lydia, could hardly contain their enthusiasm.

"What does it say, *Maem*?" Lydia asked, her eyes glowing with expectation.

Their *maem* glanced up, her cheeks flushed and a stray strand of gray hair brushing across her left cheek. Like her daughters, a few hairs had fallen free from under her *kapp* after a long day of laundry, cooking, cleaning, and gardening. "You know I'd no sooner open your *daed*'s mail than tell a lie, *dochder*! We shall have to wait until *Daed* comes in from the fields!"

A collective groan of disappointment came from the three younger girls, a groan that caused Lizzie to snicker. "Such impatience for what you already know is contained in the letter," she laughed, her big brown eyes sparkling at her younger sisters' enthusiasm.

Reluctantly everyone returned to their regular evening chores: Lizzie and Jane went on preparing the evening meal, while their *maem* fluttered about the kitchen, speculating over the contents of the letter; meanwhile the three younger daughters sat breathless on the edge of their seats. From time to time Lizzie would laugh to herself over the different ideas that would jump into their *maem*'s head and out of her mouth.

"A month," she said at one point. "Mayhaps two!"

"Oh, *Maem*," Lydia exclaimed. "Do you really think so?"

Her *maem* stopped pacing and bit her lower lip. "Or mayhaps they aren't coming at all." The thought caused her much concern and she frowned. "Mayhaps the delay in writing was because they changed their minds!" She flopped down into a chair and raised a hand, the one that still held the unopened envelope, to her forehead, striking it several times. "Oh, my nerves cannot take this much longer, I fear!" She began to fan herself with the envelope, her eyes shut. With her legs spread apart and stretched straight out before her, two dirty bare feet poking out from under the hem of her dark navy dress, she looked exasperated.

"*Maem*," Lizzie laughed. "I think your nerves would be just fine if only you'd wait until *Daed* comes inside to hear proper what the letter says."

"Oh now!" *Maem* said, waving her hand profusely at her daughter, again dismissing what Lizzie had said. "What would be the fun of that?"

As if on cue, the door to the mudroom opened, a loud squeak announcing that someone was entering. Since the entire family was already in the kitchen, the women knew that the squeak meant only one person: *Daed*, the sole individual who could end their self-inflicted torment by reading the contents of the letter. Lizzie leaned against the kitchen counter, drying a pan that Jane had just finished washing, and watched as her *daed* entered the room.

At forty-five years of age *Daed* was still in his prime. He was a nicely built man, not too tall, but not short by any definition. His mustache-less beard had started turning gray a few years back and that gave him a dignified look, especially when he was deep in thought, tugging at the beard while contemplating what others were saying. Unlike some of the other men in the *g'may*, their *daed* did not trim his beard. As a result it had become long and full, with stray hairs coming out the sides. Nowadays many of the younger men were trimming their beards, a grave issue among the elders who saw that as a trait of pride. Yet it was not against the *Ordnung*, the unwritten laws that governed each church district. Lizzie suspected it would be added into their rules at the next council meeting.

"*Wie gehts?*" he asked cheerfully as he walked into the room. His graying hair was flat and stuck to the top of his head with the bottom curling out by his ears, an imprint left behind by his straw hat that he had worn while working outdoors. "Getting warm out there, ain't so?" He crossed the kitchen and waited for his eldest daughter to move away from the sink so that he could wash his hands. When he finished, Lizzie handed him a dry towel.

"So quiet in here," he observed, turning to meet the six sets of staring eyes that watched him intently, out of speechless faces, from the sitting area. "Let me guess," he said, handing the towel back to Lizzie. "You have a letter, I reckon. A letter addressed to me but whose contents are of most interest to you." He turned and winked at Lizzie. "Am I close on that one?"

Maem stood up and hurried to him, holding the letter in both hands, as if it were a precious piece of crystal. "*Daed*," she began, "you must open this letter at once. We have all been waiting ever so patiently for you to come in from the fields."

He reached for the letter. "Patiently, you say?"

"But of course!"

Lizzie saw her father take the letter and head for his seat at the head of the table. Without being asked, Lizzie hurried over to the desk by the back wall and picked up her *daed*'s glasses. She knew that he couldn't read anything without them, and providing them to her father would only expedite the opening and reading of the letter that was causing such vexation to her mother and three sisters. "Here, *Daed*," she said, setting the glasses onto the table in front of where he sat.

"*Danke, Lizzie*," he replied.

He reached for the glasses, too aware of the expectation with which his entire family was watching him. Deliberately he took his time opening his glasses, wiping the lenses with the hem of his shirtsleeve, sliding them over his nose, and then assessing the envelope itself. Clearing his throat, he glanced up, looking over the rim of his glasses at his wife. "It's definitely from my cousin, Jacob Beachey," he announced. He looked over at Lizzie and Jane where they stood by the sink. "You might remember them. They visited here once, long ago. His *onkel* was my grandfather's cousin, if I recall correctly." He paused,

7

rubbing his chin with his finger and thumb. "Moved out to Holmes County when I was barely sixteen. Jacob came back once to check on the family farm. It has been let out ever since."

"We know that, *Daed*!" Lydia squealed. "What's in the letter?"

In a gentle gesture he turned his eyes to look at his youngest daughter. "My, my," he teased. "Such eagerness. Mayhaps I should purposefully not read this letter to teach my dear Lydia the gift of patience."

"Oh, *Daed*!" she whined, flopping back against the sofa cushion.

He laughed. Without another word he slid his finger under the back flap and opened the envelope. After withdrawing a folded piece of plain white paper, he began to read the contents, making a noise deep in his throat at one point and sighing at another. His nonverbal cues caused the others in the room to become even more anxious.

"*Ach vell*," he finally uttered, setting the letter down on the table and removing his reading glasses. "Seems that his son is being sent to tend to the farm after all. Land is scarce in their part of Ohio, and Jacob wishes for his oldest son, Charles, to take over this farm in Leola, since they already own it." He glanced up, pausing for effect. "And to find a wife."

Lydia turned to her sister Catherine, and they both grabbed each other's hands and squealed in delight. Sister Mary smiled but, as was her usual way, remained stoic and quiet. There was naught excitement that could cause Mary, the middle child, to display more than a shy smile, even in the midst of such exciting news. "I knew it, I knew it!" Lydia cried out, delighted at the news that their *daed* had just shared.

Daed held up his hand. "He's coming in late July and bringing his cousin George Wickey with him too."

"Blessed news indeed," their *maem* exclaimed, her cheeks flushed pink and her eyes boldly sparkling. "Two boys of marrying age! Heavens to Betsy," she said cheerfully. "What a perfect union for two of our girls!"

Daed held up his hand. "Now, now, hold on here, my matchmaking *fraa*. Let's not be planting celery in the rose garden just yet. We haven't even met these young men to know whether they are worthy of our *dochders*." He leveled a steady gaze at his wife. "Those Holmes County Amish boys are a bit different than our folk."

But his wife was already jumping ahead, dreaming of what was to come. In her mind, two weddings, one for each daughter. And wouldn't that just solve all of their problems? With five daughters and no sons, there was no one to take over the family farm. Most young men in Lancaster were developing skills in carpentry, shed building, even landscaping. Very few men were being raised to take over their own family farms, as land in the concentrated areas where the Amish lived was not increasing but decreasing, and it took only one son to take over the farm.

In the immediate area most farming men were already married or ready to retire, passing their farms down to one or two of their sons. As for the less fortunate sons, they tended to acquire jobs in trade or among the *Englische*. The few who preferred to farm often relocated to new communities with their families in order to farm. With four of their five girls of marrying age and few potential single farmers to court, the matriarch of the Blank family had spent many sleepless nights wondering who would take over the dairy farm when old age made it impossible for *Daed* to carry on with even the most mundane of daily chores.

Lizzie watched as her mother schemed, thinking aloud and speculating which daughter would attract which of the Beachey cousins, Jane being the obvious first choice. It didn't bother Lizzie one bit that *her* name didn't come up in her *maem*'s matchmaking plans. She was just as content to stay at home, help her *daed*, and even remain a *maedel*. While having committed to the Amish way of life and worship two years prior, Lizzie did not favor any of the young men in their *g'may* or any of the neighboring ones either. For men, there was an economic rationale to marriage: a wife bore *boppli* who would grow and help with farm work. For women, it was moral: only with a husband and *kinner* did her standing in the community rise.

For Lizzie, however, she saw it as something quite different.

Indeed, she pondered, as she listened to her mother fretting and thinking out loud. She'd much prefer to remain alone than to marry for the sake of marrying. Conformity was one thing. She had made *that* choice willingly when she had taken her kneeling vow and joined the Amish church. However, commitment to marriage without love was quite another.

❦ Chapter Two ❦

SPRING SOON GAVE way to summer, with longer days and warmer weather. But even the early sunrise of a late-June Sunday found the Blank household in full motion. Lizzie was already up and had been milking cows for an hour, her dark green work dress covered in spilled milk and hay. Since her *daed* had not been blessed with sons, Lizzie tended to the dairy cows with him while the other girls helped their *maem* with house and garden chores. While Lydia and Catherine often wrinkled their nose at Lizzie after she would help *Daed* muck the dairy, Lizzie merely ignored her sisters. A quick washing in the upstairs bathroom with *Maem*'s homemade lavender soap and a change of wardrobe and Lizzie was always prepared for visiting without a trace of odor. Besides, she countered in her mind, she was the only one who was blessed with spending such quality time with *Daed*.

Of the five daughters, Lizzie had always enjoyed a special bond with *Daed*, for her personality favored his more than the other girls. The time spent working in the dairy and helping in the fields cemented that relationship as they often discussed many topics, especially religion and philosophy. Lizzie was one of the few people who knew that her *daed* loved to read, almost as much as she did. He had a secret stash of reading material, books and journals that explored the different depths and aspects of religion as well as its importance, not just from an Amish perspective but from different perspectives encompassing all Christianity.

This had become their own special secret and one of particular joy to both.

Being that today was a church Sunday, Lizzie hurried as she moved the milking machine from one cow to the next, replacing the milking pails as needed. She would carry the full ones to the milk cooler in the back room. The gentle hum of the diesel generator, which kept the bulk milk tank cool, was always audible in the background, a noise she barely noticed anymore. The milk would stay in the tank until the truck came, on Monday morning, to collect the almost one thousand gallons that had been collected over the past three days since the last pickup on Friday morning.

As she poured the milk into the tank, she glanced around the dark room. Two buckets needed washing in order to be reused again that morning. Her *daed* must have left them there for her to tend to. Without a question or a raised eyebrow, she washed them and carried them outside to leave by her *daed*'s side.

"Best get inside to ready up for church, then," he said, his attention on the cows, not his daughter.

Lizzie didn't respond but took advantage of the extra time he had just gifted to her. She hurried into the house, leaving her work shoes, a pair of old, battered black sneakers, in the mudroom. She barely noticed her sisters and *maem*, all ready for church and setting the breakfast table, as she dashed up the stairs. Quickly she washed in the bathroom. It didn't take her long to dress in her Sunday clothing: a light green dress, fastened together with pins instead of buttons, and a crisp, white cape and apron made from organdy. She had spent time ironing it the evening before, careful to use just the right amount of starch, so that it would be ready for the morning.

Then she turned to the small oval mirror hanging over the dresser and unpinned her brown hair. It hung down to her waist in long, loose waves. Unlike her older sister Jane, she did not have blonde curls, Jane being the only Blank daughter blessed with such light, flaxen-colored hair. The other four had brown hair, although Lydia's bordered on the lighter side. Yet Lizzie didn't mind. She paid no attention to her appearance as she brushed her hair and twisted it into the typical bun that she pinned at the nape of her neck. Then, with the utmost of care, she placed her black, heart-shaped prayer *kapp* on her head and pinned it so that it would not shift from its place. Because she was a baptized member of the church but unmarried, she wore the black *kapp* on Sundays until she was married. Then she would return to wearing a traditional white *kapp*. It was a distinction that did not bother Lizzie as it did some other young women in the church district.

By the time she returned downstairs, her *daed* was washing his hands in the sink. Her sisters were already seated at the table, waiting for Lizzie and *Daed* to join them while *Maem* set down the last plate. When everyone was seated, *Daed* bent his head for silent prayer, and the others quickly followed. Only when he cleared his throat did the others begin to reach for the plates of warm food.

Breakfast on church Sundays was a quiet affair, a time of reflection and thought, not of conversation. They all knew that a three-hour church service faced them. For *Daed* and *Maem*, it was a time of soul searching and reaffirming their faith in the Creator. For the girls, especially the youngest, it was a time of anticipation of the fellowship meal, and for the four older sisters, of the evening singing with their friends.

"Heard some guests will be joining us today at Yoders' for service," *Daed* said, breaking the silence.

It wasn't unusual for guests to attend church service. What was unusual, however, was for *Daed* to know it in advance and to mention it. All eyes were now upon him. Surely these would be some important guests.

Maem tried to not look overly interested, but Lizzie saw the color rush to her mother's cheeks and a gleam shine from her eyes. Without doubt *Maem*'s curiosity was piqued. "Oh?"

Daed reached for the bread and began to spread homemade jam on it. "*Ja*," he slowly replied. "Seems Charles Beachey and his cousin George Wickey arrived last week."

The news stunned the women sitting at the table, each for different reasons. Lizzie quickly glanced at her sister Jane and exchanged a look of delighted curiosity. Immediately after, Lizzie's eyes scanned the table, amused at the suppressed energy of her two youngest sisters, who could barely contain their excitement. One could see that they wanted to ask questions; they wanted to screech in delight. However, being that it was Sunday, such a reaction would be highly inappropriate. Lizzie looked back at her *daed*, realizing that he had waited for such a moment to tell the news for exactly that reason: no overbearing hullabaloo, no public display of frenzy. He would have none of that.

Maem was the only one to challenge their *daed*. "I fail to see how you could know such a thing! Certainly you would have shared this news with your family upon hearing it! The letter we received a month ago said they were arriving in July!" she exclaimed. "How rude they must think we are if they have arrived and no one has sent over food or made introductions!"

Lizzie watched her father's reaction, delighted to see him controlling his own smile. Instead of responding, he merely continued to eat his bread. It was clear that the many questions they had would remain unanswered for the time being. As always, his timing was impeccable for tantalizing the curiosity of the women in his life. With a smile, Lizzie bent her head down and stared at her plate, playing with the food rather than eating, as she pondered the meaning of her *daed*'s game.

Twenty minutes later *Daed* helped *Maem* into their buggy and they drove down the lane. Church started at eight, but the older members of the church tended to arrive earlier, while the younger members took their time, walking to church instead of riding with their parents. Quite often there was not enough room in the parents' buggies for all of their older children, although that was not necessarily the reason why they chose to walk instead. Of greater interest was the fact that younger men might drive by in their own empty buggies and offer the girls a ride. Some girls might be inclined to accept the ride, especially if it was a neighbor boy or a friend. However, truth be told, and more so in the case of the Blank sisters, walking to church was also a great way to exercise a bit before the lengthy three-hour service.

This morning the girls walked together, Catherine and Lydia giggling in each other's ear over the arrival of Charles Beachey and his cousin George Wickey. Lizzie listened to their giddy chatter, rolling her eyes more than once in response. Jane laughed and nudged Lizzie, whispering a soft, "Oh, sister, we were like that once too, don't you reckon?"

"I take great exception to that!" Lizzie hissed. "I have never giggled and speculated about *any* young man!"

At this comment Jane laughed again. Her laughter was light and carefree, pure in nature and kind in delivery. "One of these days, Lizzie," she teased, "some young man will come along, and your heart will take heed over your head, that's for sure and certain."

"I highly doubt that," Lizzie retorted.

Behind them the all too familiar noise of horses' hooves could be heard. Without even looking back, the girls moved to the side of the road in order to give the oncoming horse and buggy enough room to pass. On church Sunday there were usually many buggies on the road, headed toward the service. The sisters were used to stepping out of the way upon hearing their approach on the hard surface behind them.

"*Nee*, indeed, I think not!" Lizzie declared after another moment's pause, her expression serious and her dark eyes flashing. "For what purpose? To cook his meals and do his laundry and have his *boppli*?" Another eye roll. "*Nee*, that's not for me. I'd much rather help *Daed* with his farm work and spend my free time at my own leisure."

"Books, I reckon!" Lydia scoffed. "You always have your nose buried in a book!" She twirled around in front of Lizzie. "I'd rather have a dozen *boppli* than spend my nights with a dusty old book filled with silly words!"

At this, Mary jumped in. "There's a lot to be said for reading, Lydia."

"Like how she pores over *Martyrs Mirror*?" Lydia was clearly not impressed, and no amount of convincing would change her opinion. "Reading doesn't land a husband!"

Mary frowned. "Books hold many treasures and should not be discredited as a leisurely pastime."

"Oh, fiddle-faddle," Lydia replied with a bored and dismissive wave of her hand. "Spoken like the true spinster teacher you will most likely come to be!"

"Lydia!" Lizzie gasped, a horrified look on her face.

There was no further time for rebuke as another horse and buggy approached from behind. It would do no one any good for a passing church member to hear them arguing, especially on the Lord's Day. Lizzie narrowed her eyes and shook her head at her youngest sister, Lydia, secretly glad that she was a year too young to attend the singing that would follow that evening. While it was true that Mary's sole dream in life was to be a schoolteacher, a dream that was about to come true in the autumn when she would assist at the local schoolhouse, to call her a spinster was a step way out of line, even for Lydia.

"Pardon me," a voice called from behind.

Lizzie was too angry with her youngest sister to glance in the direction of the voice. However, she caught a subtle movement out of the corner of her eye. Jane had turned to look and immediately slowed down her pace.

"You headed to the Yoders', then?"

It was a male voice. A *young* male voice. Lizzie forced herself to turn in the direction of the voice. Her sisters had all slowed down as an open-top buggy pulled up beside them. A young man with bright blue eyes and thick blond curls poking out from under his wide-brimmed Sunday hat smiled down at the ladies. His accent was a tad unusual and his dress clearly not from Lancaster. But he was Amish. That was for sure and certain.

Lydia and Catherine giggled, standing behind their two older sisters. It was Jane, however, who finally spoke up. "*Ja*, indeed. Church is to be held there today," she responded, her voice soft and naturally demure.

The man removed his hat and ran his fingers through his curls. "Might you direct me? I'm not familiar, you see." He paused then plopped his hat back on his head. "Charles Beachey's my name," he said, flashing a bright smile at all of the sisters, but his eyes seemed drawn particularly to Jane.

"Jane Blank," she responded, dropping her eyes, aware of his obvious attention. "These are my sisters, Lizzie, Mary, Catherine, and Lydia." When she glanced up and saw that he had nodded to the other girls but had returned his gaze to her, she added with a simple gesture, "We live over that hill there."

"Mayhaps you'd show me the way to Yoders', then?" he went on. "Seeing that we're going the same place, and if you live over that hill, we would also be neighbors!"

Lizzie watched, amused to see the color flooding to her sister's cheeks. When she realized that Jane was flustered and uncertain of how to respond, Lizzie stepped forward. "That's a right *gut* offer, Charles Beachey. But I don't reckon five sisters could fit in your buggy. However, the Yoders' is just four farms down the next road on the right. You should find it simple enough." She pointed in the direction of which she spoke. "Truly simple."

He nodded his appreciation at Lizzie, understanding the appropriateness of her response. For one of the sisters to join him, a complete stranger, in the buggy would have been forward and certain to cause tongues to wag among the church members. Lizzie wasn't certain if such behavior was acceptable in Holmes County, Ohio, but it certainly was not in Lancaster! Poor Jane, she thought, glancing over at her sister. Certainly she was embarrassed at having been put in such a situation.

"Mayhaps I shall see you sisters later, then? At the singing tonight?" He spoke to the five girls, but his eyes stayed on Jane. "Unless of course," he continued with a glance in Lizzie's direction, "Lancaster Amish don't believe in singings?"

The good-natured tone of his question caused Lizzie to laugh. Clearly there were no hard feelings from their new neighbor Charles Beachey for Jane having declined his offer of a ride to church. He tipped his hat and slapped the reins against the back of his horse, clicking his tongue to motivate the horse to pick up its speed in the direction that Lizzie had indicated.

Lydia waited until he was a good distance away before she clutched at Catherine's hand. "Have you ever seen such a handsome man?" she gushed.

Catherine giggled and nodded her head. "Those eyes! So blue!"

"Oh, why am I not old enough to go to singings yet!" Lydia lamented, dropping her sister's hands in dramatic protest. "I think having to wait until I'm sixteen is simply ridiculous! Why should I sit at home while you four have all the fun?"

Lizzie began to pick up her pace, ignoring Lydia's all too common complaints while Jane reassured her that her birthday in August would be there soon enough and, with it, plenty of years of singings and social engagements to follow.

Another buggy pulled up behind them. As they moved to the side of the road, Lizzie glanced over her shoulder, surprised to see another open-top buggy with yet another unknown young man driving, a woman at his side. They sat apart from each other, both staring at the road before them. If it weren't for their solemn expressions and the fact that the man wore no beard, Lizzie might have thought that they were a couple. At best, she figured they might be courting, but there was something distant in the manner in which they sat in each other's company that made her doubt that very much.

Lizzie paused as she walked, her eyes meeting the driver's. The buggy slowed, for just a moment, as the driver assessed the five women walking along the side of the road. Yet, unlike the previous young man, this one did not stop to ask directions. His dark eyes flashed from beneath a wave of dark hair that covered his forehead. His black Sunday hat had an even wider brim than Charles Beachey's. With a tilt of his chin, he tore his eyes from the women and stared straight ahead, not even acknowledging their presence with the customary nod or wave of the hand.

Lizzie watched the buggy pass by, curiosity in her eyes. Without a doubt the driver of that buggy was not from Lancaster. However, she questioned whether he was the cousin of Charles Beachey, for they bore no resemblance whatsoever. Instead, they were as different as night and day. Yet there was something about the man that intrigued her.

"Did you see her odd prayer *kapp*?" Lydia whispered. "So strange!"

"She must be from Ohio too!" Catherine replied eagerly. "I bet she's a sister!"

"They both looked plain miserable! I wonder that!" Lydia added, clinging to Catherine's arm as she gossiped.

"Why, he didn't even wave!" Catherine complained. "What an unlikable man!"

"And a furrow on his brow!" Lydia added. "I bet he frowns, not farms, for a living!" At this comment the two girls burst into giggles and skipped ahead, leaving Jane, Mary, and Lizzie shaking their heads at the silly antics of their two younger sisters.

It was ten minutes to eight by the time the Blank sisters entered the Yoder farm's workshop where the service was about to be held. Three families lived on the property, one who had started a farm equipment repair business five years prior. In order to work in inclement weather, John Yoder had built a large workshop that, during the spring, summer, and fall months, was perfect for holding Sunday service. With everything cleared out, the workshop easily held the two hundred members from the *g'may* as well as any visitors.

The sisters entered in single file, Jane leading the way and Lydia trailing at the end. They walked along the greeting line of women, shaking hands and leaning forward to be greeted by each of the women with a kiss on the lips, to signify their faith and friendship. When they reached the end of the line, they stood next to their peers to greet any remaining women who entered.

At less than two minutes to eight the bishop and ministers made their entrance, their expressions solemn as they walked along the line of women, shaking their hands and nodding a greeting at each and every one of them. When they had reached the end of the row where Lydia stood, the bishop cleared his throat, and the small group of church leaders walked to their seats at the center of the workshop, where rows of benches had been set, facing each other. As soon as they were seated, the eldest woman in the group led the line of elderly and married women to their seats on the right side of the room. When all of them were seated, the younger women of marriageable age followed suit. They were the last of the females to be seated.

The same procession, this time with the men, entered the room. First were the elderly, slowly and solemnly proceeding to their seats, followed by the younger married men who took their places on the left side of the room. When everyone was situated, the young unmarried men entered and filed into the back of the workshop, sitting where they could find a space. The room was silent, not a sound to be heard. Small children did not squirm or cry, despite the heat of the day prevailing in the enclosed workshop. As if on cue, all of the men removed their hats from their heads, placing them on the floor beneath where they sat. The men along the back wall stood and placed their hats on pegs that hung behind them, just above the row of windows.

And then the singing of the hymn began.

It started slowly, one man singing the first word of each line from the *Ausbund* hymn in lengthy, accentuated syllables, before the rest of the congregation joined in. Lizzie knew the hymn by heart, so instead of looking at the chunky black book that she held in her hands, her eyes skimmed the room. Her *maem* sat in the third row behind the elderly women and next to her best friend, Leah Lantz. Leah and *Maem* had grown up together, so it was no surprise that Leah's daughter, Charlotte, was almost like an older sister to the Blank girls, despite their age difference. In truth, Jane and Lizzie considered Charlotte quite dear to them, akin to a sister and a right *gut* friend.

They had just started the second verse when the bishop and the ministers stood and proceeded to exit the room. They would convene in a separate area, discussing the two sermons for the day, one long and another shorter, and deciding who would give which. While this was happening, the rest of the congregation continued singing the hymn. The ten remaining verses of the hymn would take at least another twenty minutes to complete.

During this time two men and a woman entered the room. There was a momentary lull in the singing as eyes glanced in the direction of the disturbance. It was very rare for someone to arrive late to church, and everyone was immediately curious as to whom it might be. Unfortunately no one in the congregation recognized the three strangers. No one, that is, except the Blank sisters.

Charles Beachey smiled nervously while the other man and the woman merely lifted their chins and stared ahead, avoiding eye contact with the curious gazes of the congregation. There was a shuffling noise along the back wall where the men sat as someone slid over to make room for the two men on the bench. The woman, dressed in her maroon dress and white apron with her tight-fitting prayer *kapp*, hesitated before moving toward the back of the room where all the women were seated.

Lydia leaned forward and whispered to Charlotte, who sat next to Jane, "That's the Beachey man." She bumped Jane's shoulder by accident. "He asked Jane to ride with him. He must have gotten lost after all, Lizzie." She added the last part with a quick glance in Lizzie's direction.

"Who's that with him, then?" Charlotte asked back.

"Sssh!"

Two older women in front of them cast a short, disapproving glare over their shoulders in the direction of the whispering girl. Lydia stifled a giggle and sat back up, straightening herself on the bench while trying to figure out where they were in the hymn.

Indeed, the one gentleman was Charles Beachey. He seemed nervous as he removed his hat and slid onto the bench nearest the door. The tall man next to him was the complete opposite, confident as he removed his own hat and hesitating, just for a moment, before he took his place next to Charles. His eyes seemed to dart around the room, taking in the strange faces that were obviously trying not to look in his direction. So when he noticed Lizzie, staring at him with a raised eyebrow, he paused ever so slightly and dipped his head in recognition of her attention.

Mortified, Lizzie looked away, vowing to pay no more attention to the man sitting next to Charles Beachey. He was handsome, that was quite true. But his manner was haughty and proud. She knew that from just looking at the way he carried himself: shoulders straight back, chin tilted ever so slightly in a condescending expression, and narrow eyes that seemed to be assessing the room without seeing anything. Clearly, these Amish men from Holmes County, Ohio, were quite different from the Amish men who grew up in Lancaster County, Pennsylvania.

Jane nudged her sister, bringing her attention back to the singing. Leave it to Jane, Lizzie thought with warmth in her heart. Not a godlier young woman sat amongst the congregation. Many a young man had tried to court her, for she was beautiful as well as full of faith and goodness. Yet Jane was too bashful and shy to accept rides with the Amish men, a trait that made Lizzie smile in wonder. How on earth would she ever begin courting if she didn't say yes to the traditional Amish way of initiating the courting process?

Then the first sermon began.

At the end of the three-hour long service the congregation stood for the final prayer. The women faced the wall behind them while the men did the same from their side of the room. Lizzie listened as the bishop bestowed his final words of faith and hope among the people in his district. She always tried to remember his inspiring words, words that she vowed to live by during the upcoming weeks between church services. Then, with a quick bending of the knee, the people turned back toward each other and sat while the bishop and ministers left the room.

Lizzie leaned over to Jane and whispered, "I wonder if the new men will help with the setup for fellowship." There was a mischievous glow in her dark eyes.

"Lizzie!" Jane gasped under her breath. "Behave yourself!"

She laughed at her older sister and nudged her with her

shoulder. "You watch. That tall one...I bet he's too proud to help."

Jane shook her head and clucked her tongue several times in a crescendo, disapproving of her sister's words. But she allowed her eyes to linger in the direction of the two men from Holmes County, Ohio, curiosity getting the best of even her.

It took less than fifteen minutes for the young boys to collect the chunky black *Ausbund* books and stack them neatly in the crates where they would remain until the next service, while the men moved the benches and, by placing the legs into specially constructed boards, converted them into tables. The older women were already busy in the kitchen, moving about in what they liked to teasingly refer to as "controlled chaos" as they began to set plates of food onto the tables: cup cheese and pretzels, sliced cold cuts and creamy butter, fresh bread and applesauce, chow-chow and pickled cabbage. The two long rows of tables had more than enough food to satisfy the first seating of the congregation.

Lizzie stood by the kitchen door, out of the women's way, for she knew that her job, filling the water for the men, would come after everyone was seated. The seating arrangements were always the same: The older men sat at one table and the older women at the other. Younger women with smaller children joined the first seating so that the little ones would not have to wait. The unmarried women would wait on the tables, replenishing any empty trays or bowls of food and refilling the water cups. Then, when the after-meal prayer was said, they would clear the plates, cups, and utensils and wash them for the second seating of young men and young women.

Lizzie discreetly scanned the room and noticed the two gentlemen from Holmes County standing in the rear of the room. They were speaking with the bishop. Or, rather, Charles Beachey was speaking with him while his companion stood by his side, his hands clasped behind his back and his chin tilted in the air. She couldn't help but watch him for she had never seen someone with such an air of perceived self-importance. And immediately, despite her fascination, she knew that she didn't care for him one bit.

"Lizzie, dear," her *maem* said. "You fill the men's water, *ja*? Jane, you help."

Immediately Lizzie fought the urge to roll her eyes, knowing that she should certainly not do so, especially at church fellowship. But she could see through her mother's request. As always, *Maem* was pushing her girls toward the men in the hopes of finally planting that extra celery in the garden in anticipation of an autumn wedding.

The young women waited for the pre-meal prayer before they picked up the pitchers of water and began to make their rounds of the men's table. As luck would have it, Charles Beachey sat on one side, while his dark, broody companion, sat opposite him. Jane reached for Charles's cup to fill it with water, and he turned to thank her, his eyes sparkling and a genuinely pleasant smile on his face.

"*Danke*, Jane Blank," he said.

She flushed at the attention, fully aware that he had remembered her name.

"I trust you shall be at the singing tonight, *ja*?" He didn't wait for an answer but lowered his voice. "I would be honored to accompany you home afterward, if I might be so forward to ask."

Lizzie paused, her hand lingering over the shoulder of his companion, frozen in midair as she stared at her sister in anticipation of Jane's answer. How different, this man from Ohio! In Lancaster, courtship was private and kept that way until the publishing of the wedding announcement. Yet here was Charles Beachey asking Jane to ride home in his buggy in front of other men and even before the actual singing!

"I..." She glanced around at the other men who were as

stunned as Jane and Lizzie by the openly asked question. "I...I would be happy to," she whispered.

Lizzie held back her smile, pleased with her sister's response. There was something about Jane's eyes that sparkled near this man. For a woman who was known to have rebuffed many a potential suitor, it seemed that Jane was clearly taken with Charles Beachey.

❧ *Chapter Three* ❧

THE BARN WAS lit with kerosene lanterns that hissed as they burned, reflecting bright light from their small mirror reflectors and emitting a nice area of warmth that countered the cool evening air. Lizzie stood with Charlotte and Jane, laughing as they watched the young Amish men play a round of volleyball, exaggerating their leaps and jumps in order to catch the attention of the young women. One man fell over a hay bale and, when he stood, had pieces of hay sticking out of his hair, causing a ripple of giggles from a group of girls who stood nearby. Good-naturedly the man merely plucked the hay from his hair and smiled at the girls.

"Oh, look!" Lizzie said, her eyes darting toward the open door of the building. While it was June and the evening air not too humid, the room could get warm with all of the kerosene lanterns illuminating the area, so the youths had decided to keep the doors and windows open for the evening air to cool and aerate it. "It looks like your Charles Beachey has arrived, together with his broody cousin!"

Indeed, two figures appeared in the open doorway of the barn, the one smiling and the other with a hint of a scowl showing on his clean-shaven face. A hush fell over the group. One of the men playing the game hit the volleyball over the net, which promptly bounced off of the shoulder of an opposing teammate. The two newcomers removed their hats and entered the barn, nodding toward the different groups of young Amish people and heading toward the refreshment table, where the hosting family had left bowls of pretzels, popcorn, and chips as well as three large pitchers each of fresh lemonade and fragrant meadow tea.

"That's not his cousin," Charlotte whispered knowingly to Lizzie and Jane as the room began to return to life. "I heard that's one of his friends, a farmer from Ohio."

"A friend?" Lizzie gasped. "Why, the two look about as opposite in character as a cute little pony to a big ole stout work mule! Some friend indeed!"

Charlotte and Jane laughed at Lizzie's direct statement.

"*Nee*, Lizzie," Charlotte confided, her voice low so others could not overhear. "My *daed* told me so. Apparently Jacob Beachey asked him to accompany Charles, his sister, and their cousin. His name is Frederick." She paused as if thinking. "Frederick Detweiler, I believe. And he comes from quite a line of farmers. My *daed* said that Frederick's own *daed* passed on a few years back. All the land passed down to Frederick—one of the largest farms in Holmes County. I heard it covers half of the Dutch Valley!" She paused. "I'm sure that's an exaggeration, but he even employs many other young men on a full-time schedule to help with the fields and the dairy."

Lizzie's mouth dropped, and her eyes traveled back to the man in question. He was standing with his back to her, listening intently to a lively conversation with Charles Beachey. "Employs others to work his own farm! I've never heard of such a thing!" She looked back at Charlotte in disbelief. "Why, I thought he looked very proud, but to learn that he's too proud to even work his own land?"

Jane placed her hand on her sister's arm, a gesture meant to calm Lizzie down. It worked. "You shouldn't jump to conclusions, Lizzie. We haven't yet engaged in any exchange with this Frederick. Mayhaps he is quite the hard worker and a godly man at that. After all, he came to service today."

"Apparently not Charles's cousin, George Wickey," Charlotte whispered. "We have yet to see him anywhere!"

But Lizzie was far from convinced. She glanced back to where Frederick and Charles stood, surprised to see that a few of the local men had joined them in a lively discussion. Once again it was clear that Charles was enjoying meeting new people while Frederick stood with his back straight, his hands clasped behind his back, and a dark expression on his face. *Nee*, she thought. *I don't think I shall care to engage in any exchange with that proud one.*

Charlotte made a casual gesture toward a young woman standing alone by the lantern. While she didn't look particularly friendly or even interested in being at the singing, she did look out of place with no one to engage in conversation. "That's Charles's sister, Carol Ann. I think we should go speak with her, *ja*? Mayhaps she's lonely, not knowing anyone here yet."

Lizzie followed Jane and Charlotte as they walked in the direction of the lone woman. She wore a strange head covering, much different from the heart-shaped ones that adorned the heads of the Lancaster Amish sisters. It was more cup-shaped and the strings were firmly tied, not hanging loose like the other young Amish women tended to wear them. Her dress was slightly different too. For one thing Lizzie noticed that the hem was longer, stopping just an inch or so above the ankle. The colors were a bit different, deeper and more vibrant, although Lizzie wasn't certain if she came to that conclusion only because she was too familiar with the colors that her own community wore. But the style of dress was different too. She couldn't quite put her finger on what it was, but she was certain that she was not partial to the difference.

"You are Charles's sister, *ja*?"

Leave it to Charlotte, Lizzie thought with a smile. While not the prettiest young woman in their church district, Charlotte was certainly the friendliest. She came from a large family, and her *daed* sat on the board that governed four of the nearby schools for the Amish children. With a somewhat prominent status in the community, her *daed*'s entire family had learned to be outgoing and kind, perhaps Charlotte most of all.

Carol Ann slowly turned her head and looked at the group of three women. The way her eyes narrowed, just ever so slightly, did not go unnoticed by Lizzie. "*Ja*, Carol Ann Beachey is my name," she said by way of introducing herself, and she stuck her hand straight out toward the heart of her interlocutor, for the traditional, vigorous Amish handshake.

Jane introduced herself and immediately began to ask questions about when the Beachey party had arrived and how Carol Ann liked Leola so far. With her soft, gentle voice and bright blue eyes, Jane was easy to talk to and even easier to like. Lizzie watched the exchange, half amused and half envious of her sister's ease with strangers, even one who seemed to look down her nose at their too-short dresses, bare feet, and untied prayer *kapps*.

Only once did Carol Ann let her eyes drift in Lizzie's direction, a quick assessment apparently resulting in finding her too unsuitable to engage in conversation. Lizzie was quick to take notice of this and lifted her chin to change that situation.

"I find it interesting that you accompanied your brother," Lizzie ventured.

"Brother and cousin," Carol Ann was quick to correct.

"Oh, *ja*, I had heard that there was another family member along, but I have only seen Charles. In fact, we thought Frederick was Charles's cousin."

Carol Ann smiled, a soft and secretive smile that told more than her words. "Well, *that* would be most interesting," she replied, her gaze trailing to where Frederick stood with Charles and some of the other local young men. Lizzie observed him turn, ever so slightly, and see Carol Ann watching him. He nodded his head but returned his attention to the men before him.

"Will you be staying a while, then?" Jane asked, oblivious to the exchange Lizzie had just witnessed.

"That depends," Carol Ann sighed. "*Daed* wishes for Charles to take over the farm here." She smiled at Jane, the first truly genuine thing that Lizzie recognized about the woman. "Land is getting expensive in Ohio, and since we already own the property here, it seems right silly to have tenants when we could be using the land ourselves, ain't so?"

"And Charles's cousin?" Lizzie changed the subject. "I don't believe he made service today. Is he here now?"

Carol Ann narrowed her eyes, clearly displeased that Lizzie had pointed out the obvious. "He is not here, *nee*. He has yet to take the kneeling vow."

There was no time for further questioning, although Lizzie certainly had quite a few more questions that she would have loved to ask. Why would their *daed* send both his son and his nephew when one was clearly not yet committed to the Amish way of life? Why had Carol Ann been sent along with her brother? And why was this disagreeable-looking Frederick here? To chaperone the others, or was there a courtship established between him and Carol Ann? The questions floated through her mind, and to say that her curiosity was piqued would have been an understatement. But she knew better than to pry into someone else's business, even if she was dying to know the answers.

Once the volleyball game had ended, the youths began to move to the benches, the women on one side and the men on the other. Lizzie noticed that Charles made certain to accidentally bump into Jane, reaching out to steady her with a strong hand that spoke of hard work but also gentle care. He smiled at her and leaned down, whispering into her ear words that Lizzie couldn't hear but which effect could easily be observed. The color flooded to Jane's cheeks, and her eyes, those dazzling blue eyes, sparkled like Lizzie had never before seen. Jane bit her lower lip and glanced away, but it was clear that her heart was pitter-patting. Indeed, Lizzie realized, her sister was definitely *ferhoodled*.

"Pardon me," a voice said.

Lizzie looked up, surprised to see Frederick standing behind her. "Oh," she gasped. "I'm sorry. I didn't mean to block your way."

"Indeed," he said, his voice deep and stiff as his eyes stared over her head. "I'm quite satisfied there was no ill intent."

She frowned at his words, so formal and unfamiliar. While she had plenty of family in Ohio and had cause to meet them on occasion, they had seemed no different than her own immediate family. This man, whom she judged to be close to thirty years of age, seemed too stiff and out of place. "You are with Charles Beachey, *ja?*"

He nodded his head but gave no formal introduction.

"Do you attend singings frequently, then?" she asked, trying to follow her sister Jane's advice. After all, she reasoned, everyone deserved a chance.

"As infrequently as possible," came the sharp reply.

It took Lizzie a moment to realize what he had said. She narrowed her eyes, digesting his words. If he had meant to leave an unfavorable first impression, he had truly succeeded. Between his stance and his words, there was nothing left to the imagination that this man, this Frederick Detweiler from the Dutch Valley in Ohio, thought himself too above others. And she knew that, without doubt, she did not care for him one bit.

There was nothing left to say, so she merely stepped aside, permitting him to pass, her mind still trying to understand how any one individual could be so miserable and cold. *No wonder*, she thought, *that he wears no beard. What woman would want to join with such a proud and unlikable man?*

She took her place beside her sister Jane, not surprised to see Catherine and Mary seated at the very back of the barn. Lydia was still too young to attend the singings, a fact that created great strife and tension in the house every other Sunday. While Lizzie felt sorry for her youngest sister, she was also relieved to have a few hours away from her silliness. She dreaded the day when Lydia would turn sixteen and, therefore, be able to join them at the singings. With her overly enthusiastic giggles and often embarrassing comments, Lydia was too eager at seeking attention when it was more proper to remain silent.

"What did that Charles Beachey whisper to you?" Lizzie demanded, her eyes sparkling at Jane.

"Oh," Jane replied, her hand rising to her chest. "He seems most agreeable, Lizzie. And I dare say quite handsome, *ja*?"

Lizzie lightly pinched her sister's leg. "You didn't tell me what he said!"

Jane covered her mouth to quiet her giggle. "He reminded me of my promise and said he had been looking forward to it all day."

While the youths around them sang from the hymnal, Lizzie felt her own heart flutter. She looked over to where Charles Beachey sat, while sensing a warm feeling flood over her. Handsome, charming, hardworking, and lively: *What a fortuitous match for Sister Jane*, she thought. Lizzie barely heard the words that were being sung as she lifted her heart to God and thanked Him. If anyone deserved a chance at happiness, Jane was that very person.

During a break in the singing Lizzie slipped away to use the facilities. She also needed some respite from the chitchat of the young women who, at times, seemed to talk about the silliest of things. Just once, Lizzie thought with a sigh, she wished she could find someone who shared her interest in discussing deeper issues and ideas, like the conversations she often had with her *daed*.

It was dark in the driveway leading from the house back to the barn. The moon was out, a crescent that graced the path with a gentle blue light. She could see two men standing in the doorway and quickly realized that they were Charles and Frederick. As she approached, Lizzie could see that they had yet to notice her, but she could hear them and unintentionally became privy to their conversation. Their words caused her to catch her breath and stop walking.

"You have already won the heart of the prettiest girl here, I reckon," Frederick said.

Charles laughed. "You have such a way with words, Frederick. She may be pretty to the eye, but I can see inside her soul. She's a godly woman, and I can tell her heart is pure."

Frederick made a "hmm" noise but did not respond further, a fact that made Lizzie press her lips together and bite her tongue.

"Why, Frederick, there's no need for you to ride home alone tonight either," Charles added. "Jane's sister Lizzie…she has quite a sparkle in her eye and a quickness of tongue that might just suit your temperament right *gut*!"

"It would take more than a sparkle in her eye or quickness of her tongue for me to ask her to ride home in *my* buggy. Besides," he added with a pause, "she is tolerable, at best."

"Oh, Frederick!" Charles laughed. "You are being ridiculous!"

From where she stood, Lizzie could see Frederick straighten his shoulders and glance around the room, his chin jutting forward as he said, "In fact, I see nothing redeeming in these Lancaster girls that can't be found back home in Ohio."

Lizzie pressed her back against the barn wall, aware that the shadows would hide her from view. Her heart was now pounding, and she felt her cheeks flush red. So, he had noticed her after all. Yet his opinion of her appeared deliberately poor and unfair. *How dare he*, she thought, trying hard not to let emotion overcome her. Tolerable! What an ugly word! She felt a soft rage rising inside of her and realized that it was the devil's insidious attempt at overtaking her. Pride, she thought. He has hurt my pride, and that shall not be permitted! Taking a few deep breaths, she did her best to regain her composure and typical cheerful nature. She would not let a man such as Frederick Detweiler, with his fancy farm and airs of superiority, ruin her night. She wouldn't go home in his buggy even if he would beg her. A man like that, she told herself, was destined to either a lonely life or a mousy wife.

Lifting her chin, she walked into the barn. Charles and Frederick had already returned to their places, ready for the second round of singing. She barely glanced their way as she hurried to where Jane waited for her. Reaching down, Lizzie clutched Jane's hand and smiled. "I see you have a cup of meadow tea," she teased. "I wonder that..."

From Jane's soft glow on her cheeks, Lizzie knew that her suspicion was correct. Charles Beachey had brought the refreshment to her sister. A true gentleman and a good Amish man, that was for sure and certain. Her sister's happiness was all that mattered to Lizzie, and Frederick's ugly words faded in her mind, if not in her memory.

❧ Chapter Four ❧

I**T WAS MONDAY** morning, and the Blank family was sitting around the old wooden farm table. Plates filled with scrambled eggs and sausage, toast, and cooked potatoes covered the surface. The room smelled of all the fresh foods.

Maem and *Daed* drank their coffee while Jane and Lizzie preferred hot mint tea. The younger girls were just as happy with cool water from the faucet. *Maem* was playing with the food on her plate, eager to hear how the previous night's singing went. She prodded and asked questions, but to her dismay, typical for young women, both Lizzie and Jane provided vague answers. Mary and Catherine had been too busy with their younger friends to notice any of the exchanges that their older sisters had engaged in with either Charles or Carol Ann Beachey. And Lydia seemed to be pouting, her elbow resting on the table and her hand pressed against her chin.

"So unfair," she muttered.

"Now, now," *Maem* said, pushing the serving bowl of scrambled eggs to her youngest daughter. "Your time will come, Lydia. And sooner than you think." She glanced at her husband. "Isn't that so, *Daed*?"

Daed looked up, not having paid any attention to the exchange. "What? Oh, *ja, ja*, of course, I reckon!" he replied, nodding his head demurely.

Maem scowled, and Lizzie had to hide her smile, knowing full well that her *daed* had merely answered what he thought would appease his wife or, better, defuse any potential conversation. But after more than twenty-two years together, such a

37

response was but overly transparent. "It'll do no good to have five *dochders* vying for courters, I say," *Maem* fussed, glancing at Jane.

"No one is *vying for courters, Maem*," Lizzie volunteered, a lightness to her tone that justified instant forgiveness for any perceived sassiness. "You just happen to have five *dochders* quite close together in age, ain't so?"

That answer caused *Maem* to cluck her tongue, *tsk-tsking* at her second oldest. "You have no idea of the burden I have borne from such a predicament!" she exclaimed.

"A predicament?" Lizzie laughed, her eyes sparkling as she glanced at Jane. "Five *dochders*? I fail to see how 'five *dochders*' creates a predicament. I should think that you'd be relieved to have ten extra hands to help with all the work and the house chores. Truth be told, I should think you'd find us a gift from God rather than a burden!"

Her *maem* waved her hand, dismissing Lizzie's statement. "Oh, Elizabeth!" she scoffed, which immediately made the younger girls giggle. Their *maem* only used Lizzie's full birth name when she was exasperated with her. "What would *you* know of the burdens I bear, what for having no sons and not one married *dochder* among you!"

Daed cleared his throat, setting his coffee cup down and raising an eyebrow. His graying beard was resting on the edge of the table as he leaned forward. "Ah, your burdens," he said, a teasing glow to his expression. "They are so many, and I know them so well. After all, they have been my constant companions for quite a few years, I reckon."

Maem's mouth dropped open and the fork fell from her hand. Lydia and Catherine broke into giggles while Jane and Lizzie clasped hands under the table, an unspoken support to keep from joining their younger sisters in giggling at *Daed*'s comment.

"Oh help!" *Maem* cried, with an indignant tone of voice. "I should think the burden would be yours as well. If your dear *dochders* don't marry farmers and one without his own farm, what will happen to this place? We can't keep tending the farm and the cows on our own!" She dabbed at her eyes with the corner of her apron. "To think that *Grossdawdi* put so much into keeping it!"

Daed sighed wearily and shook his head. "God will provide, *fraa*. He always does."

The conversation was interrupted by a knock at the door. At such an early hour, a visitor was most unusual. *Daed* pushed his chair back from the table and walked toward the mudroom, too aware that six pairs of eyes watched his back. *Maem* began wringing her hands, clearly fearful that the early morning visitor bore bad news. Lizzie glanced around the table, intrigued by the silence and the variety of expressions on her sisters' faces. From the mudroom they heard the squeak of the screen door and *Daed*'s low voice. Another male voice joined him, followed by friendly laughter shared by the two men.

Only a few short seconds passed before *Daed* sauntered back into the kitchen, a piece of paper in his hand. *"Ach vell,"* he said, glancing down at his hand. "Seems someone has already made a new friend."

Immediately *Maem* lightened up and leaned forward, her burdens from the previous conversation forgotten. "Oh! You must share! Don't delay the news!"

Lizzie rolled her eyes good-naturedly as Jane poked her leg under the table. Lydia's eyes were as large as their mother's while Mary seemed completely disinterested. Catherine's reaction was somewhere in the middle.

"A young gentleman has dropped off a letter," *Daed* said, dragging out the news in order to delay his wife's satisfaction. Lizzie hid her pleasure, loving the gentle teasing that flowed from her *daed* to her *maem*. "A boy."

Jane sat up straighter, but it was Lydia who blurted out, "Charles?"

"*Nee*," *Daed* said, turning the paper over in his hand. "His cousin, George."

A collective gasp went about the table and, without asking for permission, Lydia and Catherine jumped up from the bench where they had been seated and raced to the kitchen window, hoping to catch a glimpse of the younger cousin. To their dismay, his buggy was already nearing the end of the lane.

"Oh, bother!" Lydia pouted.

Maem clutched her hands together. "The letter, *Daed*. Who is the letter for?"

"*Ja, vell*," he started slowly, deliberately procrastinating as his eyes scanned the letter. "Seems it's addressed to our Jane."

A gasp escaped from *Maem* while Jane reluctantly took the letter from her father. Lizzie nudged her, urging her to open the letter quickly to put the curious out of their misery. Jane's blue eyes fluttered over the written lines, and she smiled, a soft and kind smile. When she glanced up, she blushed, realizing that all eyes were upon her.

"It's from Carol Ann Beachey," she started.

Maem sank back in her chair, unable to hide her disappointment but still intrigued.

"She's asked me to come visiting, perhaps to even show her around, take her to some of the local stores for knitting supplies and cloth. She'd like to make a new prayer *kapp* so that she fits in better with our *g'may*." Jane looked up. "She said she'd come by later to pick me up, if I have no other plans. What a lovely gesture of friendship!"

"New prayer *kapp*," *Maem* scoffed, shaking her head. Clearly she was disappointed that the letter came from the sister and not the brother. "Prideful at that! She fits in just fine with her strange little Ohio *kapp*, of that I'm sure."

Jane leaned forward and touched her mother's hand. "Perhaps

she is just reaching out to make a friend, *Maem*. Remember, she knows no one here but her brother and cousin."

"And that miserable-looking Detweiler fellow," Lizzie added drily.

Daed cleared his throat and started back to the door, clearly finished with both breakfast and conversation. "Mayhaps he's her beau, *ja*?" Taking his battered straw hat from the hook near the door, he glanced over his shoulder. "Reckon we've had enough time for idle chat. Need to rake the back pasture that we cut last week. Lizzie, you'll be out to help, *ja*?" She responded with an eager nod. There was nothing she loved more than working outside. Satisfied, her *daed* glanced at the younger girls. "And you two shall need to do some mucking in the dairy, then help rake the rows. Seems dry enough to bale later this afternoon. Besides, too much falls on your sister Lizzie while you both sit inside and crochet all day."

He slipped through the door, ignoring the imploring looks on Lydia's and Catherine's faces. They knew better than to talk back to *Daed*, but they had hoped their *maem* might jump to their defense.

Lizzie was quick to excuse herself, knowing that Jane and Mary would help *Maem* clean the morning dishes before starting on their own chores. Being Monday, laundry would have to be the first priority. After all, it would do no good to have their Sunday dresses soiled, so the sooner they were washed, the fresher they would be. Lizzie was surprised that her *Maem* had not already done the laundry. She liked to have her clothes drying on the line before breakfast so that any passing buggies would see how good and devoted a wife she was. In fact, Lizzie was equally surprised that her *maem* hadn't lamented that fact when the Wickey boy had dropped the letter off for Jane. Certainly he would have noticed, and *that* would have pleased *Maem* to no end!

It hadn't rained in a while, so the hay was ready to be mowed and then windrowed before it could be baled. Everyone would have to rake the lines of hay, insuring that most of the cut grass was ready for the baler. Their Belgian draft horses pulled all of the larger farm equipment, and driving them was one of her greatest delights. She felt closer to God in the fields than at the church services. She liked to imagine that His arms surrounded her, embracing her for her love of the land and willingness to work it with a joyful heart. From the smell of fresh-cut hay to the musky scent of the horses, Lizzie knew that God, indeed, was surrounding her with His gifts.

As they were cutting the timothy mix near the back pasture, Lizzie driving the horses with the windrower, a buggy pulled along the road on the other side of the fence. *Daed* lifted a hand to wave at the driver, a habitual gesture more than one of familiarity, but continued with his work without so much as a second glance. Lizzie, however, squinted in the early morning sun, not quite certain of who was driving the buggy until it neared her. With the driver seated on the left side, it was easier for Lizzie to see him than his companion as the buggy passed by. She stared but didn't wave, needing two firm hands on the reins in order to keep the Belgian draft in check.

Frederick Detweiler.

She would recognize that long face anywhere. He barely looked at her as he passed by, his eyes staring straight ahead. Without even having to look, Lizzie knew who sat beside him: Carol Ann. Clearly they were on their way to the Blank farm to pick up Jane. Lizzie was perplexed as to why Frederick would be driving Carol Ann except, perhaps, for the fact that she was unfamiliar with the back roads to their farm. Still, that was no excuse for not returning her *daed*'s wave or at least nodding acknowledgment in his direction. She shook her head in disbelief and returned her attention to the horses that were pulling the windrower through the rows of freshly cut hay. She was more convinced than ever that she didn't care the least for that

Frederick Detweiler or his special friend, Carol Ann Beachey, even if Jane felt otherwise about the young woman.

It was lunchtime when the subject of Jane and her visitors became the topic of conversation. *Daed* and Lizzie had just washed up and seated themselves at the large hardwood table, eager to refuel themselves for the long afternoon of baling awaiting them. Lizzie gave her *daed* a lot of credit. With the hay so dry, if he mowed smaller patches, he could bale it in the same day, thus avoiding the risk of rain delaying the process. Once the rain fell, the hay would have to be fully dried and raked in order to insure that no moisture snuck into the large, rectangular bales. Over time, moisture would smolder, and the hay often caught fire. It was the younger farmers who often lost their barns to such fires, the older ones having learned from past mistakes made by them or their peers during their youth.

The table seemed empty without Jane, but *Maem* had plenty to say to make up for Jane's absence. Lizzie only half listened, too eager to fill her stomach with the warm slices of ham, cold applesauce, and mounds of whipped potatoes. Working in the fields always gave her such a hearty appetite!

"I could barely believe that he wouldn't even step past the threshold!" she declared. "The rudest man I have ever met."

At this Lizzie looked up from her plate of food.

Maem didn't notice Lizzie's sudden interest in the conversation. "And that Carol Ann Beachey! Why, she looked around this kitchen with her nose right up in the air! As if our home was inferior to what they are used to!" She plopped a hefty spoonful of mashed potatoes onto her plate before passing the bowl to Mary. "I must say that a lived-in farmhouse is one that shows a true commitment to God. If Holmes County Amish feel differently, well, then I'm right glad we stayed put, here in Lancaster!"

"Our farm *is* in Lancaster," Lizzie pointed out.

"Fiddle-faddle!" *Maem* shook her finger at her daughter.

"You know exactly what I mean, Elizabeth. Don't be sassing me, now."

Daed ignored the banter, but his eyes continued to glance outside the kitchen window. It was Mary who noticed it first and questioned his concern. "The sky," he pointed out. "It's getting darker right quick." He pushed back his plate and quickly stood up. Walking to the window, he leaned against the counter and peered through the upper pane, his eyes full of concern as he assessed the situation. "I think it just might rain!"

"Oh, help!"

Ignoring her *maem*'s frazzled expression and the way that she wrung her hands in distress, Lizzie took one more mouthful of food. Then, pushing aside her plate, she hurried to her *daed*'s side. "Reckon we ought to bale it, then?"

She could tell from his expression that he didn't look too happy. But, as always, he tried to keep a level head. "Girls, I want you all out in the field." He glanced at his wife but didn't say a word. "Say a prayer that the rain holds off," he mumbled before hurrying to the door, Lizzie and Mary directly behind him while Catherine and Lydia lingered as if hoping to be relieved.

"You heard your *daed* now," *Maem* snapped. "I can handle these dishes by myself. Go help with the baling!"

It took less than an hour to bale the hay, the Belgian drafts working extra hard to pull the baler faster than usual. As the machine collected the dried hay and bundled it into neat, rectangular packages, the girls were quick to stack them in a wagon that was pulled behind the baler. When Lydia complained of it being too much work, Lizzie scowled at her but ignored her sister's complaint. If laziness was one of the major sins among the Amish, complaining was a close second.

No sooner had they unharnessed the draft horses, having pulled the flat wagon of baled hay directly into the barn, than the sky turned a dark gray and the winds started whipping up. Lizzie lifted her hand to the handkerchief that covered her head as she fought the wind to shut the sliding doors to the barn. The younger sisters ran toward the house, the rain beginning to pelt down upon them. Sister Mary slipped on the wet grass and landed on her knees. Lizzie hurried over to help her sister, frowning at Catherine and Lydia, who hadn't even noticed.

"Oh, help," Lizzie muttered. "You tore your dress, Mary. And I think you scraped your knees."

Mary looked up at her sister, thankful for the assistance. Of all the sisters, Mary was the frailest and quietest, often overlooked in the mix of energy from the younger two sisters. "*Danke*, sis."

Inside the kitchen it was very dark from the sudden onslaught of gray clouds. *Maem* stood at the window, her eyes lifted toward the sky and her face wrinkled with worry as she stared outside. "I've never seen any storm come so fast!" She looked over at the girls. "Where's your *daed*?"

Lizzie helped Mary to a chair. "Unhitching the drafts, *Maem*." She looked over at Catherine and Lydia, already sitting on the sofa. "Could one of you at least light the lamps?" She tried to mask the irritation in her voice, reminding herself that her sisters were younger. "And I need the medical kit for cuts, if you don't mind bringing it over here."

Maem looked over at her. "Mary's hurt? Oh, help and bother!" She hurried over to her daughter's side and lifted up the torn skirt. "I knew you shouldn't be outside helping. It's man's work, not fit for a frail thing like you."

Once the lamps had been lit, the gentle hissing of the propane filling the room with a soothing background noise, *Maem* tended to Mary's injury and Lizzie took a step back, watching through the window and assessing the situation. The rain had started to fall, a dark wall of water cutting across the fields accompanied by whirling wild winds. With such gray skies and unexpected weather, she prayed that Jane and Carol Ann were not out in the buggy, hoping that they had sensed the storm and sought shelter.

When the door opened and *Daed* walked inside, he was drenched with water. He removed his hat and hung it on the peg, droplets of rain pouring down the brim and along the side of the wall, making an immediate puddle on the floor. His hair was soaked, and his clothes looked as if *Maem* had just washed them. *Daed* ran his hand through his graying hair, drops of water splattering through the air as he entered the kitchen. Lizzie studied his face, immediately sensing his concern.

"Reckon we didn't see that coming," he muttered. "Just thankful we didn't cut more hay."

Lizzie hurried to give her *daed* a dry towel from the washroom. He nodded his appreciation and immediately rubbed it against his head and the back of his neck. "What about Jane, *Daed*?"

He glanced at Lizzie then lowered his eyes. "With wind like that, I worry."

Maem shut the lid to the small medical box that she had been using to disinfect Mary's cuts. "Worry? Worry about what?" With one tragedy averted, her attention was yet to be directed at a new one.

"Trees, my *fraa*. Limbs are down for sure and certain. I can't fetch her in this weather, and I pray to God that she had the sense to seek shelter rather than try for home if they were a-ways from the Beachey farm." He sighed, looking more worried than Lizzie liked. "Their farm is located on back roads...not all of them paved."

With something new to worry about, *Maem* wrung her hands and stationed herself at the window, muttering under her breath about having let Jane go at all. Lizzie wanted to point out that the day had started out as beautiful and sunny. How were Jane, Carol Ann, or that Detweiler fellow supposed to have known that a storm would blow in so quickly? But knowing that her *maem* loved nothing more than a good fret, Lizzie removed herself to the sofa and picked up the latest issue of the *Blackboard Bulletin*. She flipped through, her eyes scanning the short stories and recipes, but her mind still centering on Jane and the howling of the wind that sent the rain dashing against the windowpanes, the noise sounding like little pebbles instead of mere water. It was going to be a long night, she realized, one filled with concern. Yet Lizzie knew that the outcome was in God's hands; all they could do was wait until the morning to find out what had happened to her *schwester*.

❧ Chapter Five ❧

IT WAS EARLY in the morning when Lizzie awoke, surprised to see that the rain had not completely let up. She pushed back the light quilt covering her bed and swung her feet over the side. It had felt rather strange to not sleep next to Jane. She could not remember a time when Jane had not been by her side. Yet Lizzie was aware that such a sensation of loss would be something she'd have to accept, should the interest between Jane and this Charles Beachey grow into something more.

With bare feet she padded across the worn hardwood floors and peered outside the small window. Their bedroom was small, but not quite as small as the others that were located upstairs. With only three bedrooms on the second floor and one on the main floor, Jane and Lizzie had to share the room. Mary had the smallest room, the one toward the rear of the hallway, while Lydia and Catherine shared the one near the top of the stairs. There was a fourth room that had never been used for anything other than storage. Lizzie always suspected that her *maem* and *daed* had kept it empty in the hopes of being graced with a son. God had blessed the Blank family with many things and many *kinner* . . . a son, however, had not been one of them.

The sole bathroom located in the house was downstairs. It had been added to the house years ago when *Daed* had been but a young boy. Prior to that there had been an outhouse for personal needs, and bathing was done by a wood-burning cookstove in the basement. Sometimes in the summer, *Daed* had confided to Lizzie, the children would sneak to the creek with a bar of soap, preferring to bathe in secret outside in the fresh air rather than in the heat of the house basement.

Daed had been an only son, so there had been no question as to who would inherit the farm. Both of his parents suffered from the cold winter weather and had moved down to Pinecraft, Florida, settling in a small Amish community outside of Sarasota. His four older sisters had married well, two having moved to Holmes County, Ohio, where, at the time, the land was more abundant and less costly. His oldest sister had passed five years prior, refusing treatment for her spine cancer from the *Englische* doctors. Instead, she had relied on the natural cures of herbs and concoctions. Whether the cancer killed *Aendi* Ruth or it was the concoctions that did it, no one ever questioned God's will in taking *Aendi* Ruth home.

As to *Daed*'s other sister, Mary, she had married and moved to the south side of Lancaster County. Her husband was a carpenter, so they lived in a modest home in Strasburg, their own two sons following in their *daed*'s footsteps. Twice a year there would be a family gathering, usually at the old Blank homestead. Since the family was smaller than most Amish families, *Maem* always invited the neighbors, most of them people who had grown up with *Daed* and Mary.

"It's still raining, *Daed*," Lizzie said as she entered the kitchen. She wore a pale green dress with her black work apron tied around her waist. With her dark hair pulled back into a perfect bun at the nape of her neck and her prayer *kapp* already pinned to her headband, she was ready to face the day, dreary weather or not.

She took a deep breath, surprised. The kitchen already smelled of fresh bread baking in the oven. She glanced at the clock, suspecting that she might have awoken later than usual, for *Maem* usually didn't start baking until well after six o'clock, a time when Lizzie had long been outside helping *Daed* with the dairy chores.

But it was only four-thirty. Lizzie wondered what time her *maem* had arisen if she already had bread baking. Certainly she might not have slept at all, possibly sick with worry. If taking care of the family was *Maem*'s primary job, worrying was a close second. Lizzie watched as her *maem* hustled about the kitchen, touching pots and pans as if keeping her hands busy would help her stop fretting about her oldest *dochder*. As usual, *Daed* remained calm, not noticing his *fraa*'s tendency to let her nerves overreact.

For as frantic as *Maem* could become over the simplest annoyance, *Daed* seemed to always be calm and steady. In many ways they were such an unlikely couple, Lizzie often thought. *Maem* had been born to a large farming family that lived to the north of New Holland. Her own *maem* had passed at a young age and left eight *kinner* in the hands of her husband. With no matriarch in the family to guide the *kinner* and support the husband, the farmhouse had fallen into disarray and was often overlooked when it came time for the church service rotation. It was too hard to maintain the property and work the fields. *Maem* rarely talked about her upbringing, but from the few times that one of her siblings had visited, Lizzie knew that it had not been easy. The family had developed a reputation among the *g'may*, a reputation that *Maem* was quite thankful to leave behind when she was fortunate enough to capture *Daed*'s attention at a youth event so many years ago. Not caring about what others thought, *Daed* had pursued her and, within just a few months of courting, had married her, whisking her away from the slovenly farm and bad reputation that surrounded her family.

Given her upbringing, it was only natural that *Maem* would worry excessively about her oldest *dochder*'s reputation. Clearly that had kept her *maem* from sleeping well and caused her to awaken early, putting her hands to work in order to help her mind stop spinning with different what-if scenarios.

"What shall we do about Jane, then?" Lizzie asked, turning her attention away from her nervous *maem* as she bustled down the cellar stairs.

Daed stood by the counter, a large mug of hot coffee in his hands. With a deep breath he shook his head. "I checked the answering machine in the barn," he started. "That Detweiler fellow was good enough to leave a message mentioning that our dear Jane was at the farm when the storm hit." Lizzie raised an eyebrow at the mention of Frederick. "However, he left another message this morning that the bridge washed out and a tree fell onto their barn, blocking the road, I fear."

"Onto their barn!"

"*Ja*, the barn. But with them having just arrived, only the horses and buggies were inside. No damage or injuries."

Maem emerged from the basement stairs, her arms laden with jars of canned beets and chow-chow. "No injuries except for our dear Jane's reputation!" she scoffed.

"Now that's not so," *Daed* reassured her. "Detweiler is a fine man, I'm sure, and also the chaperone for the other two men. Jane is staying with Carol Ann after a horrible storm hit. Anyone who questions that, my *fraa*, has filth on their mind and gossip on their tongue!"

"I should go to her," Lizzie exclaimed, alarmed that anyone might say something against her sister. "She can't stay there alone!"

"Lizzie! I shall not have two *dochders* with soiled reputations!"

With a scowl on her face Lizzie turned to her *maem*. "My presence would salvage her reputation, and I care not a twit for my own!"

Daed stepped in. "If the rain lets up, I shall walk you there myself, Lizzie. Mayhaps we can bring her home, or at least I can see how the roads are and assist with the tree, *ja*?"

"Walk?" *Maem* exclaimed, horrified at the thought. "Why, you must take the buggy! She'll be filthy, for sure and certain!"

Her eyes were large and bewildered at her husband's suggestion. "What will the Beachey man think?"

"I don't care a fiddle-faddle about what they'll think!" Lizzie said.

"They'll think that we are a caring family who helps our neighbors and has concern for our *dochder*!" The firmness in his voice surprised Lizzie, and she noticed that her *maem*, while not happy about the direction of the conversation, immediately backed off. After all, *Daed* had spoken, and there was nothing further to argue about.

The rain began to slow down, the drops becoming a gentle mist. Lizzie helped her *daed* in the dairy, occasionally looking up from the cow that she was milking to assess the outdoor weather. While the clouds did not dissipate, the rain was all but finished by the time the last cow was milked and the herd was let to pasture. Lizzie hurried inside to grab a blue head covering so that her prayer *kapp* would not get soiled. She took a secret satisfaction in the fact that *Daed* instructed the other three girls to muck the dairy while they were gone, a job that Lizzie normally did with nary a care but one that her sisters detested.

They had walked a mile up the hill and turned down the first lane to head toward the Beachey farm. Immediately Lizzie saw why her *daed* had insisted that they walk. The roads were all but impassable by horse, buggy, or car. Many telephone and electric poles were downed, and wires were on the road. *Daed* guided Lizzie past the lines, careful to avoid as many puddles as they could for fear that the electrical current might still be active, although he suspected that the entire area was without power. Very few of the Amish farms used electricity, and those that did had special permission from the church leaders. Mostly the lines carried electric current to the non-Amish homes since all of the farms on their street stuck to the mandated diesel-powered generators and solar power. But they all had telephones. While forbidden for casual conversation and never in their homes, telephones were needed by the farmers to communicate with their suppliers, distributors, and clients. In the twenty-first century even the church leaders understood that simple concession.

"*Mein Gott!*"

Lizzie glanced at her *daed*, surprised by his expression. She followed his gaze and saw why he had spoken so. More large trees had fallen, blocking the roads so that, even on foot, they could not pass. A silo at a neighbor's farm had fallen over, and a herd of cows wandered on the road, having passed through an opening in a fence from a fallen tree limb.

"Was it a tornado, *Daed*?" she asked.

"*Nee, nee*," he replied, shaking his head. "Just a very strong summer storm." He reached over and placed his hand on her shoulder. "God is right *gut*, my Lizzie. Trust firmly in the Lord and in His wisdom."

She smiled, knowing what he meant. Damage to property was one thing; yet, God willing, no one had suffered injuries in the neighborhood. From the looks of the damage, it was nothing that the community could not swiftly recover from. She lifted her heart quickly to God, thanking Him that He had spared their family and prayed that such was the case for all the others living in their *g'may*.

Cutting through the fields took them longer than anticipated. Although the Beachey farm was a mere three miles away from the Blanks, it took close to two hours to approach it. Lizzie felt her pace quicken once she saw the white farmhouse, eager to see her sister and, hopefully, bring her home.

The lane was covered in deep puddles, and Lizzie had to hold up her skirt to jump over them. Her *daed* had wandered to the barn, assessing the damage, while Lizzie headed directly to the house.

"Allow me," a voice said, startling Lizzie as she prepared to leap over the largest puddle yet. With debris on the right and a ditch on the left, she had no alternative. When she looked up, she saw Frederick approaching from behind the debris pile. He wore his pants tucked into his tall boots, and his shirt was stained with mud. He wore a funny-shaped straw hat, different than what most Lancaster Amish men wore. She was speechless in his presence, and when he stepped forward, stretching out his hand for her to take, she could only respond by accepting his assistance.

"Did you walk all the way here, then?" he asked, his deep voice calmer and kinder than she remembered.

"*Ja*," she responded. "The roads are quite impassable, I fear."

He made a noise, deep in his throat, which she wasn't certain how to interpret.

"My *daed* went to the barn to assess the damage," she heard herself say. "I wanted to check on Jane, however." She realized he was still holding her hand, despite the fact that she had successfully scaled the puddle. "How is Jane?"

"I imagine quite fine," Frederick said. "They had just arrived as the storm hit. I fear she may have twisted her ankle, running to the house. But I leave that assessment to your tender care."

Lizzie frowned. She hadn't heard about a twisted ankle. Without the ability to walk, Jane certainly could not leave. At least, Lizzie reasoned, until the roads were cleared. Withdrawing her hand from his, Lizzie nodded her appreciation for his help. "Then I best go see to her, *ja*?" Without another look, she hurried down the rest of the lane and quickly discarded her muddy shoes on the porch, unaware that she was still being watched.

The inside of the farmhouse was surprisingly well lit and warm, not just to the skin but also to the senses. Quite an achievement, she pondered, considering that they had not been there but less than a week. The kitchen had been repainted a light pale green, and fresh room-darkening shades hung from

Sarah Price

each double-hung window. The floor was linoleum and looked freshly waxed, while the appliances appeared new and of a high quality. Lizzie stood in the doorway, staring at the room in amazement. It was clean and plain, yet refined at the same time.

"Lizzie!"

Jane's voice came from the back of the sunroom, which was attached to the kitchen. There was a dark green sofa against the wall with a matching recliner nearby. Jane was sitting in the recliner with her legs propped up, an ice pack on her right ankle. Without a thought for her bare feet, still damp from her soaked shoes, Lizzie hurried across the kitchen and knelt by her sister's side.

"Are you well? We were so worried, Jane! Tell me without a moment's delay what happened!"

Jane laughed, her eyes twinkling, despite the dark circles beneath them. "Oh, Lizzie, you are such a goose! We were fine." Jane craned her neck and looked behind Lizzie. "Weren't we, Carol Ann?"

Startled, Lizzie quickly stood. She hadn't noticed Carol Ann seated in another chair near the back corner. She was crocheting a blanket and had not bothered to make her presence known. Lizzie found that odd but forced herself to step toward Carol Ann. "I hadn't seen you there, Carol Ann," Lizzie said. "We all prayed for your safety. God was right *gut* that you escaped the storm unharmed."

"*Ja*," she said, her eyes quickly assessing Lizzie's soiled state. "Jane and I had been returning from the dry goods store. She was kind enough to help me pick out some yarn as well as material for a new prayer *kapp*."

Lizzie's eyes flickered to Carol Ann's head, secretly not surprised to see the same old Ohio *kapp* on her head.

"Oh, Lizzie, I feel ever so clumsy," Jane said lightly. "When we pulled into the lane, the buggy was stuck in a hole. George came to help push it, but I stepped out before I knew." She

56

motioned toward her ankle. "I fear I fell and twisted it." Casually she pulled the ice pack from her leg, and Lizzie had to control herself from gasping at the dark bruise that graced her sister's ankle. "I could barely walk, but Charles was good enough to come fetch me while George saw to the buggy."

"I came as soon as I heard," Lizzie said. "The roads are truly wretched. I've never seen such a storm sweep through our area, have you then?"

"*Nee*," Jane agreed. "Not in June."

Carol Ann set down her crocheting and stood up, slowly walking toward the kitchen. "I suppose I shall start the noon meal, then," she said. "The men will be hungry and need energy for the afternoon."

Without being asked, Lizzie hurried to help her. She did as she was instructed, even accepting Carol Ann's preferred manner of peeling the potatoes without comment. Occasionally she glanced over at Jane, too aware that her sister napped. It was clear that the pain from her ankle was greater than what she was letting on. Jane would never want to be seen as either a burden or a complainer. Yet the pain was evident on her face.

"I suppose we should call a doctor to look at her ankle," Lizzie whispered to Carol Ann.

"We have no phone here," she replied.

Lizzie was about to retort that Frederick had called their farm earlier and left a message. But, figuring that it was best to hold her tongue, she kept silent on the matter.

It was shortly after eleven thirty when the door opened and the men stomped inside the side room adjoining the kitchen. They could be heard removing their boots and hanging their hats before entering the kitchen. Lizzie glanced up, surprised to see three men, not one of whom was her *daed*. Charles smiled brightly at Lizzie while Frederick merely ignored her. The third man, who, by his appearance alone, was easily identi-fied as the elusive George, tilted his head and looked straight at Lizzie before stepping forward to introduce himself. As they shook hands, Lizzie noticed Frederick stiffen and turn his face away, the muscles in his jaws tightening as if he were bothered by George's introduction.

Nee, she realized as he quietly disappeared into another room. Frederick was more likely bothered by George's happy-go-lucky presence, she reasoned.

She could understand why. Unlike Frederick, George seemed to sparkle with energy. His personality was in sharp contrast to Frederick's, and, Lizzie imagined, *that* could certainly create a riff between them. However, since Frederick and Charles seemed to get on so, she was more than curious as to the cause of Frederick's obvious dislike for the younger cousin. Indeed, Lizzie found him comparable to his older cousin Charles, both in looks and charm. With curly brown hair and flashing eyes, George was quick to smile, and during the meal he engaged in lively conversation, even more than his cousin. He was not as soft-spoken as Charles but seemed pleasant enough. Yet Carol Ann seemed to distance herself from George, even as her eyes went to the kitchen doorway, anticipating Frederick's entrance. The noise of running water explained, if not excused, his absence from the table.

Lizzie watched the interactions of the household with great curiosity, too aware of the sense of the unspoken, yet too ladylike to inquire. Instead she focused her attention on her sister while politely responding to George's attention without allowing any encouragement for him to further it. Whatever was happening beneath the surface at the Beachey house was quite intense, and she certainly did not want to get swept away in the undercurrent.

The meal was soon over, and Jane had settled back into the recliner with her foot elevated before Frederick reemerged. He had washed up and changed his clothes, and he ignored Carol Ann's gesture of a plate that had been set aside. "Too much work," he mumbled, and without so much of a glance at any of the others in the room, he reached for his hat and disappeared back outdoors.

Charles knelt by Jane's side and, to Lizzie's amazement, gently took her hand as he spoke to her. "We shall work hard, Jane, so that the roads will be clear for you to return home. While your company here is..." He hesitated and lowered his voice. "Most enjoyable, I am more than certain you would prefer to be under the care of your *maem* rather than that of three bachelors and a *maedel*."

Jane blushed and smiled.

Lizzie, however, raised an eyebrow. *Maedel*? Carol Ann was considered such? Perhaps Carol Ann was not as young as Lizzie had perceived, and that could explain her sour attitude as she witnessed the gravitation toward Jane, the elder of the Blank sisters.

Charles and George returned outside to help. Lizzie stood in the center of the kitchen, feeling awkward and useless. With a deep breath she glanced at Jane, then turned her head to look outdoors. "Jane," she began. "I think I might be of more use helping the men."

Carol Ann spun around, a shocked look on her face made all the more austere because of the tight prayer *kapp* that hugged the back of her head. "Help the men?"

"*Ja!*" Lizzie replied, staring at Carol Ann as if daring her to challenge her further. "Many hands make light the work. While I might be unable to do the heavy lifting, I can move the brambles and debris, for sure and certain!" She didn't wait for a response from the open-mouthed Carol Ann before she headed toward the side room, hoping that, in the meantime, her shoes had dried at least enough to not prune her toes while she worked outside.

The sky had finally cleared, and there was now enough blue between the few remaining clouds, with a hint of a light rainbow. Seeing it lifted her mood as she walked toward the barn. The air still held a damp chill to it, but the birds were back in the trees, chirping and singing, something that greatly boosted her spirits. For a moment she stood there, letting the sunshine permeate her face and the cool air brush against her skin. She held her arms out to the sides and spun, slowly, embracing the glory of the day. After every storm, she thought, a rainbow: God's promise of renewal to mankind.

She was surprised to see many other Amish men helping to clear the lane. Her *daed* had returned, apparently bringing some neighbors to help with the situation at the Beachey farm. With eight men working with the help of several gasoline-powered chainsaws, the trees were quickly cut into manageable pieces. To her surprise, she noticed that Frederick was one of the men wielding a chainsaw, his attention focused on dismembering the tree so that the road could be passable once again. His willingness to work, and work hard at that, seemed out of character for a man who seemed to disdain everything and everyone in Lancaster, Pennsylvania.

Hard work had never been a deterrent for Lizzie. There was nothing like rolling up her sleeves and getting dirty as she worked in the fields. Today was no exception. Lizzie didn't wait for instructions to begin gathering limbs and branches and drag them away from the lane and into the pasture. Charles welcomed her help, but Frederick seemed to view the presence of a lone female in their midst with surprise and disapproval, frowning whenever she came his way. George, meanwhile, was quick to jump to her aid with some of the heavier limbs, his charming smile and light conversation making time pass quickly as they worked in unison.

Given that it was early summer, the sky stayed brighter longer than usual. For that, Lizzie and all of the men who were working gave thanks to God. However, as suppertime neared,

Lizzie's *daed* removed his hat and wiped the sweat from his brow, using the back of his arm to do so.

"Lizzie," he called out. "Best be heading back. We'll be able to see what progress the *Englische* have made on the roads."

The thought horrified Lizzie. To leave Jane at the Beachey farm yet again? Could the roads still be so impassable?

"*Nee, nee,*" Charles said quickly, leaping over the dismembered trunk of the tree. "Let Lizzie stay here with Jane. I'm sure by tomorrow the roads will be clear." He looked over at Lizzie and grinned. "If not, I shall personally carry your dear *schwester* home! But do not leave her alone." He looked back at Lizzie's *daed*. "I'm sure that Lizzie would be quite a comfort to Jane, I reckon."

Lizzie watched as her *daed* seemed to contemplate the situation. The decision laid on his shoulders and his shoulders alone. Yet Lizzie knew that her *daed* saw the sense in the suggestion from the eager Charles Beachey. The other remaining men seemed to watch her *daed* too, one or two of them nodding in agreement that Charles's suggestion made the most sense. After all, with Lizzie there, it was one more set of eyes on Jane in a house of unmarried males without parental supervision.

He leveled his eyes at Lizzie as if trying to ascertain her true desire. When she merely raised an eyebrow, he nodded his consent. "I reckon you're right, Charles. Lizzie could make Jane more comfortable, and she could continue to help clear the debris in the morning."

And so it was settled.

Lizzie watched him, thankful for his decision, as her *daed* began the long walk home. Several other men joined him, knowing that it was soon time to milk the cows and prepare for another long day tomorrow. With a sigh, Lizzie turned away from the still muddy lane and assessed the day's work. The tree had been removed from the barn, three men had patched up the holes, and five men had been busy cutting the tree into manageable chunks. It had been a productive day, to say the least.

"Tomorrow we can burn the brambles, *ja*?"

She glanced over her shoulder at George and nodded her head. "A right *gut* idea. Gives them time to dry out."

Frederick walked by, his eyes avoiding contact with both of them, but she thought she heard him make a guttural noise deep within his throat. Her curiosity was more than piqued, and she wondered if she'd be able to discover more about the obvious animosity between Frederick and George. How odd, she pondered. After all, it was her impression that Frederick was there to guide the cousins. Why on earth would he have agreed to travel such a distance and for such a long time if he did not feel the inclination to help the younger of the two?

It was after supper when she had a chance to further observe the interaction among the Beachey cousins and Frederick Detweiler. They had partaken of a rather light supper and, upon finishing their evening chores, retired to the sunroom, now lit with the glow of the propane lantern. Jane had retired to the downstairs bedroom, Charles and Lizzie having helped her hobble into the room. After Charles bade his good night, Lizzie had helped Jane into her nightgown, thoughtfully packed by their *maem* when *Daed* had returned home for the noon meal and to get more tools.

"He's *wunderbaar gut*, Lizzie," Jane had whispered. "Such a kind and charming man who is full of God's grace and love."

There was no argument from Lizzie. She could see that Charles Beachey was a good-hearted and godly man. Yet her concern about the other two hindered her from making any additional comments.

Back in the main room Lizzie quietly took her place in a straight-back chair. Carol Ann offered her a crochet hook and ball of yarn, which Lizzie gladly accepted. She felt much more comfortable with busy hands. Still, her ears stayed tuned to the conversation and undercurrents that swelled within the room.

Frederick stayed at the table, his shoulders hunched over as he pored over a piece of paper, a pen in his left hand, writing. Lizzie paid him little mind, his horrid words from the singing still ringing in her ears despite his kindness helping her span the puddles in the lane earlier today. Yet she noticed that Carol Ann continued to glance up and in his direction, her attention more on Frederick than on the blanket she was crocheting.

"Another letter?" she asked drily, although Lizzie suspected there was an attempt at humor in her tone. "You write so much for someone who has only been here but a few days, Frederick."

"There is much to share with home," he answered.

Silence.

A few moments passed, Charles poring over the worn book *Martyrs Mirror* while George lingered near the door. He seemed antsy and nervous, more interested in the outside than the indoors. He reminded Lizzie of a tomcat, wanting to explore the night more than sleep in the warmth of the house.

"Still," Carol Ann finally continued, "it is rare for a man to write so frequently. Surely it is not to the same person," she probed.

"My sister, Grace," he answered.

Lizzie tilted her head. She had been unaware that Frederick had a sister. Of course, she should not be surprised, for her exchanges with him had been so limited. Yet the fact that he would write to his sister, and apparently more than just once, surprised her. He had not seemed to be the type that would put pen to paper.

"Do share my well-wishes with dear Grace," Carol Ann gushed. "Oh, how I wish she could have joined us."

"I shared your wishes already in my previous letter," Frederick replied, stopping Carol Ann from any further flattery.

"I do hope she is faring well with her cousins Elinor and Mary Anne," Carol Ann added.

"I have no reason to think otherwise."

Lizzie had watched this banter with slight amusement, well aware that Carol Ann was vying for Frederick's attention, something he was naught ready to give to her. Indeed, she realized, had she previously thought they might have been a courting couple, she now was convinced otherwise. It didn't surprise Lizzie. After all, Frederick was too proud of himself and his status to catch or even desire a wife.

Dropping her half-finished blanket in her lap, Carol Ann stared at Lizzie. "Such horrid manners," she said, a teasing tone to her voice with a hint of seriousness lying just beneath the surface. "No wonder he is *leddich*!"

Lizzie stifled her gasp, shocked that Carol Ann had said exactly what they had apparently both been thinking. The rudeness of Carol Ann's statement gave Lizzie pause. For just that moment she felt sympathy toward Frederick and heard herself jump to his defense. "Why, I reckon he cares deeply for his sister and is focused on writing his letter," she started. "Our interruptions must break his concentration."

At her words Frederick suddenly raised his head. He looked at her, a quizzical expression on his face as he announced, "The interruptions come only from one direction, Lizzie."

She lowered her eyes and blushed, fearing that his words were a reprimand.

"I find your willingness to soften the chastisement by spreading the blame where it does not belong most admirable, a quality not often found in a woman," he stated firmly.

"And what qualities do you look for in a woman, then?" Carol Ann snapped, her own cheeks reddened, but for a different reason.

With a great display of inconvenience Frederick set down his pen and turned to face the two women. To Lizzie it was clear that Carol Ann was annoyed that his attention had gone toward the one woman rather than herself. She was amused with this reaction and watched as Carol Ann attempted to engage Frederick, at last, in a one-on-one conversation. Yet his expression clearly showed that he preferred anything but the conversation Carol Ann had started.

"A love of God and His gifts should come first," he began. "The good and the bad. A love of community and family should come second. And with that is the common sense to protect them from hurt or injury as well as guiding them toward a godly life."

"Is there a third thing, then?" Carol Ann asked, suddenly more animated and flirtatious as she was enjoying his attention. No one except Lizzie seemed to have noticed that George had slipped out the door.

"Humility with intelligence."

Carol Ann waved her hand at him, dismissing him. But he turned his eyes to Lizzie, as if waiting to gauge her reaction.

"I should think," Lizzie began slowly, "that such an ideal woman would not exist, Frederick."

He seemed genuinely curious about her statement and directed his attention at her. This shift seemed to annoy Carol Ann even further, and she rolled her eyes while walking toward the window, clearly finished with the discussion. Frederick, however, paid no mind to Carol Ann as he looked at Lizzie. "How so?"

"Only God is perfect, and what you have described…well…" Lizzie paused, not certain how to phrase what she was thinking. She didn't want to hurt his feelings, yet she knew that his ideal was so high that it could never be reached. After all, perfection could only be found in God. To even hope that any woman could come close would be to set oneself up for unobtainable expectations and enormous disappointment. In fact, to even desire such perfection went against everything in the *Ordnung*.

Humility alone countered his ideal. "You might find yourself looking for quite some time, I fear."

And then she saw it: the change in his expression; from disinterest to something else, something that she could not quite describe. Suddenly she felt nervous under the intensity of his stare and felt compelled to return her attention to the yarn held on her lap, as she continued crocheting. What could she possibly have said that would have made his manner switch so quickly?

❧ *Chapter Six* ❧

IT WAS A beautiful morning, and Lizzie awoke to the sound of birds chirping outside the window of the bedroom where both she and Jane slept at the Beachey farm. From the sound of it, she thought she could identify the pretty little nuthatches and chickadees with an occasional plain sparrow joining the song. She slipped out from under the plain white sheet, careful not to disturb Jane, who had tossed and turned a bit throughout the night. Quietly Lizzie padded to the window to look outside.

The window overlooked the back fields on the eastern side of the property. The fields were overgrown. Apparently the tenants had not used them for several years, letting them sit dormant while focusing their planting efforts on the front and western side field, away from the pasture where the cows had grazed. Birds flew through the air, dipping down and disappearing into the overgrown grasses and weeds. Lizzie leaned her elbows on the windowsill to watch, smiling at the pleasant sight, especially as the sun arose over the horizon, the sky a magnificent reddish-gold color.

It was probably close to six o'clock, and Lizzie felt refreshed at having slept so late. At this time she was normally up and working, helping *Daed* in the dairy. A momentary wave of guilt washed over her, and she wondered if her sisters were helping him so that the burden would not be too great.

Something caught her eye: movement in the field. She squinted and strained her eyes, for the movement was far toward the back fencing. It was a man, walking along the outer edge of the field as if inspecting the fencing and the amount of work that would need to be done in order to properly prepare the fields for planting crops the next year. She wondered if it was Charles, up early and assessing the farm that he was to begin working. She was fairly certain it would not be George. She had heard the door open late in the night, the hinges squeaking as they announced his arrival. While he had tried to be quiet, tiptoeing into the kitchen and heading for the stairs, she had sensed something awkward about his movements and wondered where he had been for such a long time.

With a sigh, Lizzie quickly removed the borrowed nightgown that Carol Ann had lent to her and slipped on her own dress, careful to pin it properly so that she wouldn't stick herself. She borrowed Jane's brush that she had brought with her and ran it through her long, brunette hair, pulling it over her shoulders in order to reach the ends. Then, with an expertise that came from years of practice, she twisted it into a plain bun, secured it with hairpins, and reached for her prayer *kapp*. Only when the *kapp* was firmly secured to her hair did she venture into the kitchen.

She was surprised to see Charles already seated at the table, a cup of hot coffee before him and the *Budget* newspaper in his hands. He looked up and greeted her with a broad, friendly smile. She was about to inquire as to who was walking in his field but thought twice about displaying such curiosity when, clearly, her priority and concern were tending to Jane and certainly not prying into the Beachey's business.

"*Gut mariye*," he said, smiling as Lizzie entered the room.

She returned the greeting with a simple smile.

"Coffee is on the stove," he added, pointing in that direction.

"*Danke*." She walked to the stove and, after hesitating for just a minute, opened a cabinet to try to locate a mug. She poured herself a cup then carried the pot over to the table. "A refill, *ja*?"

She heard the back door open as she was pouring the coffee

into Charles's empty mug. When she looked up, she was surprised to see Frederick saunter into the room. He left on his hat rather than hang it on the wall. Upon seeing her standing there, serving Charles, he paused and frowned.

His expression perplexed her. It was only normal that she should be serving the coffee, so she wondered why he looked at her in that strange manner. Lifting her chin, she met his gaze and raised an eyebrow. "Would you care for some coffee, then?"

Her voice must have startled him, for he merely shook his head and averted his eyes.

"Out and about so early, Frederick?" Charles asked brightly.

"*Ja*," he replied, his deep voice sounding even stronger in the quiet of the morning. "Fencing needs some fixing in that back pasture. Wire and some boards."

So it was Frederick! Lizzie couldn't help but wonder why he would be so concerned when the farm was Charles's, not his. And after all, didn't he hire his own workers back in Ohio to tend to manual upkeep and labor?

"Mayhaps we might send George to pick these up when the roads are clear, *ja*?" Charles asked.

Lizzie noticed Frederick purse his lips at the mention of George's name, the muscle in his jaw flexing. "That won't be today, I reckon. The roads are not quite opened yet," he added, stealing a quick glance at Lizzie. "I suspect your *daed* will not be able to come fetch you and your *schwester* again this day."

Charles lifted his chin, a hint of relief in his eyes as he stared at his friend. "I wouldn't dream of sending Jane home still being injured and with the roads so impassable. And such enjoyable company, especially since we do not have a dairy to tend...yet."

Frederick tensed but said not another word. Instead he turned on his heel and walked back through the door and outside. From the corner of her eye Lizzie could see him heading toward the stable. She busied herself near the window, curious as to what he was doing despite not caring one whit for Frederick Detweiler and his haughty manner. So she was further surprised to see him begin working outside, continuing to move chopped wood and broken boards away from the barn.

A few moments later the bedroom door opened and Jane appeared, limping ever so slightly but looking fresh and beautiful as always. Lizzie smiled at her sister, happy to see the rosy color on her cheeks. Charles hurried to her side, extending his arm to assist her. Jane seemed reluctant to take it, but Charles insisted and guided her to the table, pulling out a chair for Jane to sit. It did not go without notice on Lizzie's part that he had seated her beside his own place at the kitchen table.

Quietly Lizzie busied herself preparing breakfast, noticing that Carol Ann had yet to appear in the kitchen. Or, if she had, she had made herself scarce in time to avoid preparing the morning meal. Additionally George was obviously absent. Lizzie thought back to his mysterious disappearance the evening before and the noise of the door opening in the dark hours of early morning. She was learning a lot about these newcomers to their *g'may*, and not all of it was pleasant.

"I'm elated that you are feeling better," Charles pronounced, his body leaning toward Jane. "But I'm sorry that you were injured at all."

She lowered her eyes and flushed, a demure reaction that Lizzie caught out of the corner of her eye when she handed her sister a cup of hot coffee. "I'm embarrassed that I have been a burden," Jane responded, looking genuinely concerned and contrite. Clearly she was uncomfortable at having imposed on their hospitality, even if it was not something that she could control.

"*Nee!*" Charles countered quickly. "It's been our pleasure!" He paused. For as uncomfortable as Jane appeared, Charles was clearly the opposite. If she felt that she presented an imposition, Charles saw her presence as anything but a burden. Yet he was having a hard time expressing such an emotion. *"Ach,"* he stumbled across his words. "Not that you were injured, but a more pleasant patient has never existed!"

"I dare say that is high praise and undeserved at that," Jane replied modestly.

"When you do return to your *daed's* farm, I shall have to come calling," Charles said softly to Jane and just barely audible to Lizzie as she stood with her back toward them at the stove, cooking the morning eggs for breakfast. "To see how you fare," he added.

She remained silent.

"But in the meantime, perhaps we can walk a bit outside in the fresh air," he said. "To see how your ankle is holding up, *ja?"*

After breakfast Lizzie stood by the sink washing the breakfast dishes and watching out the window as Charles walked with her sister slowly up the lane. He held her arm, under the guise of assisting her, but Lizzie could tell that Jane was feeling much better. She was barely limping, at least not as much as the previous day. However, rather than resist the attention from Charles, Jane was glowing. Their heads were tipped together as they walked, talking to each other and occasionally laughing.

After the kitchen was cleaned, with still no sign of Carol Ann or George, Lizzie went outside to see about providing any assistance. Jane and Charles were returning from their walk, almost oblivious to Lizzie's presence as she approached them. With an embarrassed laugh Jane looked away while Charles pointed down the road to show Lizzie where the group of men were gathered, working on two large trees that had fallen during the storm. There still were some electrical lines down, but an *Englische* truck was there, the yellow lights flashing on top of the vehicle as a man in khaki pants and a white short-sleeve shirt assessed the scene.

Five Amish men, including her *daed*, were working at

removing a large tree. Lizzie remembered having seen it the day before when she and her *daed* had approached the Beachey farm. They had spent most of the day focused on helping clear the fallen trees from the Beachey farm, leaving the road cleanup to the *Englische*. But it was clear that the storm had taken down too many trees and lines for the cleanup to be addressed in one day. Now that the farms were taken care of, the Amish community would help their *Englische* neighbors.

Daed smiled at Lizzie as she approached. "This tree sure is a big one, *ja?*" he said.

She shook her head, startled at the huge size of the root ball that had just lifted out of the dirt, allowing the tree to topple and fall over. *What strength God must truly have*, she thought, *to merely brush His hand over such a majestic tree as if it were no more than a feather stuck in the ground.* It reminded her of the hymn "How Great Thou Art," and the tune stuck in her head.

Later that evening the household relaxed in the kitchen and its adjoining sunroom. The women were seated on the sofa and reclining chair, crocheting as the sun began to set in the sky. It was after eight o'clock, and after such a long day, they were soon to retire for the night. The men, Frederick and Charles, sat at the table, perusing the newspapers. George once again had disappeared without any explanation after supper.

"I'm hoping to get that back fence fixed as soon as the road opens," Charles said, more to Frederick than to anyone else in the room. "I'd like to go to auction next week and see about starting the dairy."

Frederick laid his paper aside and nodded in agreement. "That back field will be right *gut* for the cows to graze down and fertilize until it is time for spring plowing."

Carol Ann sighed and set down her crocheting. "I wonder why your previous tenants did not take better care of the property," she lamented. "So much work to do and on such an expansive property, ain't so?"

Her comment lingered in the air, no one quite certain how to respond. Jane looked up from her own crocheting and glanced at her *schwester* but remained silent, which did not surprise Lizzie. Jane was never one to be forward in her speech. So it was Lizzie who finally spoke up, addressing the unusual complaint.

"I am sure that the tenants did their best to maintain the property," Lizzie said slowly. She had known the previous tenants and didn't like any ill being spoken of them. While an older family, they had lived at the Beachey farm for several decades. However, as the *kinner* grew older and married, most of them moving away as they had picked up trades instead of farming, the parents could only do so much. "And, while expansive, the property seems in a right *gut* condition to produce *wunderbaar* crops. In fact, while I know little about farmers in Ohio, I do know that our farmers in Lancaster often use field rotation so that the ground has time to lay fallow and regenerate nutrients in the soil."

Another pause.

To her surprise, Frederick responded. "Field rotation is practiced in Ohio as well, of course," he started. "However, our farms are closer together and smaller. Some of those farms practice crop rotation rather than field rotation for the very reasons that you pointed out, Elizabeth."

She wasn't certain if his words were a compliment or a reprimand. She did not have a chance to ponder it for Carol Ann jumped back into the conversation.

"Indeed, our farms are not so spread out, affording our families to enjoy a bit more of life rather than working themselves to the core," she quipped.

Lizzie felt angry at Carol Ann's comment but tried to remember the Amish rule of never doing anything in anger. She had learned that all of her life, but it had been particularly stressed during her instructional, prior to taking her baptism

73

two autumns prior. "We were always taught to 'Avoid idleness as a resting-pillow of the devil and a cause of all sorts of wickedness,'" she quoted from her instructional book for baptism. "I must confess that I rather enjoy working myself to the core, as you call it," she replied. "Less time for idleness and, therefore, less time for being tempted into sin."

When Carol Ann scoffed, Lizzie felt her heart quicken and she braced herself.

"One can easily console oneself that working from before sunrise until after sunset is a way to escape the power of the devil to tempt one to sin!" she laughed, but it was not a friendly or teasing laugh. "You have to work that hard just to be able to live out here! At least if you wish to maintain a farm of any agreeable size."

"And how does that differ from Holmes County?" Lizzie asked, maintaining her composure despite wishing she could lash out at the hoity-toity Carol Ann Beachey.

"Many of our young men work outside of the home," she said. "They remain gentlemen farmers, working enough land after hours in order to maintain the family and way of life without invading it!"

"Invading it?" This time it was Lizzie's turn to laugh. "I hardly question God's will for us to work the land as a means of invading life rather than embracing it! One feels closer to God when being a steward of His earth than in doing anything else, in my humble opinion!"

"But surely you would agree that one must have time to relax and enjoy oneself," Frederick added to her surprise.

Lizzie turned from Carol Ann to look at Frederick, stunned to see that he was enjoying this conversation. The amused look in those dark eyes caused her to catch her breath. "I would," she said, ashamed that her words came out in a soft, breathless rush. "Enjoying oneself is a most agreeable reward after a long week of honoring God by tending to His animals and crops!"

She stood up, indicating that she was ending her participation in the conversation. To be truthful, she wanted to retire for the evening in order to get up early and, hopefully, be able to travel home with Jane.

"And what," he started to ask, standing up too in a manner of politeness, "would you consider being such an agreeable reward, Elizabeth?"

She looked at him, hesitating just long enough to gain the courage to say what was on her mind. With a touch of rebellion in her flashing eyes, she lifted her chin as she calmly replied, "Attending a singing, Frederick, and riding home with someone...even if that person is barely tolerable." She let her words sink in, too aware of the smugness on her face that she could not hide when she saw the incredulous look on his own. Then, with a softer expression, she turned to Charles. "I shall say good-night now," she smiled. "I suspect tomorrow shall be another busy day."

Without another word she turned and retired to the guest room that she was sharing with Jane, feeling privately pleased with herself for having proven her verbal superiority by matching wits with Frederick Detweiler and, she hoped, letting him see that first impressions are, often times, quite erroneous.

❦ Chapter Seven ❦

LIZZIE STARED AT her *maem* and three sisters as they stood in the doorway, broad smiles on their faces and their eyes roaming around the pristine kitchen at the Beachey farm. They seemed to drink in everything, from the freshly painted walls to the sparkling clean windows that Carol Ann had washed with vinegar and newspaper just a few days prior to the storm. She had made certain to comment on it several times the previous evening after supper, the setting sun casting light through the panes. She had not stopped boasting about it until Frederick finally commented on the streakless glass.

Now, *Maem* seemed overly impressed with everything, including the new sofa and recliner as well as the fancy farmer's table in the kitchen, where Carol Ann and Lizzie had just finished cleaning up the dishes from breakfast. *Maem* seemed hesitant to step into the house, not from impropriety but from being so awestruck with the grandeur. It was not usual for a home to be furnished in such a style. Items were handed down from family to family or acquired at auction or yard sales. However, no one could fault the Beacheys for having purchased new items since they had moved from Ohio, too far to bring along so many furnishings.

However, there was something else in *Maem*'s eyes that caused Lizzie to look away in embarrassment. It was clear that her *maem* was sizing up the house, her mind spinning at the thought that her own daughter, Jane, might be raising a family in that very home in the not-too-distant future. Unfortunately

Lizzie realized that Carol Ann and Frederick noticed it as well. The humiliation at her *maem*'s reaction, so transparent to the others, caused the color to pink up Lizzie's cheeks. To make matters worse, she caught Frederick watching her and knew that he had witnessed her discomfort.

"What a fine home you have started here, Charles!" *Maem* said, as she finally ventured into the room at his insistence. He gestured toward the sofa for the new arrivals to sit down and converse while Jane gathered her few things in preparation for her departure. With a broad smile and wide eyes, *Maem* stared up at him. "Such a shame that it was vacant for so long."

"*Maem*," Lizzie scowled. "You knew the family who had lived here..."

Her *maem* waved her fingers at Lizzie. "You know what I meant, Lizzie! That the Beacheys had moved away and their family has only just now started to return!" She laughed and shook her head, as if dismissing Lizzie as speaking nonsense. "It will be nice to have a *permanent* family in the neighborhood."

"Is it much different here in Leola than in Ohio?" Lydia asked, her eyes wide and her smile too big.

"You should host a picnic to meet people!" Catherine added, acting just as silly and ridiculous. Lizzie turned her head, the shame of her family almost too great to bear.

Maem's mouth dropped and she clapped her hands together, just once. "Or church service!" She looked at Charles, who had been following their banter back and forth as if watching a volleyball game, his head rotating between *Maem* on the sofa and the two girls still standing by the doorway. "Why, our very next service was to be hosted at the Millers, but he has fallen ill and is in the hospital. It would be such a relief if they didn't have to worry..." She let her voice trail off with the expectation that Charles would readily agree.

He did.

"We would be glad to do that, I'm sure!"

Carol Ann's eyes flickered and she caught her breath, but she said nothing in response to her brother's eager acceptance of such responsibility.

"We don't even have a dairy herd yet, so the service could be held in the barn with very little preparation!" he added.

Lydia and Catherine giggled and clutched at each other's hands in delight at the announcement. "And the singing afterward too?" Catherine asked.

Politely Charles joined them in their giddy laughter by nodding and agreeing to as much with a smile. "*Ja, ja,*" he said. "The singing too!"

At that moment Jane emerged from the downstairs bedroom. After greeting her *maem* and sisters, she glanced at Charles first before addressing Carol Ann. "I cannot say *danke* enough for all that you have done," she said to her friend. "I feel like I have been such a burden..."

Charles interrupted before his sister could respond. "Never a burden, Jane," he said, his eyes watching her every move. Lizzie read his expression, seeing a mixture of sorrow that Jane was leaving with a glow of infatuation that could not be denied.

"I fear the storm was more a burden than you," Carol Ann said lightly, but Lizzie flinched at the words. She glanced at Carol Ann and saw nothing but a genuine smile on her face as she said her parting words to Jane. Yet her words rang in Lizzie's ears, and when it came time to share her own gratitude with Carol Ann, Lizzie had the distinct feeling that her dislike for the Beachey woman was returned in equal volume.

Frederick and Charles walked outside with the Blank women. Charles helped Jane into the buggy so that she was situated next to *Maem*. With the other girls crowded in the back, Lizzie shook off the assistance to join her family in the buggy, declaring that she would walk home rather than risk giving her sister any discomfort.

"I shall be happy to take you, Lizzie," Charles quickly offered.

"*Nee*," she replied, smiling at his natural generosity and noting how quickly he had been willing to inconvenience himself while Frederick stood there, his hands behind his back and his lips pressed together without any indication of moving. "It's a *wunderbaar* day for walking, and I could surely use the exercise!"

By the time she arrived home, *Maem* was already fussing about Jane, who, despite her repeated claims of being right *gut*, found herself seated back in a recliner with her leg propped up and a blanket covering her legs. Mary was outside on the porch, playing with her harmonica while Lydia and Catherine peeled potatoes for the noon meal.

"Oh, stop that dreadful noise," *Maem* called out the window. "Why does that *dochder* of mine insist on playing that thing?" That question was asked to no one in particular, and therefore no one answered.

Lizzie shook her head as she walked inside the kitchen. "*Maem*, it's too hot for Jane to be bundled under a blanket!" She hurried over to her sister and quickly removed the earth-toned crocheted blanket. Folding it neatly, she set it on the edge of the sofa. "Honestly, *Maem*, she merely twisted her ankle, and she is quite fine."

The squeaking hinges of the outside screen door announced *Daed*'s appearance. He was carrying some papers and glanced around the room before sitting down at the table. He smiled at Jane and asked how she was feeling before he began to sort through the mail. Lizzie hurried over to the kitchen counter to help her younger sisters with the potatoes, rolling her eyes when she heard them whispering about George Wickey and how he had waved to them when they passed him on the road.

"When did you see George?" Lizzie asked. "I didn't pass him when I walked home."

Lydia giggled. "He was on the road walking toward the farmhouse. He's so handsome, ain't so?"

Catherine nodded and laughed with her sister.

Lizzie frowned. She hadn't seen George since the previous day, and certainly not in the morning. In fact, he had been absent quite frequently while she and Jane had been at the farm. "I cut through the field at the top of the hill," she said. "I must have missed him."

"Is he as kind as he looks?" Lydia asked, reaching out to clutch Lizzie's arm.

With a disapproving look, Lizzie freed herself from Lydia's grasp. "I certainly would not know," she retorted in a chiding tone.

"But you were there for almost three days!" Lydia cried out dramatically.

"To care for my sister, not fawn over and flirt with a man!"

"Does she have to do that?" *Maem* sighed, turning to *Daed* and gesturing toward Mary. "It's so unbecoming of a young woman. She'll never get married with a harmonica in her hand."

Daed tried not to laugh. "Unbecoming or not, I dare say that if a harmonica chases away a suitor, he was no suitor at all in the first place."

"Oh, help," *Maem* muttered, her typical response when she had nothing else to say.

"But here is some interesting news, my *fraa*." He waved a white piece of paper at her. It was a letter with small curvy handwriting, that much Lizzie could see from where she stood by the counter. "It seems we have a distant cousin coming to visit."

Maem froze where she stood, her hand in midair with a towel dangling from her fingertips. "A cousin?"

"*Ja*, that is what I said," *Daed* teased, once again drawing out the news at the expense of his wife's impatience.

"Do tell!" A new wave of excitement washed over *Maem*'s face, and she hurried to the table in eager expectation of the news to be shared. "Who, then, has written?"

"*Grossdawdi*'s second cousin or something like that," he replied, not interested in the genetic link. Lizzie watched the exchange with great curiosity as, yet again, a new relation came into their lives. "Wilmer Kaufman, bishop of his *g'may* and recently a widower."

"A widower?" she repeated with an odd sound to her voice.

"That's what I believe I said."

"And a bishop?"

Lizzie glanced over their heads to catch Jane's eyes. As usual, the two sisters shared a silent laugh between them. It was as if their *maem* were transparent, the way that her mind operated. With the wheels in motion, she would be hard to stop at matchmaking one of her *dochders* to this newly widowed bishop who was coming to visit.

"Where is his *g'may*?"

Daed squinted and looked at the letter again. "A town I have not heard of, much farther west of here and in Ohio, near the Dutch Valley. He's hired a driver so he can come meet his family in Leola, Pennsylvania," he said, exaggerating the word *family* with an undercurrent of sarcasm. "Clearly that means only one thing," he added, leveling his gaze at *Maem* and lifting an eyebrow.

"But why here?"

"We shall certainly find out next Monday when he arrives, shall we not?" *Daed* folded the letter and slid it back into the envelope, signaling that the discussion was over about this strange and distant relative, Wilmer Kaufman from a *g'may* so far away that he needed to hire a driver to come visit family that he had never before expressed any interest in meeting.

❧ Chapter Eight ❧

WHEN THE CAR pulled into the driveway Monday afternoon, *Maem* was busy cleaning the kitchen counter and directing Mary and Catherine to put away the broom, mop, and bucket. Lizzie watched her *maem* with an amused look on her face, wondering—or not—why she was so concerned about the house being perfectly immaculate. A visit from such a distant relative, even if he was a bishop, did not warrant such attention to cleanliness.

"He's here," *Maem* said, standing on her tippy-toes and craning her neck to watch the man emerge from the car.

"It's just a relative!" Lizzie pointed out. "And one who has never come before. I fail to see the importance of impressing him."

Maem glanced over her shoulder and scowled at her daughter but immediately dismissed her remark by returning her attention to the window.

Lydia hurried to *Maem*'s side and peered over her shoulder. Her reaction told Lizzie all she needed to know about this relative: he was not impressive to the eye. "Are you sure that we're related?" Lydia asked. "I see no resemblance at all!"

"Oh, hush," *Maem* scolded.

It took a few minutes for the men to settle and come into the house. By that time Lizzie was seated on the rocking chair near the open window in the back room, crocheting a doily, while Jane did the same but from the recliner. Her ankle was still sore and *Maem* had insisted that her daughter do nothing but heal until there was not a trace of a bruise or an ounce of pain. She also spent as much time as possible telling anyone who would listen about Jane's injury at the Beachey farm. Lizzie knew this as she was the one selected to accompany her *maem* to the dry goods and natural food stores the day before last.

Of course, *Maem* had also made certain to always mention that Charles Beachey had been over three times since Jane had returned to the farm. He spent a proper amount of time visiting, no more than twenty minutes. But he always came with a smile and something kind to say to everyone. Lydia and Catherine would watch from the stairwell as Charles sat beside Jane to converse during those visits.

The door to the mudroom opened and *Daed* walked in, an odd expression on his face that piqued Lizzie's curiosity. She set down her crocheting and waited for the appearance of this ever-so-important bishop. When he finally emerged from behind her *daed*, she all but dropped her crochet hook at his appearance. Indeed, Lydia had spoken the truth, for the man clearly bore no resemblance to the Blank family.

Instead of being lean and of medium build, he was short and round. His clothing was impeccable, not a speck of dust on his black coat that had hook and eyes for closures, not the typical black buttons worn by most Old Order Amish. Yet, with his rotund appearance, the jacket didn't quite shut over his protruding girth, and his white shirt stuck out from beneath it.

His straw hat looked as if he had just bought it from the store, yet it sat squat upon his head with his graying hair poking out from underneath the rim. There was a black ribbon around it, typical of the straw hats worn by Amish men, but, unlike others in the community, the ribbon also looked new: not one fray or tear in the ribbon could be seen by the bare eye.

And his beard...

"*Gut mariye,*" he said, with a nasal quality in his high-pitched voice, as if he had a cold despite it being summertime. Lizzie stared at the man's beard, which looked as though it had never been trimmed once since the day he started growing it. It was gray and frizzy, poking out in every direction. He glanced around the room, his eyes pausing on Jane for a moment, although the thickness of his round spectacles gave Lizzie reason to doubt he saw anything at all.

In a word, he looked ridiculous.

After the introductions were made, *Maem* invited the cousin to sit at the table while she bustled about the kitchen to pour him a hot tea, his preference over coffee. *Daed* did not join him but stood in the doorway, his arms crossed over his chest and that same odd expression on his face.

Lydia and Catherine ran back upstairs, giggling to themselves, which caused *Maem* to shoot them a disapproving glare.

"Why, *danke*," the bishop gushed as *Maem* set down the hot tea before him on the table. "And fresh cookies too?" Before *Maem* could answer, he had reached his hand out for not one but two cookies from the bowl sitting atop the table. Lizzie watched in amazement as he dipped the treats into his tea then ate them with great relish, claiming them to be the best peanut butter cookies that he had tasted in years. Then he reached for two more and dropped one into the teacup. With his bare fingers he fished out the drenched cookie and slurped the liquid from it.

Glancing at Jane, Lizzie suppressed her smile but saw that Jane too was trying hard not to show her amusement at this "cousin" of theirs. Almost simultaneously they picked up their crocheting and focused on it instead of Wilmer. Yet they listened with great curiosity as *Maem* continued to fluster around the cousin-bishop as if trying to impress this very peculiar man with odd manners and dubious social graces.

"Will you be staying for supper then?" *Maem* offered.

Daed responded for Wilmer. "He will be staying for a week and will attend church service with us."

Ah, Lizzie thought. Now she understood her *daed*'s odd expression. He was vexed by the idea of this man being underfoot for so many days. Surely he would not be of much help around the farm, for which Lizzie was grateful, as she could use outdoor work as an excuse to escape being trapped indoors with him for the next entire week.

"And what brings you to Leola, then?" *Maem* ventured to ask, a question which answer everyone in the room was beyond curious to hear.

Setting down his teacup onto the saucer, Wilmer used his fingers to dab at the corners of his mouth. "Christiana Bechler, the previous bishop's widow, had suggested that I should travel a bit and meet with other bishops." He tapped his finger on the edge of the saucer, a gesture that hinted far too much of a feeling of self-importance for Lizzie's taste. "During non-worship weeks it is encouraged to visit and learn what is occurring in other *g'mays*."

"Oh," *Maem* said breathlessly. "That's very wise!"

"Indeed," he replied as he lifted the teacup to his lips once again. "Christiana is quite a wise woman, as I may have already mentioned. And she was most supportive of me at the untimely death of my *fraa*."

A moment of silence fell upon the room, for it was not usual for the deceased to be spoken of, especially outside of the immediate family. Therefore, no one was certain of how to respond to the mention of his wife.

It was Jane who broke the silence by asking the bishop whether he expected to find similarities between his *g'may* and their own or if he were more interested in the differences between them. To her dismay, the bishop replied: "Indeed, my dear child, it is the latter that concerns me the most. As a man of God, I must admit to you that there have been certain rumors circulating in Berlin that disturbed me more than just a little, and I wanted to make sure of them for myself..."

"Rumors? What would these be about?" Lizzie interjected after another moment of silence, only deeper this time, that quickly befell the room.

"Well, for one," the bishop replied, "it is said that the young ladies around Leola are much more interested in their *rum-schpringe* than in adequately preparing themselves to take their baptism, to become good wives under the Lord our Savior, to raise large families, and to devote themselves to their *boppli* and their husbands as any good Christian wife would."

Lizzie stared at him incredulously, mouth gaping. Just as *Maem* brought her hand before her mouth to quickly but unsuccessfully repress an "Oh, my," Wilmer went on: "I have also heard of instances when these young ladies dress inappropriately, going as far as showing their thighs and knees while riding in the wagons, for the sole purpose of enticing young men to take them out. Several of our youth came back from visiting this area and tried to emulate the practice, you see."

"Whoever is spreading those rumors must be quite *ferhoodled*, then," *Daed* said, a slight smirk on his face, as a means to breaking the silence that, for a third time, had been brought about by Wilmer's remarks. "I have not witnessed these things, although I must say we are not happy that many of the young people crowd into the buggies, some of them sitting on the floor behind the front seat. It's dangerous, that practice. But showing flesh and enticing young men? Certainly not in *this* church district, of that I can assure you."

"I've heard about that," Wilmer fussed with his cup. "Dangerous to have them crowd so many into the buggies. However, with the rumors that our own youth claimed to have experienced the leg showing while spending time out here in Lancaster, I am most curious to try to find the source..."

"But before giving credence to those...rumors," *Daed* interrupted, obviously bored with such a conversation, "mayhaps it would be a right *gut* idea to discuss these matters with our own bishop, wouldn't you say, Wilmer?"

Wilmer lifted his head up from the bottom of his cup of tea that he had been staring at during the latter part of the exchange and glanced over at Jane. "Indeed, I was hoping," he slowly began, moving his eyes to stare directly at *Maem*, "to visit with your bishop later this afternoon. I know that my cousin has much work to do, but..." He paused as if for effect. "Mayhaps I could borrow your buggy and your elder daughter might ride along with me, to show me the way, *ja*?"

Maem glanced at *Daed* and, to Lizzie's horror, saw that *Daed* merely looked up at the ceiling. His eyes looked tired and strained. It was clear that there was more to this visit than just social niceties, and Lizzie was beginning to understand the core purpose had nothing to do with rumors, *rumschpringe*, or ruination of reputation.

"I...I would certainly agree to such an escort," *Maem* started slowly. "However, I do believe her special friend will be visiting this afternoon, as he always does."

Lizzie looked at Jane, who flushed at the mention of a "special friend" while looking relieved at the same time.

"However," *Maem* suddenly burst out, as if in a moment of clarity, "our second eldest *dochder*, Lizzie, would be happy to accompany you...to show you the way."

"*Maem*!" Lizzie hissed between clenched teeth. The thought of having to spend any time with her father's strange cousin horrified her. "You know that I help *Daed* with the chores."

Her *maem* waved her hand at Lizzie dismissively. "Now, *dochder*, it will be right *gut* for you to visit with the bishop and his family. And Wilmer will appreciate your lively company, for sure and certain."

Two hours later Lizzie found herself seated on a hard bench at the bishop's house, nursing a glass of weak lemonade that had far too much sugar and not enough lemon. The buggy ride to the bishop's home had taken only fifteen minutes from the Blanks' farm, but it had felt like an eternity to Lizzie. During that time Wilmer had cleared his throat often and spoke in stilted tones, telling her about where he lived and the state of the farm. It was quite far away from the Blank residence and in a town she had never heard of. He also had spoken at great length about his *g'may*. Rarely did he ask her a question or an opinion. When the buggy had finally pulled into the bishop's driveway, Lizzie said a silent prayer to God, thanking Him for a disruption to Wilmer's lengthy monologue.

"I'm certain things have seemed quite the whirlwind since you were chosen to be bishop of your *g'may*," the bishop's wife said as she set down a plate of homemade bread for the guests in the center of the table. "Why, I do remember when our lives changed! It came as such a surprise to us when my husband drew the lot to become bishop! For you too, I reckon, *ja*?"

"Most certainly," Wilmer said. "You see, I was quite close with Bishop Bechler. In fact, his *fraa* has been most supportive of my taking over the leadership of the *g'may*. While the church is always run by the men, of course," he continued with a strong lifting of his chin, "she is quite a persuasive woman who knows Scripture almost as well as I do! She supports the church and even counsels the other women when they are in need. I could not ask for a stronger matriarch in our district."

"Do you reside near her farm, then?"

Wilmer seemed pleased with the direction of the discussion. "*Ja*, indeed!" He smiled too broadly. "My farmette is directly across the street from their farm. She was quite instrumental in assisting me during my own *fraa*'s passing."

Lizzie fought hard against rolling her eyes, despite being curious about something he had said. If Wilmer lived on a small farm, as he had just admitted, she had to wonder from whence came his income. Living on a farmette would not bring in enough money to support him and a family, that was for sure and certain.

"A hardship, indeed," the bishop's wife replied, *tsk-tsking* and shaking her head.

"In fact," Wilmer continued, addressing both the bishop, who had just joined them, and his wife, "it was Christiana Bechler who encouraged me to come to Leola. She has a nephew that knows of the area, and when she learned that I had family here, she was most insistent on my travels." He glanced at the bishop's *fraa*. "I was especially impressed at her encouragement since I do work on her farm to help her and supplement my own farmette's income. She is most appreciative too. She is oft to invite me with my *kinner* for Sunday supper at the Bechler farm. Christiana Bechler likes to have people visit, especially since her husband passed. You see, she lives alone, except for her husband's young niece, Anna, a wisp of a young girl but certainly agreeable enough. She is quite helpful with organizing social functions for the youth." He said the last part of the statement with a lowered voice.

Lizzie was thankful that no one seemed to take notice of her presence as the two bishops began to converse more about Ohio and the differences between the two *g'mays*. She held no interest for either, bored with listening to compliment after compliment being paid to this Christiana Bechler or hearing the two bishops discuss religious philosophy. Instead she concentrated on her own thoughts, particularly the irony of so many Amish people from Ohio suddenly descending upon their small town in Lancaster County. *A small world, indeed*, she thought with an inward sigh born out of boredom.

On the buggy ride back to the Blank farm Lizzie sat as far apart from Wilmer as possible. With the doors to the buggy open, she was able to lean a bit out of the doorway, professing to be hot when he inquired about her odd position. Her answer seemed to satisfy him, for he asked no further questions.

"It is most kind of the Beachey family to host the service this weekend," he stated, breaking the silence, much to Lizzie's dismay. "With the other family suffering illness, it would truly be a hardship to have to prepare for such a great day. I am most impressed with that Charles Beachey showing such generosity."

She didn't really want to respond, knowing that to do so would only encourage more conversation. However, he continued to glance at her as if expecting a reply. When the silence became so uncomfortable that even she could not stand it, Lizzie responded with a simple, "Indeed he has shown that, *ja*."

"And I'm quite honored that your bishop has asked me to give a sermon," he continued, pride apparent in his voice, which took her by surprise. It was not unusual for visiting ministers or bishops to give a sermon. Yet Wilmer looked especially pleased with this invitation.

Again, she knew that he was waiting for a response, but she was uncertain what to say. Silently she willed the horse to walk faster, but Wilmer was holding the horse back, intentionally taking longer to get home. "I am certain the *g'may* will be agreeable to your sermon," she finally said. "It will be a nice change to hear someone new preach."

Immediately she knew that those were the wrong words, for Wilmer beamed, mistakenly interpreting her comments for a compliment.

Another buggy approached, and Lizzie stared out the open door, watching as it neared. Being that she sat on the left side of the buggy seat, it was easier for her to see passing cars and buggies...and a welcome distraction. However, as the two buggies were about to pass, she was horrified to see Frederick Detweiler at the reins, his piercing eyes staring at her. Wilmer lifted his hand in a friendly wave and Lizzie looked away, embarrassed to have been seen with Wilmer and hoping against hope that Frederick did not think she was partial to this strange, distant cousin of hers. It wasn't that she cared what Frederick Detweiler thought of her. No, that was not it. She merely did not want any speculation from anyone about her private life.

Wilmer remained oblivious to her discomfort as he returned his attention to the road. "I must say that man looked like the nephew of Christiana Bechler from the Dutch Valley in Ohio!"

Lizzie frowned and, for the first time, turned to face Wilmer. "You know Frederick Detweiler, then?"

He seemed excited. "Oh, *ja*! Indeed!" Then he paused.

"Rather, I know *of* him, I should say. He is the nephew of the former bishop. But he resides within a neighboring *g'may*. Bishop Bechler's *fraa* is Frederick's *aendi* and was quite instrumental in my being nominated to become a preaching member of the *g'may*. When her husband passed, I received the lot to take his place." He paused and sighed as if remembering Bishop Bechler with great admiration. "Mighty shoes to walk behind!"

Curiosity got the better of her, and she heard herself ask, "So how do you know of Frederick?"

"Oh, everyone knows of Frederick!" He laughed, a hollow sound that escaped his lips. She cringed at the news and was glad to see her parents' farm appear down the road. "He's quite the well-respected man in the Dutch Valley! Has helped many a young Amish man by giving them work on his farm, teaching them agriculture and enabling crop sharing. Christiana speaks quite highly of him and has hopes that he shall marry her husband's niece, Anna."

"Is that so?" Lizzie murmured disinterestedly, hiding her satisfaction. If this Christiana Bechler wanted Frederick to marry her niece, that might explain why Frederick so studiously ignored Carol Ann. Frederick certainly did not look like the type of man who would encourage the attention of one woman if it were expected that he should marry another. After all, no honorable Amish man would do such a thing, and Frederick appeared to take great pride in appearing to be a most proper Amish man. Of course, Lizzie was still quite certain that Carol Ann might have fancied such a union with Frederick and, therefore, might not be as honorable as Frederick.

When Lizzie did not respond further to his piece of news, Wilmer fell silent. Lizzie turned her face to look out the window once again, more than relieved when Wilmer no longer forced a conversation on the rest of the way back to her parents' farm.

❧ Chapter Nine ❧

LYDIA STOOD IMPATIENTLY in the middle of the road, staring back at her sisters who were lagging behind her. Jane and Lizzie were the farthest behind, talking to each other as they walked, while Catherine and Mary quickly caught up with Lydia. The sun was overhead and Lydia's cheeks were flushed. Beads of sweat formed on all of the girls' foreheads.

"I can't believe *Daed* wouldn't let us use a buggy!" Lydia complained when Catherine was near enough to hear. "It's such a bother to walk so far!"

Jane laughed. "Oh, Lydia! It's a beautiful day."

"It's hot!" she whined, fanning herself with her hand. The gesture was overexaggerated, and it highlighted the fifteen-year-old girl's tendency for preferring public drama to inner reflection, despite the unattractive nature of calling attention to oneself by complaining. "I'm sweating."

Lizzie teasingly knocked her youngest sister with her shoulder as she passed her. "It's hot at home too. So what's the difference?"

Lydia rolled her eyes and moved closer to Catherine, her special sister and one with whom she shared more in common. It was clear that Jane would not give her any compassion for her plight, especially since all five of the sisters were experiencing it at the same time. So, instead of wasting her words of unhappiness on Jane, Lydia took comfort by sharing them with Catherine.

Despite her own tendency to be the first to reprimand Lydia

for complaining or other inappropriate behavior, Lizzie secretly agreed with her youngest sister but knew better than to voice such an opinion. To do so would set Lydia off on a tirade of complaints, presuming she had an active audience and a partner in disagreeing with their parents' not permitting them the use of their horse and buggy. There had been too many complaints of young people piling into buggies, and as a result, one or two would hang out of the side. Besides the fact that this was quite a dangerous practice, the fact that the youth were still doing it, despite the reprimand of the bishop, was something that infuriated both church and parents alike.

So the girls had put on their plastic clogs and begun the long trek toward town, knowing that the walk would take at least an hour, but they wanted to look for new yarns and fabrics at the dry goods store on the outskirts of Intercourse. As usual, Jane never complained and seemed quite happy with the long walk. Her ankle had long since healed, and her eyes seemed distant and far away.

Lizzie was certain that she knew why.

Once again Charles had stopped by to check on Jane the previous day. He had also whispered to her that he wanted to take her home from the singing Sunday evening, even though it was to be held at his farm. Despite the forwardness of his request—for most young men asked the girl of interest while they were at the singing, not beforehand—Jane had shyly nodded her head in agreement. When she confided this to Lizzie later that evening, both girls had giggled and hugged each other.

"Why, you can be sure he's going to ask you for November!" Lizzie had whispered so as not to disturb the other girls who were sleeping. Most marriages took place in late October and November, well after the autumn harvest. "If he's asking you to ride home with him beforehand, that means he's considering himself your beau!"

Jane had blushed and turned her head away but not soon enough for Lizzie not to notice the smile on her sister's face.

That was how some courtships went. Lizzie envied Jane for the ease with which she befriended others and caught the attention of so many Amish men. Yet Lizzie also knew that this interest in Charles was different. Jane was not just being friendly and kind. Her heart was involved, and that made all of the difference in the world.

"Sure is a hot day for walking," a voice called out from behind them.

Lizzie snapped out of her own thoughts and looked up, surprised to see George driving an open wagon behind them, his horse just about to pass the group of walking women. He slowed the horse down and gestured to the open bed in the back. "Climb in," he offered, a broad smile on his face. "Let me take you to where you need to be."

Without a moment's hesitation Lydia jumped into the back of the wagon with Catherine close behind. "Oh, you are right kind," Lydia gushed, brazenly resting her hand on George's arm. "I was just saying how hot it is, and I was starting to regret our trip to the store! It's just too hot to walk! And then you just seemed to read our minds and stopped to offer us a ride. I can't thank you enough."

Ignoring Lydia's open flirtation with the older man, for certainly he was in his early twenties, Lizzie climbed into the wagon. With Jane, they positioned themselves in the back, waiting patiently for Mary to climb in and settle beside them.

"Which store are you headed toward?" George asked, slapping the reins on the horse's back and clicking his tongue to get the mare moving.

"The dry goods store," Lizzie answered, gesturing with her hand in the direction that they were headed. "Just down a spell on the right lane after the turn in the road."

He nodded. "Sounds *gut*. Along the way I'm headed too!"

Sarah Price

George was most different from Charles, yet Lizzie could see the family resemblance. With bright eyes and a fast smile he was just as charming as his older cousin. Yet there was also something mysterious about him. Lizzie couldn't put her finger on it but found herself wanting to find out. What exactly was behind those dazzling blue eyes?

During the short ride, for the girls had walked almost halfway there by the time George had happened upon them, he chatted with everyone about the differences between Ohio and Pennsylvania and how much he was enjoying himself. He commented on the landscapes being so different, with Leola being much flatter and spread out than where he lived in the Dutch Valley. He also laughed at a buggy that passed by, commenting that the gray-topped buggies of Lancaster County looked very fancy compared to the all-black buggies that were used in Holmes County by the Amish. He even mentioned that some church districts in Ohio refused to use the government-mandated orange reflective triangle on the back of their buggies. "But those are the most conservative districts, like the Swartzentruber Amish," he explained. "They use reflective tape instead."

Lydia and Catherine hung on his every word and giggled far too much for Lizzie's liking, but she was hesitant to say anything to them for fear of an unbecoming scene.

"What are you working on at the farm?" Jane inquired.

"The cows arrive next week," he said, a broad smile lighting up his face. "It will be right *gut* to start a regular morning routine again."

His remark struck Lizzie, for she had noticed that George had not been around during the two mornings she had stayed at the Beachey farm. She had thought she had heard him returning home in the early morning hours. Yet she wondered now if she had been mistaken. Perhaps he had truly been up so early and working already, eager to get started rather than sleep late from running around with other unbaptized young men.

When no one else responded to his comment about the cows, he continued speaking. "Charles sent me to pick up some more wire and a few boards for the back pasture. Apparently it was broken, so we are fixing it today."

This time, Lizzie frowned. Hadn't it been Frederick who had discovered the broken fencing last week? Why hadn't they fixed it until now? She could distinctly remember hearing Charles volunteer George to pick up the wire and boards once the roads were clear. Yet here it was, almost two weeks later, and just now they were getting the supplies? If that had been her own *daed*, that fence would have been fixed the next day. It was unlike an Amish farmer to postpone fixing something once it was discovered broken.

She was still pondering this mystery when he pulled into the parking lot of the dry goods store. To her further surprise Lizzie watched as George hitched the horse to the post and hurried to help the women jump down from the back of the wagon: a true gentleman. Then, without a word, he accompanied them into the store, opening the door for the five sisters and stepping inside behind them.

With his hands behind his back, he proceeded to walk alongside Lizzie. She didn't say anything to him, more curious about his behavior than anything else. Despite Lydia's and Catherine's best attempts to capture George's attention, he seemed to focus more on monitoring what Lizzie was doing and commenting on the fabrics she was selecting.

"I always liked a pretty blue," he said, pausing at the pale blue fabric on the table. He ran his hand over the material, and Lizzie noticed that his hands were small and dainty, quite unusual for a farmer.

"That blue is for wedding dresses," Lizzie pointed out pragmatically. "It's not very practical for day-to-day wear since it's

97

so light. Your Ohio women wear light blue for the weddings, *ja?*"

He glanced away and withdrew his hand. "I reckon you're right," he said and moved farther down the aisle. "But I bet you'd look right nice in that blue," he added over his shoulder, his voice low so that no one else could hear.

His words gave her a moment's pause as she lingered in front of the various fabrics. Had George Wickey been flirting with her? She hadn't truly thought of him in such a manner. However, she realized that the idea didn't seem too distasteful. She would have to pay closer attention to learn more about his character before she made up her mind, she realized, for what little she knew seemed confusing and contradictory. It was true that she did not have a lot of exposure to men, pre-ferring to enhance her mind rather than her social standing among her peers. Yet George was different, and after wit-nessing Frederick's harsh treatment of him, she was inclined to see if she could discern for herself what manner of man he was.

After the sisters had paid for their purchases, George offered to take them home if they did not mind stopping by the farm supply store along the way. Being that it was just a mile out of the way, it only made *gut* sense to ride along with him, for both the company and the convenience. It was still hot out, and no one wanted to walk back to the farm in such heat, especially after having been afforded the comfort of a ride.

This time Lydia and Catherine sat toward the back of the wagon, discussing their purchases at the dry goods store, while Mary gazed into the sky during the ride. At one point Mary reached into her pocket for the harmonica and fiddled with it, her fingers stroking the sides, but for fear of reprimand, she did not venture to play it. Despite her love of music, it was most unbecoming for a young woman to play, at least in public.

For a long moment Lizzie watched them, amazed at how different her sisters were. The silliness of the younger two seemed balanced by the common sense and steadiness of herself and Jane, while Mary floated somewhere between the two ends of the spectrum. It always made her curious to think of how the extremes in their personalities had formed, especially as they had the same parents and the same upbringing. It was a most peculiar question that she had never been able to answer.

A buggy was passing by, and by way of habit, Lizzie glanced to see who was driving it while lifting her hand to wave in greeting. To her surprise, she recognized Frederick as the driver, but he must not have noticed them for he merely stared straight ahead, not once even glancing in their direction. *Peculiar personalities indeed*, she thought, wondering how on earth Charles Beachey found anything in common with that man.

"Sure is hot for June, *ja*?"

George's words interrupted her train of thought, and she looked at him. She and Jane were seated beside him rather than in the back of the wagon. "June tends to get hotter as it approaches July, *ja*," she responded. "What is Ohio like?"

"*Vell*," he began, holding the reins in one hand and wiping the sweat from his brow with the back of the other, "hot, but not quite like this, I reckon. It's definitely more humid here, that's for certain."

"It was nice of you and Frederick to accompany Charles to help him settle into Pennsylvania," Lizzie said, knowing that she was opening a doorway to get some of the answers to the questions that were lingering in her mind without looking too curious.

George smiled. "It was natural for me, I suppose," he started. "You see, I was practically raised by Jacob Beachey."

Now this was news! Even Jane turned her head to listen to the conversation. Lizzie shook her head and encouraged him to continue with his story by saying, "I had not known that."

"*Ja*," George affirmed. "I was an only child, the firstborn, and my parents were killed in a buggy accident when I was just a small boy. Naturally, my *onkel* raised me, so Charles and I are more like brothers than cousins."

At his news Jane gasped. "I'm so sorry," she whispered, ever the tenderhearted one of the sisters. "I hadn't heard that your parents were deceased." Even Lizzie felt a pain in her chest at the thought of a young boy being left parentless at such a tender age.

"*Danke,*" he replied politely. "It was Jacob's hope that I would help Charles and settle down out here, mayhaps on the Beachey farm in the *grossdawdihaus* at some point until I could establish my own farm. I was to have one in Ohio, you see. A property left to me by my parents. It was just land but adjacent to my *onkel*'s. They had planned to build their own buildings on it when they had more children. When they died, it became mine. Legally, anyway. While I was too young to farm at that age, I had intended to do the very same thing when I became a man and had the resources to do so." There was a momentary pause, and he sighed. "But I fear that it was not meant to be."

"Why ever not?"

He shrugged and looked forward, his eyes on the road. "Frederick managed to buy the property away from me as it abutted his own."

Both women caught their breath, and Jane laid her hand on Lizzie's arm, a warning to tread cautiously with this conversation. Lizzie had been more than vocal at home about what she thought of Frederick, with his proud demeanor and disapproving looks. Yet Lizzie was not about to let the conversation stop without learning more.

"That does not sound like a very kind thing to do," Lizzie started, trying to pick and choose her words carefully. "Certainly there is more to the story than that."

George shook his head. "*Nee,*" he countered. "Not much, I'm afraid. You see, his family worked the property while I was too young. When Frederick's father died, he took over farming the land. Naturally." No one could argue with that point. Still, Lizzie held her breath to hear what George was holding back from them. "When I was to come of age and could begin working the farm, he refused to relinquish the land to me. Claims he had been paying the back taxes for years and therefore it was no longer mine."

All five sisters were listening now, Lydia and Catherine with wide eyes and their mouths gaping open in complete disbelief.

"It's not in our nature to argue or sue," George sighed, referring to the Amish. "So it was best that I'd search for a new farm. When I heard that Charles was coming to take over the old Beachey farm here in Pennsylvania, I thought it would be a *gut* opportunity to start fresh in a new place."

Lizzie frowned. "Surely the bishop could have gotten involved!" she declared.

Another casual shrug. "It is not for me to disrupt the *g'may*," he said softly. "Old Bishop Bechler did not like strife among his church members."

"That's just downright horrid!" Lydia exclaimed. She crossed her arms across her chest. "No wonder he looks so miserable all of the time! It's a wonder he can live with himself, such a selfish and heartless man!"

Jane shot her a glance, but Lizzie did not. She stared straight ahead, trying to digest the words that George had just spoken. If true, Frederick Detweiler was certainly a very proud man with more focus on personal elevation than spiritual! It also explained a lot, especially the very obvious bitterness between the two men. However, she couldn't help but wonder why Jacob Beachey would have entrusted the care of his son, daughter, and nephew to such an awful man as Frederick Detweiler!

❧ *Chapter Ten* ❧

THE LONG ROW of gray-topped buggies greeted the Blank family as they walked down the lane. Since the storm, Charles had hired some *Englischers* to pave the driveway so that there were no longer dips and ditches or risk of pockets of water. Since none of the Blanks had been at the Beachey farm since after the storm, it was the first they had seen the fresh-topped macadam. With the buggies along the side, it was a grand entrance to the farm with freshly painted barn, stable, and house. Impressive to say the least, Lizzie thought with a moment of tender feeling toward her elder sister. One day Jane might raise her *kinner* on this well-maintained property and with a truly godly man as Charles Beachey.

Because of the heat the service was to be held in the empty room above the stable. That too had been freshly painted. With the windows open on three of the walls, there was enough of a breeze to keep the room light and airy, although Lizzie suspected that it would become warm after everyone arrived and was seated. As it was now, the women were inside, approaching Carol Ann Beachey and offering their assistance with all the preparations for after the service. Lizzie noticed that her own *maem* lingered far too long in the receiving line, gushing to Carol Ann about how wonderful it was that the Beacheys had offered to host the service on such short notice.

Carol Ann merely smiled, her eyes glancing over *Maem*'s shoulder at the next person in line that waited to greet her with a handshake and simple kiss on the lips. Lizzie clenched her teeth, dreading having to greet Carol Ann in a similar fashion.

She had observed on far too many occasions that Carol Ann seemed to look with disdain not just upon the Blank family but also on the entire *g'may*. Today was no different. While she was polite and proper, there was no air of either cordiality or interest emanating from Carol Ann Beachey.

When it was Lizzie's turn to greet Carol Ann, she extended her hand and, with some satisfaction, noticed that Carol Ann barely held it as they greeted each other. Instead of planting the familiar kiss on Carol Ann's lips, Lizzie stopped short and pulled back, a gesture noticed by no one but the intended recipient. Lizzie merely lifted an eyebrow and continued down the line, not one word exchanged between them. If anyone noticed besides the two women, nothing was said.

During the second hymn Lizzie held the *Ausbund* in her hands, closed. She had no need to reference the chunky black hymnal, for she was well aware of the words to the *Loblieb*. It would take almost thirty minutes to sing the verses, and this gave her time to peek around at the members of the *g'may* as well as to reflect on her own thoughts. The words flowed from her lips without the need of much consideration.

Since the service was being held at the Beacheys' farm, Charles and Frederick sat in the first row of men. Lizzie took a moment to study both men, too aware of how different they seemed. Charles was singing with sparkling eyes, enjoying the song and pleased with the attendance at his first church service in Leola, Pennsylvania. In complete contrast Frederick was quite serious singing the *Loblieb*, his deep baritone voice resonating in the gathering room. Not once did his eyes falter from the bishop as he sang. Despite not caring for him, Lizzie had to admit that he appeared to be a very godly, if not also a very intense, man.

And then Wilmer stood up to give the second sermon, the longer of the two sermons at the church service. Lizzie sat between Jane and Charlotte, noticing that both women stiffened when he stood up and took his spot in the middle of the room. With his wiry gray beard and deep wrinkles in his brow, he looked much older than Lizzie knew he was. But it was his black vest that caught her attention. She had to hold back her laughter. In a way she felt sorry for him, but only because he was too proud to realize that he had long ago outgrown the vest and two of the hooks had popped open, exposing his white shirt beneath it.

As he began to preach, his voice cracked, and Lizzie could tell that he was trying to hide the fact that he was nervous. Beads of sweat began to break out on his forehead as he paced, his words being spoken in a singsong-like manner with clipped endings to each sentence. She realized that she was listening to his every word, not because his sermon was interesting, for that was clearly not the case. Indeed, she wasn't even certain what he was talking about...something about how good Christians communicate with each other. No, she was listening to how he spoke, with a delivery that lacked confidence. Several times he paused to clear his throat, looking around nervously. At last Frederick stood and left the meeting room only to return a moment later with a glass of water for the preacher.

The gesture surprised Lizzie.

Her eyes trailed from Wilmer back to Frederick as he resumed his place next to Charles. Once again Frederick maintained a stoic look as he watched the preacher, listening to his every word, despite the lack of structure to the sermon and the odd speech pattern. Lizzie wondered if this was how Ohio Amish preached or if it was only unique to Wilmer. If it was typical, Frederick would be familiar with such a preaching style. However, if it was unique, he was being a most polite and attentive listener.

That was when she realized that, once again, George was not in attendance.

Charlotte pinched her leg, and Lizzie glanced over, realizing that Wilmer's sermon had ended and it was time to pray. The congregation stood up and each person turned around, before kneeling down to pray against the bench or chair upon which they had just been seated. Lizzie followed suit, quickly dropping to her knees and placing her forehead on her clasped hands. As she knelt with her hands on the hard wooden bench, she glanced at the crossed feet of the young Amish girl that was praying on the bench located directly behind hers. She was a younger girl and her black boots were scuffed on the heel. She had a nervous tick to her foot and kept wiggling it. Lizzie quickly shut her eyes and prayed, asking God to help her be a better Christian and to honor His laws. She prayed for the strength and wisdom to both recognize and avoid sin. She prayed that He would bless her labors and help her maintain a joyful spirit in all that she was instructed to do. Finally she prayed that God would continue to guide her against being prideful, for the Bible often spoke that no sin was ever to be punished more severely than pride.

When the silent prayer was over and she was seated again for the final hymn, she felt her cheeks flush from the heat of the room. Because of the heat, summer services were often harder and seemed longer than the services held during other seasons. She wished that she could fan herself but knew that it would be inappropriate. And that was the moment she sensed that he was looking at her.

She felt his eyes on her, an intensity in his gaze, when she glanced around the room and found Frederick watching her. Until this moment she had not seen him look anywhere except at the preacher or the *Ausbund* in his hands (and even that, not quite often).

Following the service, Lizzie busied herself helping the women prepare for the fellowship meal. While most of the food was ready, being mostly cold cuts, canned food, bread, and jams, the younger women scurried about, carrying the plates to the long tables that were made from the wooden benches used for the service, while the older women quickly set the two tables. Men would sit on one side while women sat on the other.

As was tradition in their *g'may*, the younger women over the age of sixteen served the men while the married women serviced those seated at the women's side. Lizzie paid no attention to the men as she placed plates of food before them. They were talking about the weather and their plans for the upcoming week. With such delightful weather the hay had grown faster than usual and most farmers had bumper crops, so haying and baling seemed on top of most to-do lists for the upcoming week.

"Might I have some more water?"

Lizzie almost didn't hear the request, the voice being so soft. Yet the tugging at her skirt caught her attention at once. She turned, surprised that someone would be so brazen to single her out in order to request more water. Usually the men waited until the girls walked around the table with a pitcher to refill cups.

"Excuse me?" she asked as she turned, too aware that her voice was louder than intended.

It was Wilmer, holding up his cup, which she had filled only moments before his request. They hadn't even said the pre-meal prayer yet. But sure enough, his cup was empty. Clearly he was sending a signal to her and a very public one at that. Such requests were usually saved for courting couples.

Color flooded her cheeks, and she tried not to look around as she took his cup and hastily backed away from the table, embarrassed that too many eyes were watching her. She would be the talk of many on the Amish grapevine, a thought that horrified her for sure and certain.

And then it happened. She tripped on an *Ausbund* that had not been properly packaged in the crate set aside for the next church service in two weeks. It was always the job of the young boys to collect and stow the books in a wooden crate. After the fellowship meal the tables would be dismantled and stowed in a long boxlike wagon with the crate of hymnals before being taken to the farm that would host the next service in two weeks. Obviously one of the boys had overlooked a lone *Ausbund*, which was lying on the floor. Not expecting to step on something, Lizzie felt her ankle twist and she began to fall, the cup flying out of her hand and a gasp escaping her throat.

She felt his arms grab her before she realized that her fall had been stopped in midair. Everything had happened so fast that Lizzie took a second or two to gather her bearings. The room was silent, all eyes now watching as Frederick held onto Lizzie, his tall figure looming over her. His hold lingered on her, keeping her steady as she collected her balance.

"*Danke*," she whispered, avoiding his dark eyes.

"*Gown shanner*," Frederick responded. Glancing around the room, he caught Carol Ann watching and motioned toward Wilmer. "Mayhaps you might refill his water, *ja*?" Then, releasing Lizzie, he leaned down and said to her in a soft voice so that no one else could hear, "Take a moment outside, then. Collect yourself."

Without arguing, Lizzie left the large room and escaped outside through the side door. Leaning against it, she willed her heart to stop beating so rapidly. While infuriated at Wilmer's presumptuous and overly public request, Lizzie found herself disturbed more by having been saved from a fall by none other than Frederick Detweiler. The embarrassment was too much to handle, as were the conflicting emotions that she was feeling.

How could Frederick Detweiler be such a cold and unemotional man one moment yet attentive and caring the next? Clearly he had been watching her, and clearly he had directed her outside in order to save her the embarrassment caused, not by the near fall, but by Wilmer! Yet she couldn't imagine why he would do such a thing. She felt as though she knew his character, from the moment they had first met to his rude insult at the singing to his lack of conversation at the Beachey farm. Still there were moments when something else shimmered through the man's exterior...a softness that she couldn't quite fathom.

"Are you hiding?"

Lizzie turned around and smiled at Charlotte. "Mayhaps," she replied, a teasing tone on her face. "Did you see that Wilmer Kaufman?"

Charlotte laughed. "Oh, *ja, ja*! We all saw Wilmer Kaufman, indeed! However, it was the look on his face when Carol Ann brought him fresh water that we saw!"

Joining her friend in laughing, Lizzie reached for Charlotte's hand. "How appropriate for both! Yet I wonder who was more horrified, Wilmer or Carol Ann!"

For the rest of the fellowship hour Lizzie steered clear of the tables. Instead she busied herself with washing plates and cups as the table was cleared for the second sitting. Her own appetite was gone, so she preferred not to eat. She chose, instead, to linger near the older women, listening to their early afternoon banter, most consisting of speculation about who might be getting married in the upcoming season, a topic of increasing preoccupation to the women in the *g'may*.

"Lydia Esh has an awful lot of celery growing in her garden," one woman remarked. "I suspect she plans to see two weddings in November!"

Maem was the next one to add a comment to the conversation. "I hadn't thought to plant extra celery," she offered, although Lizzie knew that this was not exactly true. There were plenty of celery plants in her *maem*'s garden, only tucked along the back rows so that anyone who passed by or visited would not be able to notice. The planting of celery, a staple at Amish wedding feasts, was traditionally a notice to the community that a *dochder* was destined for marriage in the upcoming wedding season. However, some families hid the plants in the back of the garden when they didn't want to draw attention to its presence, as it was often merely an indicator of wishful thinking rather than impeding nuptials. This year, however, *Maem* had reason to hope that the celery would be put to better use than just stuffing and soup throughout the winter months.

Maem continued, "But we fully expect that our *dochder* Jane will be given an offer!"

Several women raised an eyebrow and looked at her. Only one leaned forward and whispered, "The Beachey boy?"

"Ach vell," *Maem* said, her eyes searching the ceiling as she tried to elude the question in a falsely demure fashion. "I wouldn't want to whisper a name, not until it is official, of course," she remarked. But the gleam in her eye spoke otherwise, and everyone nodded their heads, glancing over at Charles Beachey who was standing with several of the other young men just outside of the door in the fresh air.

Lizzie shook her head and walked away from the group of women, conscious that her *maem* should not be speaking of such things. It was indeed too soon and could raise hopes that risked being dashed to the ground; it was like building castles in the air. After all, courtship among the Amish was a private matter. While many women liked to speculate and gossip, it was frowned upon by the bishop as well as the younger women who wanted to avoid any possible embarrassment from broken relationships.

Looking for Charlotte, Lizzie wandered outside. A small group of women were standing under the shade of a small tree outside of the Beachey house. Jane and Carol Ann were talking, standing a bit to the side of the group. For a moment Lizzie observed them, wondering why Carol Ann seemed so comfortable with Jane but uncomfortable with the other women. As she approached them, it became clear that Carol Ann was doing most of the talking while Jane was her attentive listener.

"I find the services here much more focused on practical rather than spiritual guidance," Carol Ann said, her tone quite condescending. "I didn't care for that sermon about communication one bit!"

Never one to complain, Jane did not respond. However, Lizzie felt compelled to make her presence known. "That's interesting, Carol Ann," she said lightly. "I thought Wilmer was the bishop in your very own *g'may*!"

"*Nee!*" she responded too quickly. "He is the bishop of Frederick's *aendi*'s *g'may*."

"Isn't that in Ohio?" Lizzie asked, straight-faced and with a perfectly even tone. "Or do the Ohio services differ so drastically from district to district?"

There was no chance for Carol Ann to respond to Lizzie's obviously sardonic question. They were interrupted as Lydia and Catherine came running over, laughing as they bumped into Lizzie. "*Maem* and *Daed* say it's time to leave," Catherine managed to state between giggles. "Asked to fetch you both."

For the rest of the afternoon the Blank family relaxed at home, *Daed* sitting in his recliner for a short nap while Wilmer read Scripture aloud from the family Bible. Since the church leaders did not permit crocheting and knitting on Sunday, the girls had no choice but to sit there and listen to Wilmer, his voice droning on and on as the afternoon heat began to feel more and more oppressive.

Lizzie's eyes felt heavy, and she found herself slipping into a light sleep as she sat next to Jane on the sofa. Mary played with her harmonica, spinning it on the table, for she could certainly not lift it to her lips in the house, especially on Sunday. Lydia and Catherine looked bored, seated on the opposite side of the table from Mary while *Maem* pretended to do some light work at the kitchen counter.

"Can we play a game of Scrabble, then?" Lydia sighed, her voice clearly indicating her high degree of boredom.

Wilmer looked up from the Bible, a scowl on his face as if waiting for *Maem* or *Daed* to reprimand her for interrupting him.

"That's a right *gut* idea!" Catherine chimed into the conversation. "Mary, will you play?"

Their desire for a fourth player rested on Jane or Lizzie, neither of whom wished to play. Still, the prospect of listening to Wilmer continue with his high-pitched singsong voice convinced Lizzie to take the bait, and she crossed the room to join her sisters.

Wilmer's mouth fell open. "Such games to play on a Sunday?"

Having been awoken by the renewed energy in the room, *Daed* scratched at his head and shook away the sleep. "Games played together are acceptable on the Lord's day," he confirmed and stood up. He stretched and glanced over at his daughters, who were sorting through the Scrabble pieces. "I fear it's time to milk the cows soon," he said, his eyes leveled at Lizzie. "Mayhaps one game, then you might join me, *ja*?"

It was shortly after seven when the five Blank daughters walked back to the Beachey farm. Despite not being sixteen yet, Lydia had insisted upon joining them, for the walk at least. She had promised her *maem* that she would turn around and walk back alone, but she wanted the fresh air (and to escape the house where Wilmer was still prattling on about the importance of Scripture, not games, on Sundays).

The air was cooling down after a fairly hot June day. With July just around the corner, the summer heat was to be expected. Several buggies passed the group of women as they walked, the driver and occupants waving hello in recognition of their friends. Occasionally a single Amish man would drive by in an open-top buggy and Lydia would giggle next to Catherine, knowing full well that the driver intended to ask a girl to ride home with him.

"You'll never get asked home if you continually giggle like a little schoolgirl," Lizzie reprimanded her.

"Good thing I have a few more weeks to practice!" Lydia replied, skipping down the road to further tease her older sister. "And I often see you walking home with the others. Maybe you should giggle more, sister Lizzie!"

"Lydia!" Jane gasped in defense of Lizzie. "You be kind!"

"Well, it's true!" Lydia said smartly, a defiant look in her eyes. "I intend to be asked to ride home with a boy on the night of my very first singing!"

"I'll be certain to have *Daed* ready with his buggy, then!" Lizzie snapped back, knowing that the sarcastic comment would only further infuriate her youngest and most foolish sister.

Later that evening Lizzie and Charlotte sat together on a bench, a plastic cup of meadow tea in their hands. With Charlotte working the vegetable stand at her parents' farm, it was hard to visit during the summer, despite the longer days and evenings. Only at the church services and the ensuing singings did the two young women have time to catch up.

For years they had been friends. Charlotte's *maem* had grown up with Lizzie's, and as a result their families often got together, more so when the *kinner* had been younger. Now that Charlotte's older siblings were married and with their own *boppli*, there was less time for visiting friends than family. Still, despite their age difference, Lizzie enjoyed Charlotte's company and considered her a special friend, almost as dear to her as Jane was. It had always baffled Lizzie why Charlotte had not already married. She came from a good family and had a reputation for being quite godly and modest as well as a hard worker.

Despite these facts, at almost twenty-five Charlotte had yet to court a young man and had few, if any, prospects on the horizon.

Sarah Price

"It's because she is so plain!" her *maem* had commented one day when Lizzie had mistakenly said something to that effect.

Lizzie had laughed. "We are *plain* people, *Maem*!"

"That's not what I meant, and you know it, Elizabeth," her *maem* had retorted. "She's plain to the eye and plain to the personality. Does nothing to make herself stand out whatsoever! And, besides the singings, one never sees her anywhere! She doesn't have a chance of being naught more than a *maedel* and burden to her siblings, mark my words!"

Horrified at her *maem*'s words, Lizzie had immediately shown her disapproval by leaving the room. Yet those words rang in her ears, and from time to time she caught herself wondering about her friend and how anyone could be prejudiced against such a kindhearted and faith-based woman!

Now, as they had time alone at last, Lizzie and Charlotte whispered and giggled softly over the latest news. Without prying eyes, Lizzie was able to tell Charlotte about their stay at the Beachey farm and how in love Charles seemed to be with Jane. Charlotte lifted her hand to her mouth, hiding her surprise but not the sparkle in her eye.

"She must encourage it, then!"

Lizzie was taken aback by Charlotte's words. "What do you mean by that, I wonder?"

"She's such a sweet and kind woman, Lizzie, for sure and certain," Charlotte whispered. "But Charles is quite sought after by the young women. In fact, I heard that Maddy Fisher has her eyes fixed on him!"

"Maddy Fisher!" Lizzie frowned and waved her hand. A local young woman who was older than Jane, but not as old as Charlotte, she had a reputation for desperately searching for any man who was still *leddich*. "She has her eyes fixed on several young men!"

"*Ja*, but she always gets asked home in a buggy," Charlotte pointed out. "She encourages the attention in order to learn more about their character."

"But we know about *his* character," Lizzie countered. She had seen enough of Charles to form a very strong impression. From what little she knew, there was nothing to question or doubt about that man. "He's an upright and fine man with his eyes on God more than girls! But he clearly has a tender spot in his heart for my sister. His character is, in a word, clearly unblemished."

"Mayhaps that is true, but does he truly know her character? Remember that he has only just moved here, ain't so?"

Lizzie was stunned by Charlotte's words and realized that, shocking as it might be, there was a point of reality underneath her friend's statement. After all, what did Charles really know of Jane's character? Jane was shy and quiet. The little amount of time they had spent at the Beachey farm had not been together but apart. Charles had been helping to clear the roads during the day and, in truth, had spent more time with Lizzie than Jane.

"Excuse me," a deep voice said from behind them, immediately disrupting Lizzie's thoughts.

Both Charlotte and Lizzie turned simultaneously in the direction of the voice, surprised to see a stoic and unsmiling Frederick Detweiler standing there, still wearing his Sunday suit. It was all black: the pants, the jacket, and a vest. Underneath the vest was a white shirt. Despite how warm it was, he did not look to be uncomfortable.

Before that moment Lizzie had not noticed him at the singing and had presumed that he, like George, had chosen not to attend. While she was surprised, and mildly disappointed, that George was absent, having somewhat enjoyed his company the other day when he had given them a ride both to and from the store, she felt the complete opposite about not having seen Frederick.

He nodded at Charlotte, but his eyes lingered on Lizzie. As always he looked far too serious and his dark eyes far too piercing. "I noticed that you did not have a ride here this evening," he said, his voice flat and emotionless.

"I did not," Lizzie replied, her cheeks flushing with the humiliation of his having pointed out that she had walked to the singing when so many other young women were driven by a young man, even if it was only a *bruder* or neighbor. While she normally would not have minded, the fact that it was Frederick pointing it out made the matter more demeaning on a personal level. His next words, however, changed everything.

"Then I shall waste no time in requesting that I might be allowed to take you home after the singing," he said, his eyes quickly looking over her shoulder. "If that is agreeable to you."

Without a moment's pause Lizzie heard herself reply, "It is. *Danke*." The words just popped out of her mouth, and she could scarce believe that she had said them. Frederick did not give her a chance to rescind. Instead he nodded again at both women and hurried away. Her eyes followed him as he walked not toward the men but out the door of the barn. Indeed, she realized, he was *not* attending the singing but had arrived merely to ask for her to ride home with him.

Stunned, Lizzie turned and stared at her friend. "Did I just agree to ride home from the singing with this Frederick Detweiler?"

Charlotte smiled and nodded her head. "I heard you myself, Lizzie."

"What on earth...?"

Leaning over, Charlotte whispered into her ear. "Mayhaps he has a crush on you after all."

"Or merely wishes to torture me some more with words about how tolerable I may or may not be!"

At this statement both women stared at each other, and then, whether from nerves or teasing, they started to softly laugh and reached out to clutch each other's hands in a gesture of close friendship.

True to his word, Frederick approached her toward the end of the singing. He stood beside her, his hands behind his back and his chin jutting out, just a touch, as he cleared his throat in his usual fashion and met her eyes. Without a word she excused herself from her friends and followed him outside of the barn and toward the buggies. She glanced at the sky, noticing that there was no moon, which left the blackness full of twinkling stars.

"It's a beautiful evening," she commented.

"Indeed."

"I prefer moonless nights," she continued, listening to the crickets chirping and the sound of the gravel beneath their feet. "The stars are so much more interesting to study, don't you think?"

He stopped before a buggy and slid open the door. Holding out his hand, he waited for her to take it and place her foot on the black round step-up to get into the buggy. Unlike Charles, Frederick had not brought his open-top buggy. Instead he had the traditional gray-topped closed buggy this evening. She was relieved when he left the door open so that a nice breeze would keep them cool.

The silence that followed felt awkward. To be fair, it took Frederick a moment to get the horse and buggy backed up before they could begin the short journey to the Blank farm. Yet when the silence remained, Lizzie frowned and spoke up. "I do believe it is your turn to begin a conversation, Frederick. I have already commented on the evening," she quipped.

"What is your pleasure?"

"I should think you would have something to say," she remarked. "After all, it was *you* who sought *me* out for the ride home."

The battery-operated headlights cast a soft reflecting glow

inside of the buggy. She thought she saw him smile, but it was too dark and shadowy to know for certain. He paused at the end of the lane, and rather than turn right toward her parents' farm, he turned left. She was about to comment on this when she became aware that he intended to take a long route home in order to spend more time with her, a realization that made her heart flutter in a moment of panic. What on earth was Frederick Detweiler up to?

"Speaking of rides, then," he began, "are you oft to accept rides when heading to the store?"

Ah, she thought. Now *this* was getting interesting. "By that question I presume you mean George." She paused and waited for a response. When none came forth, she presumed that she had guessed accurately. "I find it curious that you inquire about my accepting a ride home with George Wickey when I was walking with my sisters." She wanted to add that he did not inquire about having seen her riding in the buggy with Wilmer the day she had been forced to accompany him to the bishop's house, but her own self-preservation forbade her from even bringing up that embarrassing matter.

"It was just a question," he replied.

"A question, *ja*," she repeated. "I would have not thought you even noticed any of us, for when you saw us, you barely did more than nod in acknowledgment. One would think you were perfectly estranged from the man rather than sharing a home."

A long pause.

"And it seems an odd question since it appears that we shall be neighbors. And from how busy George Wickey has been, rarely at home and socializing outside of the youth groups, it seems that he is doing quite well at making new friends, and that's something to be admired, *ja*?"

The twitch by his eye told Lizzie to stop talking. She could see his expression in the glow from the lights—just enough to tell her that her words had hit a nerve.

"It is a good trait of a godly man to make new friends, indeed," he said slowly. "But it is a godly trait of a good man to be able to keep them."

She had to think about his remark for a few long seconds. There was some merit to what Frederick had said, and she certainly could not argue with him. However, his words hinted at an underlying problem. "I take it from your comment that he was unable to keep your friendship, and therefore you do not consider him a good man," she remarked.

Frederick exhaled, the only indication of any vexation on his part. "The only comment that I can make to your statement is that if George Wickey and I had been on friendlier terms at one point in time, we are no longer. You see, I have a flaw in character that, once lost, my good opinion of someone is lost forever."

She wanted to laugh at his statement but realized that he was sincere in what he was saying. A flaw in character? Did he not realize that he had many more than just one? "*Vell*," she said sharply, "that does not sound like a display of a very forgiving nature. It would seem to hint to a greater character flaw, if you asked me."

At this, Frederick glanced at her. "Forgiveness is one thing, Elizabeth," he scolded her. "That is a character trait of all good Christians. I do not *judge* George Wickey for things that he has done, but I certainly do not *condone* them either, and I choose to no longer be acquainted with him."

"And you will never change your opinion of him?" she cried with a light laugh to her joke.

"What is the meaning of these questions, Elizabeth?" he asked, ignoring her question.

"Why, merely to try to understand the meaning of *your* character," she admitted. "I hear such conflicting things about Frederick Detweiler that I'm both puzzled and mildly curious. Unlike you, I do not form prejudice as easily."

"Nor I!" he exclaimed.

"Ah, but you said that once lost, your good opinion of someone cannot be changed," she tossed back at him. "What a shame, for by this reasoning, if I have not already received your favorable opinion, I will surely never have it. Your own words claim that to be true, ain't so?"

With a deep sigh Frederick shook his head. "I would wish that you would not try to analyze my character right now, Elizabeth. As for listening to conflicting reports, I suspect you already know to use caution in believing what you hear and in judging from whose lips such words are spoken."

"I do believe I am a good judge of character," she confessed, an edge to her voice.

"And never prone to prejudice?"

"I have never been accused of having such an unchristian trait," she admitted. "I let my opinions of people develop from real experiences, not from hearsay. I can assure you that, unlike others, my opinions are never *preconceived*, that is for sure and certain." The way that she proclaimed that last statement sounded harsh and condescending. Clearly she was accusing him of having preconceived prejudices, despite not saying the actual words. Immediately she wished that she could take her statement back, for it had sounded haughtier than intended.

"I see," he said, turning the buggy down a lane toward the back of her *daed*'s farm. "Well, now that we have *that* established, it appears that we have arrived at your *daed*'s home." He stopped the buggy by the side of the house and stepped on the brake. He leaned back in the seat for a moment, letting the silence stand between them.

From the fields crickets chirped, creating a choir of music. There was no moon, and the stars twinkled in the sky. In the distance the rolling noise of another buggy could be heard, along with the rhythm of the horse's hooves hitting the macadam.

Another couple going for a drive after having attended another singing, no doubt.

Frederick slid open the buggy's door and stepped down, the boxlike vehicle shifting as he did so. He reached his hand inside for Lizzie to take, and to her surprise, it was with care and tenderness that he helped her step down and onto the driveway. He stood there and glanced at the sky, almost as though he was going to make a comment. Then, thinking better of it, he looked at Lizzie and nodded his head.

"*Danke* for the company." That was all that she heard him say before he took a proper step back and waited for her to turn toward the house.

Without a word Lizzie turned and hurried into the darkness, putting as much distance between her and Frederick Detweiler as she could. Once inside the house she shut the door and leaned against it, wondering about her own behavior. She had never met a man as insufferable as that man. Still, that did not excuse her insolence toward him. She could only shut her eyes and pray to God that not only would He forgive her but also she would forgive herself.

❧ *Chapter Eleven* ❧

ONDAY MORNING DURING breakfast Wilmer walked down the stairs, dressed in his Sunday's best as if to impress someone. The unfortunate part was that no one was paying attention to his entrance. Instead, plates were being passed around the table while *Maem* fussed over Lydia's complaints regarding being just three weeks shy of turning sixteen and why could she not attend the next singing?

Clearing his throat, Wilmer tried to gain their attention. However, the noise of seven people seated around the table was too great for anyone to hear him.

"But then I'll have to wait almost a month, *Maem*!" Lydia whined.

"It'll be here soon enough, *dochder*," *Maem* tried to reason.

With a pout Lydia refused the plate of eggs that Catherine tried to hand over to her.

"Is this a hunger strike, then?" *Maem* scolded. She lifted her eyes to meet her husband's, visibly exasperated with her youngest *dochder*. "Lydia won't eat now!"

"Which is exactly why she's too young to attend singings, my *fraa*," he retorted casually. His remark had its intended effect, and Lydia snatched the plate of eggs and dished some onto her own. With a satisfied smile *Daed* raised an eyebrow at his wife and returned his attention to his own breakfast.

Once again Wilmer cleared his throat, a little louder, which this time caught the attention of Jane, who nudged Lizzie. Within seconds everyone was quiet and staring at the small man in his dark suit that was quite out of place for a Monday morning on an Amish farm.

"Are you to go visiting today, then?" *Daed* asked to break the silence. "Before breakfast?"

Wilmer held his black hat in his hands and shuffled it nervously. A sense of dread washed over Lizzie, and she reached under the table to grab her sister's hand. Squeezing it, Lizzie tried to stare straight ahead, hoping that, by not making eye contact, the inevitable would not happen.

She was wrong.

"I should like to speak alone to Lizzie after breakfast," he finally said.

Silence.

Outside a dog barked, and in the distance a horse neighed from its stall. *Maem* and *Daed* stared at each other while Lizzie clung to Jane's hand, refusing to look at anyone. Lydia's mouth fell open, and she stared at her sister before a giggle escaped from her lips, despite Catherine elbowing her sharply in the ribs. Mary seemed perplexed, looking first from Wilmer to Lizzie then to her *maem*.

"I think we are all done here," *Maem* finally said, slowly rising to her feet. "Lizzie, you go with Wilmer now. He wishes to speak to you."

The color drained from Lizzie's face. "I'm sure *cousin* Wilmer can speak to me here," she said between clenched teeth, emphasizing the word *cousin*. "There is nothing so private that cannot be shared."

As if *Maem* had not heard her words, she bustled about the kitchen, plucking plates from the table and carrying them to the counter. If breakfast had not been over beforehand, it was over now. Lydia and Catherine quickly stood up from the bench and began gathering the dishes, their shoulders touching as they whispered into each other's ears.

Lizzie stared at her *daed*, her eyes pleading with him.

However, he seemed more puzzled at why breakfast was suddenly over and his plate whisked away from under his raised fork. When he realized that his wife meant business, he sighed and stood up. "I have chores to tend, then," he mumbled and disappeared through the kitchen door.

Maem came over to the table, standing behind Lizzie for a moment. "You should go speak with Wilmer," she urged, her hands placed on Lizzie's shoulders and strongly pulling her daughter to her feet. "To the porch, Lizzie."

"*Maem*," she whispered. "Please don't make me..."

"Hush, Elizabeth!"

Outside on the porch Lizzie sat on the bench and folded her hands on her lap. She crossed her bare feet at the ankles and tucked them under her dress, more to avoid the urge to run than to appear demure and proper. Wilmer stood before her, his hat still being nervously shuffled between his hands. He seemed to be thinking for a moment, each second of silence drawing on her nerves and causing her heart to beat faster. She felt faint and said a quick prayer to God, asking Him to make her wake up from whatever horrible nightmare she was to experience.

"You are aware," he began in his nasal voice, "I have recently become a widower."

"That is most unfortunate," she managed to say.

"Indeed. Yet being a practical man and leader of my *g'may*, I recognize that I must not linger in the past but move forward. I have three small *kinner* who are still in need of a mother. It is not good for my older sons to be entrusted with their upbringing, and my older *dochders* have already married."

Another pause.

"From the moment I arrived," he continued, "I have felt a bond with you, Elizabeth Blank. You have impressed me with your good manners and godly ways. As a bishop I must be most careful and selective of the people I bring into my life, so

125

I have observed you with the gravest of interest and have come to the conclusion that you will not only be a wonderful *maem* to my *kinner*, but you shall be quite efficient in helping me in my role as bishop of the *g'may*."

"Wilmer, I..."

He interrupted her. "I should like to request that you return with me to Ohio, to become my *fraa* and help with my *kinner*. It will be a good change for you," he stated, his eyes roving around the porch as if the chipped paint and torn screen were beneath him. "My farm is not as large as your *daed*'s, but with sons working it, it is..." Pause. "Better maintained."

"I have to say..."

Again he interrupted her. "Of course, I am agreeable to a few more *kinner*." He smiled at her. "I know every woman wishes for her own *boppli*."

His words and the expression on his face caused her to blush. "Wilmer, please!"

"I know you will enjoy the Dutch Valley. It's a lovely town with rolling hills. It's not quite so spread out as here," he said, almost with a hint of disapproval to his statement. "Much easier to visit with each other, I dare say." He breathed in deeply, as if tasting the air. "*Ja*, you will have a much better life and enjoy the new scenery, for certain."

"I have not given you my answer!" she finally managed to say as she jumped to her feet.

He looked puzzled and took one step backward. "Answer?"

Lizzie tried not to scowl. It dawned on her that Wilmer had never asked her a question. He had merely stated what he wanted to happen, and to her further displeasure, she realized that it had never dawned on him that she might have a choice. "My answer to your request that I'd marry you," she snapped. "And as it is a question, Wilmer, not a mandate, I shall have to inform you that I will not return to Ohio with you."

The furrows in his brow deepened. "You will not?"

"*Nee*," she said firmly.

And then, he smiled again. It was a strange smile, especially given what Lizzie had just said to him. Yet when he spoke, she realized that he had misunderstood what she meant. "I see," he said. "It is too soon for you. I have taken you by surprise!"

"*Ja*, I am a bit surprised," she mumbled. He did not hear her for he continued.

"And I see your point, being such a modest young woman. It would not be proper to return to Ohio together unless we were married already!" He clapped his hands in delight. "I should have realized that!"

"*Nee!*" She held up her hand to stop him. "I will not be going to Ohio with you at all."

At this he seemed genuinely perplexed. She watched the smile and happiness fading from his face as he stared at her, trying to digest her words. Behind him a blue jay chased away the plain little sparrow while two nuthatches landed on her *maem*'s feeder. Lizzie wished she could have wings like the nuthatch and simply fly away to any place other than her parents' porch, where she was subjected to the proposal of such a man as Wilmer Kaufman.

"I don't understand," he confessed.

She tried to soften her tone. "Wilmer, I am honored by your request, but I can assure you that I would not have a better life nor would I enjoy the scenery of Ohio, not for want of your provisions, which are most honorable, but because my heart is not in such a journey or life. I am far too inexperienced to raise your *kinner* and quite inadequate as a Christian to be the wife of an established bishop."

"You are being too modest, Elizabeth," he said happily. "Another admirable trait that just furthers my decision that you are meant to be my *fraa*."

"*Nee*," she said, shaking her head. "I am not meant to be your *fraa*, Wilmer, for there is something more that you must know."

She took a deep breath and blurted out, "I don't love you and never could, not in the way a *fraa* should love her husband."

For a moment the reaction on his face seemed as if he had been slapped. He blinked his eyes and pressed his lips together as he contemplated her words. "Love? What has love to do with a godly marriage?"

She laughed, only there was no mirth in the sound. "And that is a perfect example of why I could never marry you, Wilmer. Nor should you wish to marry me. I'd never be happy, and I can assure you that you would find fault with me soon enough to hinder any chance of your own happiness."

"You are being coy."

She saw it was his last effort to make an excuse for her refusal. "*Nee*, I am not being coy," she stated. "I simply will not marry you, Wilmer." Without another word she turned on her heels and hurried off of the porch, scurrying to the barn where she knew that she could escape, unbothered by Wilmer or her *maem*. She didn't look back as she darted into the open barn door and headed immediately for the ladder leading to the hayloft. She needed a moment to be alone, to digest what had just happened, and to escape from the reality that she would, no doubt, hear about this decision for the rest of her unmarried life from her *maem*.

However, it did not take long for her hideaway to be discovered. She could hear her *maem* well before she saw her head pop through the opening in the floor. With a scowl *Maem* glanced around the hayloft until she caught sight of Lizzie, sitting on a hay bale. Her eyes narrowed and she completed the ascent. Behind her trailed a sullen-looking *Daed*, his cheeks drawn and tense.

"What is the meaning of this?"

Lizzie looked up. "I will not marry that man!"

"And why ever not?" *Maem* placed her hands on her hips, staring down Lizzie with a fierce and determined look on her face. "He's as good a man as any other! And I see no others willing to even escort you home from singings!"

If Lizzie wanted to blurt out that Frederick Detweiler had brought her home from the singing the previous night, she kept her mouth shut. It would do no good to have her *maem* catch wind of *that* information.

"He's ridiculous!"

Maem tossed her hands into the air and turned to stare at her husband. "Do something with her!"

Daed put his hands into his pockets, his shoulders slumped forward as he faced his wife. "What would you have me do? She's quite right about this. He *is* ridiculous."

At that declaration *Maem*'s eyes bulged from her head and she gasped. "Would you have her become a *maedel* then? A burden to whom? Us? Her sisters?"

He tried to smile. "She will not become a *maedel*, my *fraa*. I can assure you of that."

"This is a perfectly agreeable match!" *Maem* turned back to her daughter. "I insist that you accept this offer and marry Wilmer. And if you do not," *Maem* said, straightening her back and lifting her chin, "I shall shun you, Elizabeth Blank!"

"*Daed*!" Lizzie stared at him, pleading with her eyes for some interference.

Her father took a deep breath and nodded his head. "I see where we have quite a problem here, my *dochder*. You shall have to make a decision today that is quite difficult in nature." He ignored the tears that were welling up in Lizzie's eyes. "Your mother shall shun you if you do not marry Wilmer Kaufman, and I shall shun you if you do!"

Maem gasped and spun around as Lizzie hurried to her father and hugged him, clinging to him for giving her the reprieve. Regardless of *Maem*'s insistence, it was *Daed* who had the final say. Now that he had spoken, there was nothing that

Sarah Price

her *maem* could say to counter it. To do so would be to disobey and disrespect her husband.

"*Danke, Daed*," she whispered into his ear. To her delight she felt him squeeze her arm in support of the decision. Then, without a moment to waste, Lizzie hurried down the ladder to escape from any more words from her *maem*, who was sure to give her a deeper tongue lashing once *Daed* would return to his chores and be out of earshot.

Once she was out of the barn, Lizzie ran down the lane and toward the road. She knew that she couldn't go back to the house. Things needed to simmer down and that would take time. Once she hit the main road, she stopped running, her feet beginning to ache, and began walking, catching her breath as a whirlwind of thoughts and emotions jumbled in her mind: the strange buggy ride home with Frederick, the unexpected proposal from Wilmer, the outrageous demand from her *maem*. *When had life become so complicated?* she pondered, her eyes staring straight ahead but seeing nothing. Was it her fault that she was not interested in the Amish men from her *g'may*? She had grown up with most of them and felt a love for most of them as if they were brothers, not potential husbands.

Lizzie sighed and lowered her head. Was it wrong for her to want more from a marriage than simple convenience? She didn't want to be just a gardener, baker, and *boppli* maker! She wanted to be a companion, and she wanted to love her husband. She wanted a friendship that would carry her through the years. If she had to choose between not having such a marriage and being a *maedel*, she'd prefer the latter!

"Early for a walk today, *ja*?"

She looked up, realizing that she had already walked three miles. At that rate she was passing the Beachey farm. Her cheeks flushed as she saw George waiting for her by the railing of the fence. "*Gut mariye*," she said sheepishly, embarrassed that she hadn't noticed him in advance. If she had, she certainly would have turned in order to avoid engaging in a conversation. She much preferred to be alone at the present moment, but as chance would have it, she had been too involved in her thoughts to see him in the paddock.

"So deep in thought," he commented with a smile. He was leaning against a fence post. She wondered how long he had been watching her.

"You were missed at the singing last evening," she replied. "It was a right *gut* time. And at your own home!"

He shrugged. "I had a prior engagement."

She was fairly certain that his absence had to do with Frederick, yet he too had been absent beyond his brief appearance to ask to take her home. Still, she understood that George might have felt uncomfortable just knowing that Frederick might show up. However, she reminded herself that he had also missed church service too. Again. It was one thing to miss the social activities, but quite another to never attend worship or fellowship.

"*Ja, vell*, I see that your current engagement is keeping you outdoors today," she replied lightly, not certain how to move beyond the awkward silence that had followed his statement.

He glanced around and sighed. "Just checking the fence line. The cows are being delivered later today." He placed his hand on the wire and gave it a good shake. "Looks right *gut* to me," he said.

As they were speaking, a car pulled out of the driveway, stopping for a moment at the end before turning left and away from where Lizzie and George stood. She could see three people in the car besides the driver. Lizzie raised an eyebrow but asked no question. There was no need, for George volunteered the information.

"Heading back to Ohio," he stated, no emotion in his voice.

At first Lizzie didn't think that she heard him properly.

The words echoed inside of her head. Ohio? Heading back? Whatever was George saying?

He nodded his head, reading her mind. "Jacob Beachey had a heart attack last night. We received word just this morning. Neighbor brought us word since we don't have a telephone yet," he said. "The three are returning home to tend to him."

"Three of them?" This was surprising news. "Is Jacob going to be all right then?"

Again, George shrugged. "Only God knows," he replied.

"Of course, of course," she whispered, staring in the direction of the car as it disappeared from view. How terribly sad for the Beachey family, having just gotten established in Leola only to be called home by such horrible news. "I'll make certain the bishop knows and we pray for Jacob."

On her way home she realized that of the three people that had returned to Ohio, only two were related to Jacob Beachey. She wondered why Frederick had not opted to stay behind to accept delivery of the herd of cows so that George, the self-professed unofficial son of Jacob Beachey, could help care for him. Curious indeed, she thought as she cut through a pasture that led to her *daed*'s farm.

"A heart attack?" Jane gasped when she heard the news. The color drained from her face. "Oh, how dreadful!"

They were huddled together near the barn, whispering to each other so as not to draw any attention from their *maem*, who, according to Jane, had collapsed in a fit of tears when Wilmer had borrowed *Daed*'s buggy to go visit the bishop. Clearly he had been humiliated by Lizzie's refusal to marry him and just wanted to get away from the Blank farm.

"How long is the drive back to Ohio?"

Lizzie shook her head. "I don't rightly know," she replied honestly. "Six hours? Mayhaps seven?"

"Poor Charles," Jane said, more to herself than to Lizzie.

From the expression on her face Jane was clearly thinking of him more than of his father. It dawned on Lizzie that she was seeing, firsthand, the look of love. Despite the solemnity of the moment, she felt her own emotions well inside of her: feelings of hope and joy for her sister's future happiness with Charles Beachey. In thinking this, she laid her hand on Jane's arm and tried to reassure her. "Everything will be fine, *schwester,*" she said. "You'll see."

Jane lifted her eyes and stared at Lizzie. For a moment, Lizzie couldn't tell what emotion her sister was feeling. It was a mixture of worry and fear. Did Jane fear more for Jacob's health or for Charles's return?

❧ *Chapter Twelve* ❧

To Lizzie's great relief, she saw very little of Wilmer during his final days staying at the Blank farm. In fact, most mornings he was gone before she had returned to the house following morning chores, and quite often, she was already asleep upon his return in the late evening. Where he went, she never once inquired. To be perfectly honest, she frankly did not care as to where he escaped.

As the week progressed, there was no word from Charles Beachey or his sister. Since the Blanks had a phone on their farm, it was not unreasonable for Jane to expect a message, explaining his absence and updating her on the condition of his *daed*. After all, they were special friends, and it had been suspected that a fall wedding was imminent.

After four days had passed with no word, Jane began to withdraw into herself. Lizzie was the first to notice. Jane began to linger around the barn where the phone was kept. She offered to help sweep the dairy and even took to milking the cows. And her eyes continually drifted to the machine near the telephone as if willing it to blink red, indicating the presence of a message.

Additionally they were all quietly surprised that no letter arrived from Carol Ann, the self-professed friend of Jane. It was a common practice among the Amish, especially those who lived farther away, to write letters to each other. In fact, in the evening there was always a letter or two to write so that in the morning it could be taken to the mailbox. Telephones were not meant for socializing, just important news that could not wait. So letter writing was still in great practice among the different church districts.

Jane finally broke down and wrote a letter to Carol Ann. Lizzie had frowned while her older sister spent a painful hour, writing and then rewriting the missive. Reluctantly, for Lizzie could almost guess how this was going to play out, she took the letter to the mailbox the following day and pushed the little red flag up so that the mailman would know to stop and pick up the letter.

On Saturday two surprises occurred, almost simultaneously.

First was an unexpected visit by Charlotte. It was unusual for her to visit the Blank farm as she ran the family farm stand on Saturdays during the busy tourist season. When Lizzie saw her friend come down the lane, using her foot scooter, she immediately presumed something had happened and hurried in her direction.

"Charlotte!" she cried as she approached. "*Wie gehts*? Is everything all right?"

Charlotte avoided looking at Lizzie's eyes but nodded her head, reassuring her friend with a simple "*Ja, ja*, everything is right *gut*."

"You scared me!" Lizzie said with a light laugh, pressing her hand to her chest. "I can't remember ever seeing you visit on a Saturday in the summer. I was quite afraid you had some bad news to share."

"*Ja, vell*," Charlotte began. "That's just the thing…"

Lizzie cocked her head to one side. "What is the thing?"

"I do have news. Only it is good news, not bad news."

The frown disappeared from Lizzie's face, and she smiled. "Why, do tell me then! Don't delay and keep me in suspense, Charlotte. Good news would be quite welcome around here since *Maem* isn't speaking to me and Jane is moping around for her dear Charles!"

Charlotte hesitated and averted her eyes. For having such

good news, her expression spoke otherwise. Lizzie's smile faded as Charlotte began to speak. "I shall be moving to Ohio," she started.

"Ohio!"

"*Ja*," Charlotte affirmed and tried to look Lizzie in the eyes. "That's what I said."

"Whatever for?" Ohio seemed like the farthest place on the planet to Lizzie. And there was no particularly clear reason why her friend would be moving there. Her family was here in Leola...not Ohio!

"I will be marrying Wilmer Kaufman."

There was no amount of repeating the words in her head that made them sensible to Lizzie. At first she thought she had misheard Charlotte. Such a match was not only ridiculous, it was unfathomable to Lizzie. Hadn't he just proposed to *her* on Monday? Then, as Charlotte pursed her lips, bracing herself for Lizzie's reaction, the reality of the situation broke through the surreal clouds of doubt. As impossible as it seemed, Charlotte was, indeed, intending to marry Wilmer!

"But why?"

Charlotte laughed, a laugh filled with nervousness, not cheer. "Don't do that, Lizzie. Please," she said softly. "This is hard enough as it is. I need your support."

"But he's ridiculous!" Lizzie cried.

"Lizzie!"

"It's true! And you know it."

For the first time since Lizzie had known Charlotte, her friend took a deep breath and faced Lizzie with a confidence that had previously never existed. "He is to be *my husband*, Lizzie," she said solemnly. "I ask that you remember that."

The reprimand stung, and Lizzie looked away. She was embarrassed, but for many different reasons, not just having been reminded that she had overstepped a line of propriety by being overbearing. When she felt Charlotte's hand on her arm, she forced herself to look back at her friend.

"I'm not like you," Charlotte said softly. "I have to be practical, Lizzie. My parents cannot provide for me forever, and I know how it goes with *maedels* as they age. My siblings will have their own families to care for, and, in turn, to care for them when they become elderly. Who cares for *maedels*?" She laughed before answering her own question. "You and I both know that *maedels* must fend for themselves. I don't want to be that old spinster woman who becomes a burden to all and family to none."

"Charlotte..."

Her friend held up her hand and shook her head. "*Nee,* Lizzie," she said. "It is not oft spoken of, but it is true. You know it. And I'm too old to keep notions of romance and love in my dreams. At my age I will have to accept what comes my way or become *that* woman..."

And Lizzie suddenly realized that it was true. While Charlotte was a lovely young woman with a hard work ethic and great devotion to God, she was not particularly young anymore. In her mind Lizzie could see her friend age and become the old *maedel* that was tended to by the *g'may*, forgotten at holidays, and visited only by reminder. She would no longer attract young, unmarried men, only widowers who needed help with *kinner* and farm work. To marry Wilmer, a bishop with an established home, family, and community standing, was definitely a more acceptable alternative for Charlotte, Lizzie had to admit.

"Oh, Charlotte," Lizzie started to say, wanting to wish her friend well but not able to form the necessary words.

"I'm leaving tomorrow," she said. "So I came to say good-bye. But I wanted to extend an invitation, Lizzie. I want you to come and visit. Please say that you will, so that I can leave here knowing that good-bye is really just a 'see you in a few weeks.'"

Lizzie nodded her head, unable to trust herself to speak. She was too close to tears at the thought of losing her dear friend to such a distance and at the realization that the only option for a possible future for Charlotte rested with Wilmer Kaufman. "I shall pray for you daily," she managed to gasp before hugging her friend.

The second surprise that caught Lizzie off-guard was a letter. When she retrieved the mail and saw a letter that was addressed to Jane and postmarked from Ohio, she had a moment of hope. That lasted only as long as it took for her to flip the envelope over, for with great disappointment Lizzie saw that the letter had been sent by Carol Ann Beachey, not her brother Charles. Still, she felt a shred of hope as she delivered the letter to her sister, thinking that they might receive some word about Charles's doings.

Jane set aside the sewing she had been doing and eagerly opened the letter. So determined was Jane to think the best of all people, she started to read the letter aloud, eager for its contents, which, she presumed, would include an estimated return date for Charles. But as the letter progressed, her voice trailed off. With tears in her eyes she tossed the unfinished letter on the table and quietly excused herself.

Snatching the letter from the table, Lizzie's eyes scrutinized the neatly written words, searching for the place where Jane's voice had faltered. She read the rest of the letter, the color draining from her face, and she looked up, taken aback by the four sets of speculative eyes watching her.

"What is it, *dochder*?" *Maem* gushed nervously.

"Carol Ann states that when they return, Charles will most likely be bringing a wife," Lizzie whispered. She let the piece of paper slide from her fingers. It floated through the air and landed on the floor. Lizzie stood there, frozen in the middle of the kitchen as she tried to digest this horrible news. "A

wife," she repeated under her breath. "By the name of Grace
Detweiler!"

A gasp escaped *Maem*'s mouth, and she looked as if she might
swoon. Catherine and Mary were beside her and reached out to
steady their *maem*. Gratefully *Maem* leaned against Catherine,
her head on her *dochder*'s shoulder and her eyes shut. Her lips
moved in silent prayer.

Mary spoke first. "What does this mean?"

"It means that Charles Beachey is to marry Frederick
Detweiler's younger sister," Lizzie said, her eyes still unfocused
as she stared at the wall.

"But..."

Lydia nudged Mary to stop her from stating the obvious. It
would do no one any good to hear the word spoken out loud:
betrayal.

"I have to go find Jane," Lizzie whispered and slowly walked
toward the door, cringing as she heard a sob escape from her
maem. She could well imagine the disappointment that her
maem felt at the thought that Charles would not be returning
to marry Jane. But her biggest concern was for her sister, who,
despite her usual outward appearance of calm goodness, was
surely experiencing a pain in her heart way beyond that which
her own *maem* felt.

She found Jane standing in the garden, her back toward
the house and her head hung back with her face lifted toward
the sun. Lizzie walked around her, giving her a wide berth
to respect her privacy until she could gauge Jane's reaction.
Immediately Lizzie noticed that Jane's eyes were shut and her
hands clasped before her chest. She was praying, that much
was clear. Yet the look on her face was serene and peaceful.

"It's God's will," she said without turning to look at Lizzie.
"I will be happy for Charles and Grace, not bitter."

Listening to her, Lizzie was amazed. How could her sister

accept this news with such faith? How could she not cry and need comfort?

"What if it is not true, Jane?"

At this question Jane turned her head to look at her sister. "Then that too is God's will." She smiled, a pure and genuine smile. "Who am I but a mere sinner to question His plan?"

❦ *Chapter Thirteen* ❦

THE BLANK FARM was quiet for the month of July and into August. Besides two hay-cuttings, one in the front pasture and one in the side, and a family picnic in Ephrata, the long, lazy days of August seemed to drag out, hot and humid, sticky even into the nighttime hours.

The only excitement was the occasional visits paid by George Wickey, who seemed to appear at least once a week around the evening supper hour. He appeared much more relaxed, having become familiar with the area and, apparently, having made quite a few friends. However, during the weeks that had passed since Charles, Carol Ann, and Frederick had left, he had never made an appearance at any of the Sunday worship services. Lizzie ignored the gossip among the women as to why George Wickey did not attend service and fellowship, for with his new herd of cows to tend, he certainly had enough work to do at the farm without any helpers. And, from comments that he had made at their home during the supper hour, she suspected that he had never taken his kneeling vow, anyway.

While his appearance at their house brought with it a lightness and new energy, Lizzie did not suspect for one moment that he was calling on her in particular. Indeed, he would direct most of his conversation at her, at least when he was not talking to *Daed*, but she took his presence to be a neighborly visit out of boredom and loneliness rather than an interest of any romantic nature.

He also kept her family updated to the health situation of Jacob Beachey. It was clear that Jacob would live, but his recovery would be slow. There was never any mention of Frederick and only a casual mention of Carol Ann. However, Lizzie clearly noticed that George was quite anxious to have Charles return, as he made several comments about how working the dairy was rather cumbersome. Even her *daed* raised an eyebrow at his lighthearted complaints. Rare was the Amish farmer who found fault with the practice of farming!

In mid August a letter arrived from Charlotte. Her parents were coming to visit her for a week, and Charlotte wanted Lizzie to come along with them. Lizzie sat under an oak tree in the cow paddock, rereading the words. The words seemed so inviting, although the six-hour car ride did not. Yet the aura of doom and gloom that hung over the Blank farm seemed like more than enough reason to leave, even if only for a week.

In addition Lizzie wondered if she could pay her respects to Jacob Beachey in order to find out what, exactly, was keeping Charles from returning. She also wanted to verify that, indeed, he was intent on marrying this Grace Detweiler!

She approached her *daed* rather than ask her *maem*. Knowing her parents, *Daed* would be more inclined to grant permission while *Maem* would be horrified at the mere thought of Lizzie leaving, even for a short time, especially given that it meant one or two of the other girls would be recruited to help with barn chores. Mary was preparing for the upcoming school year, her first as a teacher aide, so she was of little help to *Daed*; as to Jane, while trying to maintain a positive facade, she was clearly still hurting inside from the knowledge that Charles had misled her into thinking that he had harbored serious feelings for her.

"Why, that's a right *gut* invitation!" *Daed* said. "And well deserved for all the work that you do around here. Although of any of the *dochders* to leave, you would be the last I'd like to send away. Mayhaps Lydia might accompany you?"

Lizzie smiled at his joke. "And miss her first singing?"

"Ah, that's right!" *Daed* replied, pointing a finger in the air as if he had just remembered that. "Her first singing is next Sunday, *ja*?" He sighed. "I shall have to relive it at least twice, I'm sure...once from her and once from your *maem*!" He leaned against the handle of the pitchfork and wiped a piece of straw from his cheek. "If you are wise, Elizabeth, and I know you to be so, I would run to Ohio to escape your sister on *rumschpringe*!"

As expected, *Maem* fussed and complained at the injustice of Lizzie leaving when, clearly, it was Jane who needed time away after the loss of her beau. But it was *Daed* who stood firm, accepting nothing of an argument against his having decided that Lizzie would accompany Charlotte's parents, William and Leah, to visit her in Ohio.

They left at seven in the morning on a Saturday in order to arrive before late afternoon. They shared the van with another Amish man, Gideon King. Despite having never met before, Lizzie found him good company, at least for the first hour. Even William engaged in conversation with him, happy to learn that they had some common acquaintances in Lititz.

By the time the second hour of their journey rolled around, Lizzie drifted to sleep, surprised to find that the gentle rolling of the vehicle actually aided her in her sleep. Charlotte's *maem*, Leah, spent her time knitting a sweater from thick brown yarn, most likely a present for one of her sons for an upcoming birthday. William merely stared out of the window, his head nodding at times, an indication that he too slept during the trip. And Gideon seemed content with his own company, speaking only general pleasantries when the driver stopped, once for lunch and once for gasoline.

As they entered Ohio, Lizzie began to pay more attention to the scenery. It was different from Pennsylvania, that was for sure and certain. It looked hillier than Leola with long, rolling mounds of green that spread as far as the eye could see.

However, unlike Leola, the farms were closer together, and because of the hills, there were a lot of rises and dips in the horizon. Most of the farms were white, although she spotted a few with red painted barns. It was a pretty country, and she enjoyed observing the differences and similarities while the van made its way through the meandering roads.

By the time the van pulled into the farm, Lizzie could barely wait to stretch her legs. The house was smaller than she expected and more contemporary, clearly a former *Englische* home that had been retrofitted to the Amish way of life. Yet there was enough land for gardens and small crops that had been well tended and were bountiful enough to yield food for the Kaufman family, that was for certain.

"You have arrived!"

Lizzie turned around at the sound of her friend's voice. The front door of the house was shutting behind her as Charlotte hurried across the porch with her arms extended and a smile on her face. Quickly she hugged both of her parents, blushing when her *daed* commented on how much she had changed.

"Must be running your own household, *ja*?" Charlotte's *maem* suggested. "Gardening and tending to *kinner* can do that to a woman."

After inquiring about her siblings and stealing one more embrace, Charlotte turned her attention to Lizzie. She reached for Lizzie's hand and squeezed it. "I'm so very glad to see you!"

Lizzie smiled back, trying to take in this new Charlotte who was so very different from the one she had last seen not even six weeks prior. She wore the clothing typical of the Ohio Amish, including the cup-shaped prayer *kapp* that hugged the back of her head. The fabric of her dress was looser and shaped a bit differently than what Lizzie was familiar with. It dawned on Lizzie that, despite looking different, Charlotte was at home while Lizzie was the outsider.

"You are looking well!" Lizzie managed to say to her friend.

It was true. Charlotte looked happy, with her rounded cheeks that were flushed with color. Her eyes were literally sparkling, and there was an air of confidence about her that Lizzie had never seen before. Or, she wondered, had she just never noticed it?

"Come inside," she insisted. "Leave your things there. I'll send the *kinner* to bring them to your rooms."

Inside the front door Lizzie stared at the pristine home with shiny hardwood floors and white painted walls. Unlike the houses that Lizzie was familiar with at home, this one had the kitchen in the back of the house, something that was most unusual for farmhouses. There was a small entrance hall with two rooms off the sides: one was a larger gathering room and the other a smaller room that appeared to be used as an office. At the end of the hallway was the large, airy kitchen with windows that looked out over a rolling field.

Lizzie entered the kitchen, aware of the linoleum floor that looked as through it had been freshly waxed. Everything shone from cleanliness and love. It was a welcomed vision. She felt Charlotte touch her arm.

"It's so *gut* to see you, Lizzie," Charlotte gushed. "And to have you in my own home!"

"Do you feel at home then?"

Charlotte nodded. "Oh, *ja!* It's *wunderbaar gut* to run my own home, and the *kinner*..." She smiled. "They have been most respectful and kind. I was worried about that."

"Where are they?"

Charlotte looked around and shrugged. "Likely helping Wilmer outside or at the Bechler farm."

There were four bedrooms upstairs and two downstairs, one being the master bedroom and one a small guest room. Lizzie was situated in the small guest room and spent a few moments unpacking her things as she tried to organize her thoughts. It felt strange to be in a home that was run by her

Sarah Price

friend Charlotte...even stranger considering that Charlotte was living in Ohio, not down the lane from the Blank farm in Leola, Pennsylvania.

It was only an hour later, when the door opened and Wilmer Kaufman entered the house, that the extent of how surreal everything truly was hit Lizzie. Wilmer greeted his *fraa* with an air of formality that only slightly hinted at the familiar. Yet Charlotte beamed at the three young boys who obediently followed their *daed* into the house. A fourth one, an older son, trailed behind, his long legs and arms indicating that he fell into that gangly stage somewhere between childhood and manhood.

"Ian, David, and Peter," Charlotte said by means of an introduction of the three smaller boys. "These are your new grandparents, my *maem* and *daed*, Leah and William." She glanced at the older boy. "John, after you have shaken hands, mayhaps you could bring their bags inside, *ja?*"

"I want to help too!" the smaller boy named Peter said, jumping up and down eagerly.

Wilmer seemed to puff out his chest, watching the scene with a sense of pride over his small family. "I trust the drive was right *gut, ja?*"

To Lizzie he seemed just as ridiculous as ever. However, she knew that her friend was happy, living a life that was far better than any prospect she may eventually have had in Pennsylvania. If originally Lizzie had been disappointed in her friend for having settled for Wilmer, she at least understood better Charlotte's decision to achieve a marriage to fulfill her position in life, both now as a wife and a young mother and in the future. It was also evident that Charlotte had given herself over to her role as *fraa* and *maem* with a clear conscience and a willingness that came from the heart. And it pleased Lizzie to see that Wilmer's sons appreciated Charlotte's efforts, rewarding her with not just the respect due to a *maem* but also

148

the tremendous compliment of love. She knew that it couldn't have been easy for Charlotte or the boys, but their willingness to work together and unite as a family was clearly a success.

Later that evening, shortly after supper, Wilmer explained that he had been down with his sons at the Bechler farm, helping Christiana with the late August haying. Since Wilmer did not have enough land to farm, he had the time and inclination to help Christiana with hers.

"We have been invited to Sunday dinner at the Bechler farm tomorrow," Wilmer said, glancing at his three guests as if they should be impressed. "It's a visiting Sunday, and as bishop, we often are invited to others' homes for the noon meal."

Charlotte nodded from the plain rocking chair where she sat, a lukewarm cup of tea in her hand. "Christiana is quite generous with her invitations," she explained.

"Indeed," Wilmer stated, taking charge of the conversation once again. "A more generous woman has never graced God's fine earth. Her willingness to let my *kinner* work her farm is also a true testament of her godliness. They will learn farming while doing God's work helping a fine woman who has been left alone in this world."

"No *kinner*?" Leah seemed horrified at this prospect and shook her head. Lizzie, however, saw a different reaction from William, who seemed to realize the predicament that Christiana Bechler faced and was simultaneously relieved that his own *dochder* had avoided the same.

"She lost those that she had and then, sadly, was never able to conceive more," Wilmer replied. "She has, however, taken her husband's niece into her care, a poor girl who was orphaned at a young age. I imagine that whoever is to marry Anna will inherit the entire Bechler farm."

"Oh, my," Leah gasped.

"An advantageous marriage for some young farmer," William quipped.

"And the Beachey farm?" Lizzie dove headfirst into the conversation. "I should like to know how Jacob Beachey fares, all these weeks having passed since his illness befell him and whisked our new neighbors away from Leola."

"Interesting that," Wilmer said, leaning forward in his chair as he removed his glasses and wiped the lens on the edge of his sleeve. "There is talk that Charles may not return to Leola but may, in fact, marry Frederick Detweiler's young *schwester*." He placed his glasses back onto his face and blinked twice. Satisfied that he could see better, he turned to look at Lizzie. "With Frederick's encouragement, I have heard."

Had she heard him correctly? Lizzie felt her heart lurch inside of her chest, and she fought the urge to jump to her feet. "At the encouragement of his own friend?" She looked to Charlotte, who merely lowered her gaze, too aware that Charles had openly courted Jane, a fact that Frederick was certain to have known. "Such matters are meant to be private, ain't so?"

"Times change," Wilmer said with a simple shrug. "I heard that Frederick was not impressed with Leola for Charles's future. In fact, Charles was intent on returning, more so for a young woman than the farm, or so I heard. However, his friend convinced him to stay here and not return to Pennsylvania."

"Indeed!"

Immediately recognizing the mistake that he had made, Wilmer apologized profusely. "No insult was intended, my cousin. My own *fraa* is from Leola. I do believe that he meant from a *farming* perspective. However, truth be told, the culture of the Pennsylvania Amish is different than this of Holmes County. It would be better to marry from within one's surroundings," he said with a serious look on his face before adding, "for not all men can be as fortunate as I to find such a suitable and mindful companion from so far away."

Lizzie knew that her cheeks had flushed red, more from the humiliation of the insult than anything else. If she did not care for Frederick Detweiler before she had learned of his treachery, she knew that she would have to pray for forgiveness for simply despising him now. If Christiana Bechler was the most generous woman who ever walked God's good earth, clearly Frederick Detweiler was the most despicable man.

For the next half an hour Lizzie barely heard any of the conversation that was shared among Charlotte, her parents, and her husband. When enough time had passed, she excused herself to escape to her small room, retiring for the evening. After changing into her sleeping gown, she forced herself to kneel by the side of her bed and pray to God, asking for forgiveness for the darkness that had consumed her heart, all the while knowing that it would take more than a prayer to God for such darkness to be lifted off her soul.

❧ Chapter Fourteen ❧

IT WAS LATE Sunday morning when the five adults and four *kinner* headed down the lane to cross the road in order to walk to the Bechler farm. While Wilmer had professed that it was located directly across the road, that had been more of an exaggeration as the property was rather expansive, even for Ohio. The walk took almost twenty minutes, for they had to walk along the road rather than cut across the fields as Wilmer and his sons typically would do.

Lizzie felt numb, still reeling from Wilmer's disclosure of the previous evening. She had wanted to write immediately to Jane but knew that such news was better presented in person. Besides, the letter would only make it back to the farm a day or two before Lizzie. There was no sense in further upsetting her dear, special sister until she was certain of the facts.

The Bechler farmhouse was small and quaint, tucked on the edge of a hill. Everything looked neat and tidy, no display of ostentatious flowers or decoration. In fact, it was the picture-perfect Amish farm: clean and well tended yet plain at the same time. The driveway was long and winding with paddocks and pasture on either side. Everything was well maintained, despite the lack of a man to tend to the property. Wilmer, however, was quick to point out all that he and his sons had done over the past few months to assist Christiana Bechler in her time of need.

Upon approaching the house, Wilmer pointed out that a buggy stood beside the stable, although no horse was harnessed to it. Clearly someone was visiting and had been invited for the noon meal besides Wilmer Kaufman and guests. However, nothing could have prepared Lizzie for what she saw upon entering the house: standing immediately before her was the very same man that she had determined to loathe for the rest of her life.

Without even waiting for a proper introduction to Christiana and her niece, Lizzie narrowed her eyes and stared at the man before her. "Frederick Detweiler!" she said, her voice sounding both surprised and irritated at the same time. Of all the people in the world whom she might have expected to see standing before her, he was the last on the list.

A mild silence befell the room, and Frederick took the opportunity to clear his throat and nod his head at her, acknowledging her presence but remaining silent.

Wilmer tried to make a proper introduction, but the older woman seated in the rocking chair lifted up her hand for him to stop. Her dark eyes flashed from behind her glasses, as she stood and walked toward the newcomers. "I see you know my nephew, then," she said, her eyes quickly assessing the young woman from Leola who stood before her. It was clear that she did not like what she saw. "From Pennsylvania, *ja?*"

Ignoring the way that Christiana had uttered the word *Pennsylvania* as if it were a disease, Lizzie turned to face the woman and immediately reached out her hand. "I am Lizzie Blank," she replied, introducing herself while trying to regain her composure and improve her behavior. She was not only surprised to see Frederick standing in the same room, but she was also taken aback by how old Christiana was. With her black dress and tight-fitting kapp, she looked austere and stern, far too old to be such an essential influence in her niece Anna's life. "I trust you are well on this lovely August day, *ja?*"

The older woman's eyes flickered, first to Frederick and then back to Lizzie. She was trying to determine something, that much was apparent. However, she merely lifted an eyebrow in response. "I much prefer autumn weather," she stated sharply. "The crisp morning air suits me better."

Wilmer moved forward, introducing his in-laws and thanking Christiana for her generous hospitality in hosting him and his guests for Sunday dinner. His abundance of praise left Lizzie feeling awkward and embarrassed, sensing that even Christiana found his tribute to her kindness overbearing. She did, however, notice that Charlotte seemed immune and merely stood there, her hands clasped before her and a small smile plastered on her face.

In order to avoid speaking to Frederick, Lizzie stayed glued to Charlotte's side. She tried to stand with her back toward him but felt the heat of his eyes boring a hole into her shoulders. Twice she managed to glance in his direction and was not surprised to find him watching her.

There was little doubt that she would not escape the visit without sharing a word with him. When the opportunity finally arose, Lizzie took a deep breath and approached him, too aware that he was still standing in the same place, one hand behind his back while the other held a glass of tea. His dark eyes seemed piercing and bold, following her every movement as she neared.

"I'm rather surprised to see you here, Frederick," she said, trying to sound light and cheerful rather than angry.

"I should say that I am equally as surprised," he replied, his voice even as usual.

"Charles's father must be in quite a state of ill health for Charles to stay away from his Leola farm," she dared to say. "I do pray for Jacob's speedy recovery."

Frederick seemed curious about her remark, but as always managed to keep a straight face. It was the tilt of his head and look in his eye that Lizzie caught, knowing that she had captured his attention. "Jacob is faring quite well, Elizabeth," he said. "I shall extend your prayers and words of goodness."

Lizzie frowned, feigning confusion despite the growing anger within her regarding his role in keeping Charles in Ohio. "Then if he is well, Frederick, what keeps Charles from returning?"

There was no time to respond, for Christiana called them to the table. Yet he managed to stare at her for a long moment, and she knew that he was wondering how much she had been informed about his role in separating Charles from Jane. Without another remark she turned and headed toward the table, pleased that he was aware of her knowledge.

As luck would have it, Frederick was seated next to Christiana and opposite Anna. With Wilmer at the other head of the table and the *kinner* on the bench beside Anna, Lizzie had no choice but to sit between Frederick and Charlotte. The silent premeal prayer gave Lizzie time to collect her thoughts before giving a quick word of gratitude to God for their safe trip the previous day and the food on the table that had been provided by Christiana.

"You are most fortunate to have encountered such fine weather for your visit," their hostess said, starting the conversation prior to passing around the plates of food. "Just the week prior it was rather hot, was it not, Wilmer?"

He readily agreed, affirming that, indeed, it had been unusually hot. Lizzie had the distinct feeling that, had Christiana mentioned that a blizzard had passed through the previous week, he would have agreed to that too.

"It's been rather hot at home as well," Lizzie offered. "But August is usually rather hot and muggy. Our haying, however, has certainly been bountiful. God has blessed our farmers, for sure and certain."

Christiana raised an eyebrow. "Do you work in the fields, Elizabeth? Where are your brothers?"

Setting her fork down beside her plate, Lizzie shifted her weight so that she was facing Christiana. "We have but five *dochders* in the family. I prefer the outdoor work, so I do help my *daed* with the crops, including haying."

"No one from the community helps your *daed*? No hired boys who could learn farming?"

Sensing that this was a horrifying admission, Lizzie merely shrugged her shoulders and shook her head. She wasn't going to engage in a discussion that hinted of negativity and differing opinions, especially with someone like the woman seated before her.

"Five *dochders*, you say?" Christiana seemed to digest this information. Surely it must have seemed bittersweet to a woman who had lost all of her children at young ages, if she had been able to birth them at all. "Are any of them married?"

"*Nee*," Lizzie admitted. "Not one."

"And you are the..."

Lizzie knew where this conversation was headed and inwardly cringed. "The second eldest."

"I see," Christiana said, tapping a wrinkled finger against the tabletop. "And the youngest?"

"She turns sixteen this week," Lizzie admitted.

With her eyes riveted on Lizzie, Christiana seemed to find this prospect completely unnatural. "Five *dochders*, all of marriageable age, and yet not one with a prospect?" She looked down the table at Wilmer first, and then Frederick. "No prospects at all? Why, I must admit that is a most unfortunate situation."

The offensive comment all but bounced off of Lizzie. She was astonished by the pompous nature of this woman that Wilmer had regarded as being so generous of heart and spirit. She witnessed no generosity in Christiana Bechler except for her generosity with insults and unwanted opinions. "I find it rather fortunate, don't you?" Lizzie offered, knowing full well that she was being sassy to this elderly woman, despite the sweetness of her tone. "The youngest shall learn from the eldest, and a sisterly bond will be had by all. I think we are fortunate indeed, and I am quite happy with my family situation and upbringing."

"You speak most freely," Christiana observed, her eyes narrowing as she studied the young woman before her. "Most freely for a young, unmarried woman…with no prospects."

"*Aendi*," Frederick interfered suddenly, interrupting the conversation and handing her a plate. "Your favorite: pickled red beets!" Without waiting for an answer, he began to dish some of the food onto his aunt's plate. "I stopped at the market just yesterday to make certain you had plenty of these for today."

Distracted, Christiana pushed several of the red beets onto her plate before passing the dish to her niece, a quiet and timid mouse of a young woman who rarely spoke unless a question was directed at her by her *aendi*. Lizzie managed to take a few short breaths to calm her beating heart and took advantage of the shift in conversation to watch Anna, trying to see how a match with Frederick and the pale, frail woman would manage to succeed. Anna's personality was clearly lacking, whether from poor health or low self-esteem, Lizzie could not guess which. With Frederick's composure and reserve, she could scarcely think of a better match for him, she told herself, knowing that the thought was something about which she'd have to pray later for forgiveness.

After the meal was served, Lizzie quietly excused herself and, without being asked, began to clear the table and tend to the dishes. Charlotte joined her, and the two women worked side by side, washing and drying the plates and utensils while the formidable Christiana proceeded to question Wilmer about his plans with the church regarding the new tendency for young girls to hang out the side of the buggies, their dresses blowing and exposing their bare legs to indicate their "availability." She caught the insinuation in Christiana's voice that such a practice must certainly have come from the youth being exposed to the

Amish of Lancaster. She even berated him for not having found a solution after his trip to Pennsylvania almost two months prior.

Lizzie rolled her eyes and almost giggled, but both she and Charlotte kept quiet, pretending to focus on the task of drying the dishes. Instead they were eagerly listening to Wilmer stuttering and fumbling with his words as he tried to address this most serious of concerns from Christiana Bechler, the wife of the late bishop. It was clear that he preferred to gauge Christiana's outlook on any situation before he ventured his own opinion, for he wanted to please the elderly woman by appearing to take her advice or simply to agree with her perspective.

With permission, the Kaufman brothers excused themselves and disappeared outside, the younger ones racing across the paddock and scurrying under a fence while John, the older son, followed behind, his hands shoved into his pockets and his shoulders slumped forward. Anna, however, remained seated at the table, her pale hands pressed together and placed primly on her lap. If she had wanted to go outside—something Lizzie would have highly recommended, for the girl was paler than fresh snow—Anna gave no indication of it.

Wilmer and Christiana were deep into discussion when, with the plates cleaned, dried off, and returned to their cupboard, Lizzie indicated to Charlotte that she too wanted to go outside and enjoy the fresh air. Slipping out the door, Lizzie took in a deep breath, shutting her eyes for a moment as she felt the sun on her face. Inside, Wilmer was still stumbling around how to address the situation of the Amish girls exposing their legs when sitting on the buggy's floor. She smiled to herself, shaking her head as she began to walk down the porch steps and head down the driveway and toward the road.

She was amazed about how familiar everything looked while showing some slight differences at the same time. Most of the farms were painted white, just like at home. Many of the larger farms had windmills, and she loved hearing the gentle whirling of the blades in the breeze. However, there were not as many tall silos as she was used to seeing back home, and that took her by surprise.

"Mind if I stretch my legs with you?"

She was startled to find Frederick walking to catch up with her. She had not heard him following her, and when he spoke, he was only a few strides behind. Her surprise was so great that she could not answer but merely kept walking as he fell in stride with her pace.

For a few moments they walked in silence. Lizzie held her breath, waiting for Frederick to speak. He seemed comfortable with the silence, however, his hands tucked into his pockets as he walked alongside of her, his eyes straight ahead and his expression devoid of any emotion. Determined to wait for him to be the first to speak, she continued to walk as if nothing was amiss.

Twenty minutes had passed, and she felt him pull back. Stopping, she looked up at him, realizing how much taller he seemed. She had never noticed how large in stature he was, with such broad shoulders and long back. *Handsome* could not but describe him. Still, the realization that, despite the exterior, his interior was lacking brought her back to reality.

He did not see her studying him as he glanced at the sky then over his shoulder. "We should turn back, *ja*?" He didn't wait for her response before he turned and started walking back, hesitating for just a moment until Lizzie had done the same and was now walking beside him.

To her further surprise, the return trip to the Bechler farm was the same as going: neither spoke. When it became apparent that Frederick was walking for the sake of exercise and not for company, Lizzie relaxed a bit and let her mind wander as her eyes took in the new surroundings. Things seemed greener in

Ohio, although she wondered if that was not her eyes playing tricks on her. With the rolling hills of green, it seemed more alive and interesting to the eye than Leola. There were pockets of trees everywhere, something else that was not familiar to Lizzie. And the farms, indeed, were much closer together.

Charlotte and Anna were seated on the porch when they walked down the driveway. Anna was staring into the distance, not once lifting her eyes to seek out Frederick's. Charlotte, however, smiled when she saw her friend and jumped to her feet. She hurried to meet the two approaching figures.

"They are still discussing the buggy issue," she said lightly. "Dare I say there may be no resolution?"

Frederick exhaled sharply. "Of course there is no resolution. To forbid the youths from doing it will only make them want to do it anyway, and without their being members of the church yet, who is to stop them?"

"And if you ignore it?" Lizzie challenged, wanting to hear his logical answer to that question and engage him in a verbal sparring match.

"You are merely accepting it by omission of complaint. Either way, the practice will continue. The least amount of strife is in ignoring it for now."

Lizzie looked at Charlotte, annoyed to see her friend's amused expression. "That seems very brazen, however. Showing their legs on purpose! Why, I'm surprised the parents would allow such a display!"

"Mayhaps the parents are unaware of their behavior," Frederick responded drily. "Have you considered that?" He paused, as if allowing Lizzie time to think about what he had said before he continued. "In which case, should the youths be blamed or the parents?"

"It's different here," Charlotte said quickly as if to avoid a heated debate between the two. "I can't explain it, Lizzie, for I have yet to fully understand it myself. However, I know that it

161

is still a right *gut* place to live." She glanced at Frederick then back to her friend. "It just takes some getting used to, is all."

"I give you a lot of credit, Charlotte," Lizzie quipped lightly. "Brazen girls and parents lacking control over their *kinner*...I can only imagine what other changes you will need to get used to."

Charlotte laughed lightly. "I think getting married is change enough, Lizzie. The actual community does not matter so much, even if they are quite different. It's being in a godly marriage and being happy in it, at that."

"Why, I couldn't have said it any better!" Lizzie wished she could clap her hands in delight at Charlotte's statement. "If only the rest of us could be blessed with the same: a partnership and friendship with a love of God. *That* is the foundation of a right *gut* marriage."

With a sly glance Lizzie observed Frederick's reaction. He barely flinched at her words, but Lizzie could tell that he was dwelling on them. She wondered whether he was thinking of Charles with his sister or himself with that frail mouse of a girl, Anna. Perhaps, she realized, he had swayed Charles from returning to Leola and, ultimately, to Jane, because he was selfish and did not wish his friend so far away from him. Nor did he want him happy, it appeared.

It certainly said a lot about his character and further reinforced her very reasons for not caring for him...not one bit.

❧ *Chapter Fifteen* ❧

IT WAS EIGHT o'clock Monday morning. Charlotte and her parents had gone for a walk with the boys to the schoolhouse down the lane. The younger ones were starting their first day, and Charlotte had wanted to show her parents where their future grandchildren would study. Lizzie had suspected that she also wanted to show them some more of the area. Wilmer had disappeared immediately after breakfast, hitching the horse to the buggy and driving it down the road.

With the house to herself Lizzie had time to write to her sister, patiently trying to think of interesting things to say while avoiding the unmentionable: Charles Beachey and Grace Detweiler. Lizzie was seated at the table, tapping the end of the pen against the piece of paper. She had made a promise to herself not to write anything about what she had heard from Wilmer. After all, to spread such a story was gossip and hurtful at that. The last thing she would ever want to do would be to say something in a letter to her special sister that might upset her, especially given the chance that it might not be entirely true. Despite being the bishop, Wilmer was most likely not the most reliable source of information, she suspected. Or, rather, she hoped.

For a long moment she sat in the quiet of the kitchen, pondering what to actually write. There was only so much she could tell about the weather and the different types of landscape. She did admit that it was very beautiful and that, even in Lancaster County, she had never seen a blue sky the same brilliant color as in the Dutch Valley. She started to write about her visit to the Bechler farm the previous afternoon, but she set her pen down and paused. For some reason she felt hesitant to mention that Frederick had been there. She certainly did not want to tell her about how he had joined her for a walk after the meal. He had seemed so at ease and comfortable, despite not saying one word to her. She had to admit that there was something about him that made her feel confused, and until she figured it out, she certainly didn't want to put pen to paper about it.

"You are alone?"

Lizzie looked up, startled to see Frederick standing in the kitchen doorway. She hadn't heard him enter the room and wondered how long he had been standing there. Had he been watching her? The thought unnerved her, and she flipped over the letter before she turned to face him. He held his hat in his hand, spinning it slowly as he grasped it. With his dark pants and a crisp white short-sleeved shirt, he looked ready to work, yet everything was too clean for doing so.

"You frightened me," she said, half laughing.

He didn't apologize for having frightened her but looked about nervously. "No one else is home then?"

"I'm afraid not," she confessed, glancing around the room as if to prove the truth behind the statement. "The others have left, but I suspect Charlotte should be returning momentarily. I can't speak for Wilmer, however." Frederick stared at her, his hair swooping over his forehead and his eyes wide. When he made no further attempt to comment, she gestured toward the chair. "You are welcome to wait for them."

He stood still, not moving from the doorway. The expression on his face was like nothing she had ever seen. Nervous and tense. And this coming from one of the most overly confident men she had ever met.

"Frederick?"

"*Nee*," he said, shaking his head and looking at her again. "I came to see you."

"Me?" The word came out of her mouth with the utmost surprise, sounding like a squeak rather than a word. Without thinking, she exclaimed, "I cannot imagine for what reason!"

He glanced at the window and seemed nervous. "It's a lovely day, *ja*?"

Setting down her pen, Lizzie leaned back and stared at him. Had he gone addle-brained? "It is a nice day, *ja*," she replied slowly. She hated to admit it to herself, but this side of Frederick Detweiler was so different from their previous interactions that she was genuinely amused and a touch curious. "Would you care to sit? We can further discuss the delightful weather if you'd like. And I believe there is still coffee in the pot. I'd be happy to warm it."

He lifted a hand to stop her. "*Nee, nee*," he mumbled. "But *danke*. I did not mean to intrude or be a bother."

"Intrude? Bother? I must confess that I am confused, Frederick," she managed to say. "I don't quite understand the meaning of any of this."

He nodded his head and took a step backward. "I must be going, then," he said. "Cutting hay this morning." Without another word he turned and left the house.

Stunned, Lizzie stood up and walked to the window. She leaned against the counter, watching as Frederick resumed his usual air of self-confidence and pride as he sauntered over to his horse and buggy, which he had left tied to the hitching ring on the side of the barn. As the buggy passed the house, he never once even turned to look back, such was his determination to leave the Kaufman property with his pride intact after what was, clearly, a disastrous visit on his part.

She was still standing there, her mouth all but hanging open, when Charlotte reappeared after having walked the children to school.

"*Wie gehts?*" Charlotte asked, a concerned look on her face. "You look pale."

"The strangest thing just happened," Lizzie confessed, keeping an eye on the window so that she could see when Charlotte's parents were approaching. They had walked over to admire the garden upon their return from the schoolhouse. When she was convinced that they would not be interrupted, Lizzie turned to stare at her friend. "You won't believe this, but Frederick was just here."

"Frederick Detweiler?" Charlotte seemed as amazed as Lizzie had been. "Why, I haven't seen him visit with Wilmer since I've been here!"

"That's the funny part," Lizzie said. "He told me he came to see me!"

"You?" Charlotte laughed but not unkindly. "Whatever for?"

"That's what I said, and he had no good reason. He commented on the weather and then left!"

"Oh, help," Charlotte whispered, the laughter gone from her eyes and voice. She stared at Lizzie with an expression of complete wonder. "He's *ferhoodled*!"

Ferhoodled? Lizzie caught her breath, wondering how such a thing could possibly be true. Indeed, there had been times when he acted as if he might possibly be interested in Lizzie. Even she had noticed that. Yet his cold mannerism and expressionless face spoke nothing of feelings or emotions. Instead, that part of him was left to the imagination, since he was usually nothing more than a proper Amish man.

And then there was the Charles situation. Why would Frederick be opposed to a relationship between his closest friend and Jane, having witnessed firsthand their fondness for each other, encouraging him instead to marry his own sister, if he, presumably, had feelings for Lizzie? The nature of such a complex situation was too convoluted for Lizzie to even begin to consider grasping it.

She also remembered what George had told her. Any man that would steal another's birthright was not a godly man and certainly not a man whom Lizzie could ever be interested in courting.

"Don't say such a thing!" Lizzie hissed. "I don't want a man such as Frederick Detweiler being *ferhoodled* on my account!"

"Why else would he visit, Lizzie?" Charlotte asked kindly. "Tell me that? And he went walking with you yesterday. And, if my memory recollects properly, was I not seated beside you back in Leola when he asked you to ride home in his buggy, despite the fact that he not only did not attend the singing but he lived on the very farm where it was being held!"

"I don't want Frederick Detweiler to be *ferhoodled*...," she whispered.

Charlotte shook her head as she reached for her work apron to tie around her waist, in anticipation of the morning's chores. "*Ja, vell*," she answered. "Mayhaps God has another plan for you, Elizabeth Blank. You can't be in control of everything, I reckon."

"But...Frederick Detweiler?"

The two women stared at each other for a minute, digesting this amazing news, one with admiration in her eyes and the other with fear. And then, just as Charlotte's parents crossed the driveway to head toward the house, both young women began to laugh, the idea of Frederick Detweiler with his piercing eyes, stoic expression, and rigid posture actually caring for Lizzie seeming too far-fetched and ridiculous to be taken seriously.

❧ *Chapter Sixteen* ❧

T HE FOLLOWING DAY, after Lizzie helped with the breakfast chores, Charlotte shooed her outside, encouraging
her friend to take a nice walk along the winding roads
behind their house. While reluctant to leave Charlotte alone
with so many other things that needed to be done, Lizzie
agreed with her friend's generous suggestion, as she was eager
to explore her new surroundings and take in some fresh air.

At the end of the short driveway Lizzie took a deep breath
and started walking down the road. She was still enthralled
with how different the landscape was in Holmes County, Ohio,
when compared to what she was familiar with back in Lancaster
County. And the cultural differences of the few people that she
had met certainly intrigued her. Clearly there was no cookie-
cutter Amish person, either religiously or individually.

It was a humid morning, quite different from the previous
day. With low clouds and dampness to the air, it felt as if it
might rain. She didn't mind that the air felt sticky. And rain
would certainly help the farmers, even at the end of August.
Besides, her mind was still preoccupied with all that had happened in the three days since she had arrived to visit with her
friend.

The one thing that pleased her greatly was the contentment
with which Charlotte carried herself. What Lizzie could never
have imagined possible, Charlotte had made a reality: happiness. Certainly it was an advantageous marriage for Charlotte
on many accounts, and as Lizzie could see that her friend was
not affected or bothered by the silliness of her husband, she felt

that Charlotte had done quite well in making a decision that, at the time, had seemed to be rather rash.

The road curved to the right by a small hill that was over-grown with trees. The branches hung over the dirt road, casting shadows in the morning sun. There were thin tracks in the dirt made by buggies that had driven by either earlier that morning or the previous night. Unlike in Leola with its long roads and flat landscape, Lizzie couldn't see what was around the corner. It felt like she was on a secret treasure hunt, unsure of what she would see next.

To her delight there was a path between two paddocks leading down the hill. She could not see what was at the end of that path and decided to explore, imagining that the over-hanging branches were similar to a jungle in a faraway land. Birds flew overhead, chirping and greeting the morning. She watched them as she walked, smiling to herself. Soon it would be fall and, with the start of that season, the migration south of the summer birds. Left behind would be the plain brown sparrows, which contrasted so sharply with the brilliance of the winter red cardinals, if Ohio was anything like Pennsylvania.

"Elizabeth!"

Hearing her name called out startled her, and she spun around in a moment of panic at the interruption. To her amaze-ment she saw Frederick walking down the path behind her.

"Were you following me, Frederick?" she asked breathlessly, her hand covering her heart. The last thing she had expected was to run into anyone, never mind *him*, while walking down this secluded road. "You should have made your presence known! You near gave me a fright!"

He did not apologize as he caught up with her. Once again she noticed that he was wearing freshly laundered clothing, no tears in his pants or stains on his shirt. His shoes had been cleaned and bore no trace of dirt or manure. She couldn't help but wonder what type of farm he ran that he was never in soiled clothing.

"I must speak with you," he said solemnly when he finally stood before her.

Considering that the day before he had unexpectedly stopped at Wilmer and Charlotte's house to visit her but had nothing to say, Lizzie was equally surprised that he had, once again, sought her out. "I trust it is not about the weather, then?" she quipped. "For that would be a long walk just to ask about something that appears to be bordering on most unpleasant!" She stared at the sky, missing the brilliant blue sky with fluffy white clouds from the previous three days.

He did not seem amused by her teasing comment. Or, rather, he may not have even heard her for he appeared determined to say what was on his mind. He cleared his throat and stood before her, unaware that she was watching him with great curiosity.

"These past weeks have been most difficult," he began slowly. She had the distinct feeling that he had practiced his speech. "And I have struggled in vain to convince myself that my infatuation with you is naught but a passing fancy."

There was nothing he could have said that could have surprised her more. She was so stunned that she could not think of anything to interject when he paused.

He quickly continued. "Our cultural upbringings are so different that any type of relationship would clearly bring extra hardships, especially given the differences in our family backgrounds and financial standings." He stopped for just a moment to catch his breath. "I have fought against my family expectations as well as against my better judgment, hoping that distance would calm my feelings, but I stand before you today to express my sincere desire to have you agree to end my torment."

"I do not understand you," she whispered, her heart beating

inside of her chest and her eyes wide as she stared at him, looking so forlorn and miserable after his short speech.

"I love you, Elizabeth Blank." He lifted his eyes to meet her gaze, the piercing darkness of his typical expression having softened. "Most fervently."

Silence.

"I wish that you'd marry me, Elizabeth."

For a long moment they stood there, facing each other. Frederick looked pained, waiting for her response, while Lizzie tried to comprehend exactly what had just happened. The words seemed to echo in her head. Had she just been proposed to by this man? He was, after all, a man she barely knew, and what little she did know was not flattering.

"I...I don't know what to say," she heard the words slip from her mouth. "I find this most...unexpected."

"Do me the honor, Elizabeth. My heart is pained in anticipation." And he did look pained. His cheeks were pale and his eyes wide as he waited for her response.

"I certainly meant you no pain," Lizzie managed to say. "That was never my intention."

He took a step forward. "I did not mean to insinuate..."

She cut him off. "But I certainly must decline and for reasons that you are well aware of, Frederick."

"Reasons?" Clearly that was not the response he had been anticipating.

Lizzie took a deep breath, the shock of having been proposed to suddenly giving way to the underlying anger that had been dormant. "Indeed! You claim to love me despite having fought your feelings and despite our very different backgrounds, both familial and financial! Had you been so eloquent about your feelings for me instead of the reasons why you should not have such feelings, perhaps I might have been inclined to consider such an offer. However, there are other reasons why I cannot accept!"

He seemed confused. "I wish to know these reasons!"

"How could I possibly marry a man who has worked so hard to destroy the one bit of happiness for my dearest sister?"

"Jane?"

"Do you deny that you have kept Charles Beachey in Ohio, encouraging him to court your sister rather than return to Leola where a young woman sits, brokenhearted at the rejection of your best friend?"

At this question Frederick glanced away. "I cannot deny that."

Lizzie's mouth fell open at his admission, but no words came to her lips.

Frederick quickly tried to explain. "I cared enough about my friend to not wish him to experience emotional distress, for it was my observation that she did not return his ardor. She barely talked to him."

"She's shy!" Lizzie cried. "And yet you interfered!"

"Only to protect my friend, not to hurt your sister," he explained.

"Were you protecting George Wickey then?"

Immediately, at the name of George Wickey, Frederick stiffened and lifted his chin. His eyes narrowed and acquired the familiar piercing darkness that represented the Frederick Detweiler she had come to know. "What about Wickey?"

"Do you deny having stolen the land of his birthright from George, leaving him landless and without a means of earning a living now that he has reached age?"

"Is that what you heard?"

"Indeed! How callous and prideful a man you must be! Why should any good Amish woman wish to align herself with such a man who would destroy the happiness of two people, only for his own selfish gain?"

He took a step backward, his eyes glaring as he stared at her. "This is your opinion of me, then? The character you tried so hard to discover?" Straightening his suspenders and placing his hat on his head, he returned to his formidable self. "Your explanation is most sufficient, despite the overbearing tone of pride that you have..."

"Pride?" she cried out. "You speak of *me* having pride?"

"Your pride has tainted your eyes, Elizabeth Blank!"

She laughed but out of disbelief, not joy. "From the first moment I met you, you have done nothing but display a pride in your own position in life while looking with complete disdain at those around you. Nothing could be good enough for the proud Frederick Detweiler! Such arrogance and contempt! Why, from the first words out of your mouth I knew that you would be the last man on earth that I could ever be prevailed upon to accept an offer of marriage!"

Her final words changed his expression once again to that of pain. With his hat shielding his eyes, she could only see the way his mouth trembled, just a touch. He tilted his head to stare at her, the lower parts of his eyes visible and full of sorrow. For a moment Lizzie wished she could take back her words, so hurtful and accusatory. Yet the thought of Jane sitting at home, pining for Charles Beachey, gave her a feeling of vindication.

"I shall leave you now," he mumbled. "Thank you for your time, Elizabeth."

Without another word he turned and began to walk up the path toward the road. She watched him until he disappeared. Then, once he was out of sight, she let the tears flow from her eyes, and she covered her face, ashamed at her own behavior and wondering if there had been a hint of truth to Frederick's words.

Had she too been as prideful as him?

❦ *Chapter Seventeen* ❦

LIZZIE SPENT THE rest of the day quietly crocheting in the kitchen of the Kaufman home. She could barely speak, for her head was filled with words that sent conflicting messages between her conscience and her heart. Charlotte was busy baking cookies for the *kinner* who would return from school in the early afternoon, having given up trying to engage Lizzie in any sort of conversation. Charlotte's parents had gone visiting some former friends from Pennsylvania who had moved to a neighboring town almost ten years prior. So the house remained quiet, for which Lizzie was thankful.

"That's the third time you have unraveled that row," Charlotte observed gently. "Do you want to talk about what is bothering you?"

"*Nee, nee*," Lizzie replied, pulling at the yarn. It came apart easily, but she was too irritated to roll it back into a ball. She sighed and tossed it onto the seat next to her and exhaled loudly.

"Mayhaps you need some fresh air, then?" Charlotte glanced out the window and smiled. "The clouds are breaking, and I think we shall get blue skies and sunshine within the hour!"

Lizzie shrugged noncommittally. After a few more moments of silence she excused herself to retire to her room, commenting that she felt a headache in her temples.

In the solace of her room she stood at the window, staring outside at the hill behind the house. At the top of the hill was a cluster of trees, and she wondered what was beyond them. Most likely the edge of another farm. For a long time she stared at the trees, unable to keep her mind from returning to the confrontation with Frederick. Somewhere, she thought, on the other side of those trees, someone might be staring up and wondering what was on *her* side. Perhaps they too imagined an expansive farm instead of the small farmette that was occupied by Wilmer Kaufman and his family.

Different perspectives engender different realities. She sighed and turned away.

For most of that day Lizzie stayed in her room, her head spinning and her temples throbbing. She emerged briefly for supper and to help Charlotte with the dishes, still remaining quiet and aloof, unresponsive to her friend's attempts to converse. No one else seemed to notice as Wilmer talked about the splendor of the day, working on the Bechler farm with his son John and, later, his younger sons, who had joined them after school.

While the sun set behind the house in the evening hours, Lizzie sat outside on the porch, her crocheting on her lap but her hands stilled from working the yarn as she watched the golden orb descend behind the hill. On a whim she stood and began to walk behind the house and up the hill. She wanted to pass through the trees to see what, indeed, was on the other side. Was it a farm? Or merely another hill?

Her feet became damp with dew, but she ignored the uncomfortable feeling as she walked on. The fence line stopped just before the trees, and Lizzie bent down to slip between the two boards that made the split-rail fence. Her skirt caught on a splintered piece of wood, and she yanked it free, annoyed to see a hole near her hem.

At the top of the hill she paused and stood, her arms hugging herself as the evening air was becoming cool now that the sun was setting. Instead of an expansive farm as she had imagined, she found herself looking down at another farmette and, just beyond that, a road that curved between another pocket of

First Impressions

trees. On the other side of the road were more contemporary houses, most likely belonging to *Englische* families, not Amish.

"If you please spare me one moment," a voice said behind her.

Lizzie turned, not frightened this time by the intrusion. Indeed, she realized that she had almost expected Frederick to appear. He was now standing before her in the same clothing as before, still perfectly laundered and with nary a spot. She wondered if he too had been tormented all day, reliving their conversation and the feelings brought about by the conflicting emotions that she had experienced.

"I would not dream of repeating any of the words that were met with such repulsion earlier today," he said solemnly, taking a step forward. He held a white envelope in his hand, which he proceeded to reach out and hand to her. "However, I did wish to request that you take this and, when feeling the urge of curiosity, read my words as an answer to the two charges against me that you spoke of earlier."

Reluctantly Lizzie reached out her hand and took the envelope, feeling the weight of multiple pages within it. She stared at it for a moment before looking up at Frederick. She had no words to say. Or, rather, she couldn't speak for the forlorn and miserable look on his face, one that reminded her far too much of Jane's expression upon learning that Charles was destined to marry Grace Detweiler.

"I shall bother you no more," he whispered, bowing his head and turning to retreat back down the hill where his buggy had been parked, near the stable on the Kaufman farm.

She waited until his buggy disappeared from view before she turned around, facing the setting sun, which had begun to barely brush against the horizon, its great orange rays peeking through the clouds and forming a colorful quilt in the sky. Slipping her finger under the flap on the back of the envelope, she opened it, ashamed to see that her hand was shaking as she withdrew its contents.

Sarah Price

Unfolding the letter, her eyes quickly flowed through the lines, her heart racing with each word that was laid before her in Frederick's neat and precise handwriting.

Dear Elizabeth,

I shall not repeat words of sentiment in this missive, but I would request your indulgence in permitting me the opportunity to respond to the two charges against my character, which you laid before me this morning.

While I am under the impression that your acquaintance with George Wickey has been but just peripheral, I can assure you that mine has not. Upon the death of his daed, George was, indeed, granted a rather large parcel of land that abutted my own property. It was never my intention to acquire it but rather than wish to farm his land and worship with his community, George chose to engage in a most unusual rumschpringe.

His onkel, Jacob, tried most everything to set his ward, George, on the track of godliness, but George refused baptism and began to spend his free time with other young men, less reputable and clearly not men that would join the church.

When he began to disappear for days at a time, there was naught that could be done to find him. His farm sat unworked and his bills began to accumulate. And then came the news that George had acquired a gambling habit, one that brought with it much debt.

Jacob Beachey was beside himself and vowed to pay the debt. However, with so many kinner of his own, several that had come of age and

178

were in need of their own farms, Jacob Beachey did not have the extra funds to save George from his own sins. There was talk of selling the land, but being that it was landlocked and without much by way of a farmhouse, there was not much interest from anyone besides developers, a most undesirable outcome.

It is true that I offered to purchase the property in order to save George Wickey from his terrible debt and to save the community from having valuable farmland turned into housing for the *Englische*.

While George should have been grateful, he was not. Instead he asked me to turn it back over to him...which I refused. It was shortly after that when I learned he had begun taking my sister, Grace, home from singings. She was just sixteen and unwise to the world of courtship. Within just weeks he had begun to arrange for an elopement with her, an elopement before baptism and one that would certainly have been her ruination.

Thankfully she confided in me before that unhappy event could occur. You can only imagine how devastated she was to learn of George's deception, having only wanted to marry her for her access to land, the very land he had so willingly abandoned for want of a dice and a card game!

As for the charges against me in regard to your sister, Jane, of that I cannot beg anything more than forgiveness. My observation of Jane was that of casual friendship and circumstance, not of romantic interest in Charles. I feared for

*his heart and distracted him with the suggestion
that he might wed Grace and have the tract of
land that lies between his father's farm and my
own. The conversation went no further, and no
courtship has ensued, however.*

*Had I suspected that Jane truly felt emotions
for Charles, mayhaps I would have been less
inclined to interfere. Still, there was the issue
of the expectation of marriage from your own
maem, a story that was spread throughout
Leola before Charles's bags were unpacked upon
arrival! It was distressing to think of Charles
Beachey marrying into a family where the maem
was prone to gossip and the younger sisters to
such silliness.*

*If I offend you by these words, I do apologize.
I write with an open heart and with truth, in
order to explain myself. While I cannot hope to
redeem my favor in your eyes, I do hope that
these words set the story straight so that you
think less ill of me, now that the facts have been
shared.*

*With much blessings,
Frederick Detweiler*

Lizzie stood there at the top of the hill, the letter in her
hand and her eyes watching as the sun finally dipped down
below the horizon. The colors of the sky changed from orange
and reds to dark purples and blues. She watched the quilted
pattern of colors shift behind the random scattering of clouds,
which began to fade as day rapidly dissolved into nighttime.

If the contents of the letter gave pause, she showed no outward signs. Inside, however, she could scarce make sense of
what she had just read. Was it possible that George Wickey

had lied to her? His character certainly was in grave question, given that he had not attended one single worship service in Pennsylvania and had certainly not thought much about returning to Ohio to attend to his *onkel*.

As for the other matter, Lizzie tried to recall the two nights spent at the Beachey house. How could Frederick have presumed that Jane was indifferent to Charles? It was true that the men had worked outside of the house on most days. Frederick had certainly failed to witness Charles's attention to Jane and her response when the house was quiet in the early morning hours. As for the evenings, Lizzie recalled that Jane had, indeed, sat quietly crocheting, rarely engaging in conversation when other people occupied the room.

With her face tilted toward the sky, Lizzie shut her eyes and prayed. She prayed for God to forgive her for having rushed to judgment and having formed a first impression that was so far from the truth. She had let the tongue of one man speak ill of another without questioning the motives behind such evil words. And to think that George Wickey had tried to cajole a young Grace to betray her faith and elope with him, all for the want of land that he had gambled away to begin with!

❧ *Chapter Eighteen* ❧

IT WAS TWO days later when William and Leah insisted that both Charlotte and Lizzie accompany them on a buggy ride to explore the countryside. They were to leave the following Monday morning to return to Leola, a slight delay in their plans after Wilmer had pressed them to stay for church service.

With a free day of leisure, a buggy ride had seemed like a natural course of pastime. Lizzie barely cared what they did or where they went. She was merely counting down the days until she could return home and disappear into the routine of life on her *daed*'s farm, far away from the confusion she felt from her time spent at the Kaufman farm.

She had tried to remain upbeat but found it increasing hard as she repeatedly replayed the scene with Frederick. She thought back to having met him and his horrible words about her. She remembered his disapproving looks and proud mannerism at the Beachey farm. She couldn't forget their words in the buggy ride home from the singing. And yet...

She remembered him helping her over the puddle in the driveway after the storm. She recalled his look of hidden curiosity when she had tossed his horrid words back at him. She could feel him standing next to her when she walked down the road each morning.

Despite the mixed feelings, she realized that she found it hard to forget the very things she wished not to remember.

She was barely paying attention, knowing not where they were, unaware of the direction in which the horse and open-topped buggy went. So oblivious was Lizzie that she neglected to see Charlotte watching her and failed to notice William turn down a particularly long lane.

"I believe this is the place, ain't so, Charlotte?" her *daed* asked.

Charlotte glanced over her shoulder and, after taking a moment to recognize where they were, nodded her head. "*Ja*, this is the Detweiler farm."

At the mention of Frederick's last name Lizzie snapped out of her daydream and looked around at her surroundings. Plush green fields with a plain wooden fencing kept the horses grazing on the hilltop while two perfectly painted white buildings stood in the dip of the valley. A windmill was stationed behind the one building, spinning slowly in the midday breeze. As far as the eye could see were rolling hills of pasture and crops, all carefully manicured. The horses that frolicked in the one pasture were gorgeous Standardbred horses, several with gangly colts beside them.

Everything was clean and pristine. She could not imagine the amount of work that it took to maintain such a property. Many farmers dumped old pallets or garbage behind the outbuildings. But there was no sign of anything amiss at Frederick's farm. It was, in a word, immaculate. She felt in complete awe as she stared at the house and barns, amazed that one man could take such good care of a property.

"I dare say we should not intrude on Frederick," Lizzie said, her eyes pleading with Charlotte to implore her *daed* to turn around the buggy and continue down the road. Charlotte returned the plea with a quizzical look of her own, not quite understanding Lizzie's sudden animation about being at the Detweiler farm.

"Nonsense," William said dismissively. "He invited us to see his farm on Sunday last."

"But our visit is unannounced!" she cried, desperately hoping that her friend's *daed* would change his mind. What on earth would Frederick think if she showed up at his house after all that had so recently happened? The thought horrified her, and she continued with her plea. "He will be working and we will be an interruption and bother."

Charlotte laid her hand on Lizzie's arm and leaned forward, whispering in her friend's ear. "Wilmer mentioned a special auction today. All of the men are there, and it is located across town." She leaned back and smiled reassuringly.

Indeed, when William stopped the buggy and hitched the horse to a simple ring on the side of the barn, he helped his *fraa* and *dochder* before extending a hand to assist Lizzie. Reluctantly she took it and stepped down from the buggy. No one had come to greet them, and by all appearances, the farm was empty of any human occupants.

Disappointed, William insisted on knocking at the door, just in case someone resided inside. The three women stood by the buggy, watching to see if anyone was home at the farm. When the door opened, Lizzie caught her breath. For a long moment she dreaded the realization that Frederick would, indeed, have stayed home.

"Be still," Charlotte said softly. "It is his *aendi* who stays here to tend the home."

Exhaling, Lizzie's eyes flew to the door and took in the sight of an older woman who greeted William. Within minutes he had waved the small gathering of women to join him on the porch, where he confirmed that Frederick had gone to the auction and the hired men were baling hay on the back field, which could not be seen from the dip in the valley where the house was located.

Frederick's *aendi* invited them inside, delighted for the company. Lizzie entered with a sense of dread, feeling as though she was invading his privacy and wishing that she had claimed illness rather than accompanied her friend's parents on this ill-fated journey. *At least*, she thought with a sense of calming, *he is not here to know firsthand of the visit.*

The *aendi* hustled about the kitchen, insisting that the visitors sit down and enjoy a cup of tea prior to returning on their way. She seemed genuinely happy for the company and joined them for a brief respite and fellowship.

"Such a shame that my young niece Grace is not also here to greet you," she said, shaking her head. "She is visiting her cousins Elinor and Mary Anne!" She laughed good-naturedly, the noise sounding like music. "And Frederick is away at auction. He loves to attend and buy well-priced equipment that might be of help to his neighbors in the *g'may.*"

Lizzie frowned, listening to the unexpected praise bestowed upon Frederick by his dotting *aendi.*

"Such an impressive property," William managed to say between bites of a cookie that the *aendi* had set down on the table. "Yet he's not married and has no sons." He shook his head in disbelief. "He must work very hard."

"Oh *ja, ja,*" the *aendi* said, smiling at the unexpected guests. "Never seen such a hardworking man. But he does not maintain the farm alone."

At this, Lizzie seemed surprised. "Who helps him?"

"Why, he hires other Amish youths to help," his *aendi* said proudly. "Many of them come from big families, you see. I imagine it's the same in Pennsylvania. But without a lot of land, they would be forced to take jobs among the *Englische.* Our Frederick hires them to work here, helps them learn to farm while earning money. And they even share the profits from the crops."

Leah looked impressed. "That's very kind of him!"

The *aendi* nodded her head. "Oh, that's my Frederick. Not a kinder and more generous soul has ever walked the earth."

For a moment Lizzie wondered if they were talking about the same man. While she could see that Frederick was hardworking from the way he helped during the cleanup from that storm, *kind* and *generous* were not the two words that she would have used to describe him.

"In fact, besides buying farm equipment for the neighbors to use," she said, leaning forward to whisper the next part, "he even helped a young couple with some very steep medical bills." She leaned back and fussed with her cup. "I shouldn't share that with you, but it's common knowledge now. When the *g'may* collected for the bills, it was Frederick who quietly paid the balance."

Lizzie stared at the *aendi* with a mixture of curiosity and disbelief. "Did he tell everyone about this?"

"Oh, heavens no!" The *aendi* laughed and waved her hand at Lizzie. "He was mortified when the story became known. You see, the minister's *fraa* has a gossiping tendency. Frederick was quite put out that people learned about what he had contributed." She glanced nervously at Charlotte at the mention of the wife of a minister in their *g'may*, even though it was a different church district.

Lizzie was stunned. Within minutes she had learned that Frederick hired young men to work his farm, young men from larger families who would otherwise be forced to work in the community among the *Englische* workforce. Not only did he pay them for their time, but he also shared the profits from his crops with the workers and, as a result, had helped several young men save enough money to buy their own small farms in nearby villages and towns.

In addition, he had a reputation for breeding outstanding horses and made quite a strong living from it. His *aendi* was quick to inform her visitors that her nephew was able to help his community by purchasing farm equipment that he permitted others to use. He asked nothing in return for the usage of the equipment. His kindness and generosity were well known throughout the area and beyond, something that Lizzie wondered why neither Wilmer nor Christiana had mentioned before. In fact, a young couple whose husband was working for Frederick in his breeding operation had just experienced mounting medical bills from the premature birth of their third son. Frederick had taken care of these as well.

His wealth had come from his *daed* and his generosity from his *maem*, the *aendi* went on. Yet he was the least proud man despite his ability to buy more land or hire more workers. He had even taken in his *aendi*, a fact that delighted her, for she was naught more than a *maedel*, the youngest sister of his *maem*. He had refused to let her live alone and insisted that she'd occupy the *grossdawdihaus* in order to maintain some degree of independence in her old age.

Even Charlotte seemed taken with this new image of Frederick Detweiler. Having lived in the neighboring *g'may* for almost two months, she had yet to become privy to these stories. His other *aendi*, Christiana Bechler, had never mentioned all of the good deeds that were being attributed to the elusive and quiet Frederick Detweiler. Without having heard these stories, Charlotte had been unable to share them with Lizzie. She looked as stunned as her friend. They caught each others' gaze, a look of wonder and awe in their eyes as they listened to even more praise about his kindness to the local schoolchildren by purchasing new books and a fresh blackboard just this past year.

It was too much for Lizzie to comprehend, the image conflicting so greatly with what she had harbored within herself. If the *aendi* wasn't so pleasant and kind, Lizzie would have trusted none of her words.

"I...I think I need some fresh air," Lizzie said abruptly as she quickly retreated outside, hearing Charlotte excuse her to the *aendi* by stating a recent bout with migraines.

Lizzie wandered the lane, her mind not able to comprehend this very different version of Frederick Detweiler. Generous and kind? Modest and caring? This was not the man Lizzie had met in Pennsylvania. Had she met such a man, she wondered, would her reaction have been different the other day on the lane?

She was just about to turn a corner along the fence line when she saw a figure approach her. To her deep embarrassment she realized that it was none other than Frederick. They saw each other at the same time and stopped in midstep. For the first time Lizzie saw him in work clothes, soiled pants, and a shirt that was unbuttoned at the top. His straw hat was tattered and his hair clung to his forehead from sweat.

"Frederick!"

He seemed uncomfortable, and his eyes darted around as if looking for an escape.

"I'm so terribly sorry," Lizzie whispered, avoiding looking at him. She felt the color flood to her cheeks, and she could barely find the words to speak. "Your *aendi* said you were at the auction..."

"I...I was headed there, but I changed my mind," he managed to say. "I decided to help the men with the baling."

"I see," she responded.

"You are here alone?" he asked, finally lifting his eyes to meet hers.

"*Nee, nee,*" she quickly replied. "Charlotte's parents took us for a buggy ride to see the area. It was William who came calling." She chewed on her lower lip, hating the shakiness in her voice. "I never would have invaded your privacy had I known you were on the property." She glanced around. "Your farm is most pristine and well maintained!"

"*Danke,*" he managed to say, averting his eyes. He was uncomfortable with the encounter, and Lizzie could hardly blame him. He seemed to shuffle his feet and stared past her toward the house. "I must excuse myself," he said before he walked on and hurried in the direction of the house.

Lizzie stared after him, wishing she had found the proper words to say, something, anything to correct the prejudice that she had shown by misjudging him so poorly. Yet, from the way that he hurried, she knew that the days of cordial meetings, no matter how infuriating the discussion, were over.

She tried to walk farther but found that her mind was too preoccupied. She felt sick to her stomach, realizing how her appearance at his farm must have looked to him. It was as though she was showing off her delight at having rejected his offer of marriage, which truly was not the case. Her thoughts distracted her, and she felt compelled to return to the house in order to insist that they leave at once. Her feet could not carry her there fast enough, and when she finally approached the front door, she was further disturbed to hear laughter from within, one laugh in particular most distressing, for it belonged to Frederick.

He had changed. He no longer wore his work clothing but his regular attire: clean black pants and a freshly washed and ironed white shirt. His boots were not the dirty ones that he had just been wearing. In their place he wore fresh boots that had been cleaned, or simply never soiled. His hair was neatly combed and the dirt washed from his hands and face. This was the Frederick she was used to seeing, and she realized that his discomfort in seeing her on the path was more at his appearance than about her rejection.

Something about that realization caused a warmth to grow within her heart.

"Lizzie, come!" William said when he saw her standing in the doorway. "We have the great fortune of the company of Frederick Detweiler! He did not attend the auction after all!"

"I see that," she murmured.

There was something casual about Frederick as he stood beside his *aendi*. She had never witnessed a laughing and cheerful Frederick. The change was remarkable and captured her attention. He offered them dinner, which they declined, but he demanded that William permit him to show him the new foals, an offer that was accepted by all except Lizzie, who stood there in stunned silence.

He walked in leisure, asking questions of Charlotte about her move and adjustment to the different lifestyle afforded in Ohio. It was clear that even Charlotte could scarcely believe the transformation of the man who stood before her and kept glancing over at Lizzie, who was just as stunned as she was. He then addressed William and Leah, asking what they thought of their *dochder*'s new surroundings and inquiring as to their time spent in Dutch Valley.

Only when they reached the fence line surrounding the horses and foals did Frederick fall back enough to walk in step with Lizzie. He walked in a comfortable silence beside her, his eyes gleaming as he saw the foals in the middle of the paddock. When one began to frolic and play, leading the other into a game of chase, he laughed and pointed out their antics to a still speechless Lizzie.

"He'll be a good stepper, no doubt," he said cheerfully, his face glowing with happiness at the sight.

On their walk back toward the house William and Leah stopped to admire the gardens with Charlotte, leaving Lizzie alone with Frederick for a few minutes. Again the silence between them grew long, and despite his evident comfort with the lack of conversation, Lizzie felt compelled to once again apologize for having intruded on his time and farm.

"Don't be concerned," he said lightly, his dark eyes searching hers. "It was a welcome respite from work." He hesitated before adding, "The most tolerable of company."

She flushed at his remark, and he laughed.

"Have I rendered you speechless? At last!" he said teasingly. "I would not have thought it possible."

Leah and William rejoined them, oblivious to the color on

Lizzie's cheeks and joy in Frederick's eyes. "What gardens you have, Frederick! I should only hope that Charlotte could imitate a quarter of what you have done!" Leah said.

"They are kept by *Aendi*, I fear," he said, sobering at the compliment and deflecting it. "She loves to garden and is helped by Grace as much as possible." He cleared his throat. "Without a *maem*, Grace needs some guidance and oversight from a woman who can teach her the things that I cannot. Perhaps one day," he added, his eyes avoiding Lizzie's, "I may boast of being blessed with a *fraa* to help take over where *Aendi* cannot. After all, *Aendi* is older and quite unaware of the proper ways of a young Amish woman in today's world, *ja*?"

"What a *fraa* that would be," William said somberly. "To take on the care of this place would be most intimidating and require a *fraa* with extensive experience at maintaining a large farm."

Lizzie looked away, uncomfortable with the direction of the conversation and too aware that Charlotte was watching her. Knowing this, Lizzie tried to act natural and not respond to the undercurrent in the discussion, but she knew that her discomfort was far from unapparent to the ever-watchful eye of her friend.

Another hour was spent in Frederick's company, each moment increasing Lizzie's further feeling of confusion. She continued to remind herself that the man standing before her had separated Jane and Charles, albeit out of an abundance of caution for Charles's feelings and an understandable dismay about her *maem* and *schwesters*. There was no amount of forgiveness that could change that situation, even if she *had* been mistaken about George Wickey.

When they finally parted company, Frederick made certain to help the women step into the buggy. When it came time to help Lizzie step up, his hand lingered for just a moment, barely noticeable to anyone save her. She lifted her eyes and met his gaze, surprised to see his eyes dancing and sparkling at her in a way she had never seen prior to this moment. Stunned, she took her seat next to Charlotte in silence.

"What a fine fellow, that Detweiler!" William said as they drove down the lane toward the main road. "Why, it is remarkable what he has done with his property, helping so many young men. And to think that he was thought so proud when he was staying in Leola!"

His wife shook her head, clicking her tongue in disapproval. "People can be such poor judges of character, ain't so?"

Lizzie remained silent, staring into the scenery and feeling the breeze on her face. The trees that bordered the road shielded the sun's heat from them, and the day was rather pleasant. Yet, despite the beautiful surroundings and perfect weather, Lizzie was unaware of anything except this new side of Frederick that she had experienced while in the Dutch Valley of Ohio. While she knew that the truth would always be known in the end, she still felt a battle of emotions at having her previous view of the circumstances so unexpectedly and strongly corrected.

❖ *Chapter Nineteen* ❖

AFTER CHURCH SERVICE on Sunday Frederick Detweiler drove his black-topped buggy into the Kaufman's driveway. He hitched the horse to the same ring at the stable as he had the evening when he had delivered the letter to Lizzie. Only this time he did not walk up the hill but proceeded to walk to the door. He knocked once, twice, then stepped back, allowing time for someone to answer it.

Once inside the kitchen he let his eyes adjust to the dim light before nodding his greeting at the family gathered around the kitchen table. The boys were outside playing, their older brother John tossing stones at a hollow tree by the road.

"Why, Frederick Detweiler!" Wilmer said, jumping up from his seat and gesturing toward the recliner in the sunroom. "I dare say this is a most welcomed surprise! Come, sit for a spell."

"I wanted to wish everyone well on your journey back to Pennsylvania," he said politely. "I am headed to my *aendi*'s for Sunday supper and thought I'd take a moment to wish you well."

"That's most kind!" Wilmer gushed.

"I also thought to inquire if you might care to join us at the Bechler farm once again," he said. "It would be our pleasure, especially since Grace has returned from her visitation with her cousins Elinor and Mary Anne." His eyes fell upon Lizzie in particular. "I should like you to meet my young sister before departing."

Lizzie looked at Charlotte, her mouth almost falling open at the unexpected request. Instead, she managed to maintain her composure and tilted her head in acknowledgment of his request. "I should like that very much," she said. "If it is not too much trouble for Christiana or Charlotte."

Wilmer laughed, the noise distracting Lizzie for the moment. "No hardship whatsoever on my *fraa*. I'm sure she has yet to prepare an evening meal for us."

They had no sooner arrived at the Bechler farm a few hours later—Wilmer boasting once again of how generous Christiana was to host them for a meal, not once but twice, during their stay—than Frederick appeared at the porch with his younger sister beside him.

Lizzie could only stare at the angelic-looking girl with blonde hair that highlighted her large, dark eyes—eyes that seemed far too familiar. She was petite and fragile, quite the opposite of her tall and muscular brother. It was clear from the look on her face that she was all innocence and propriety, not a blemish to her character to be found.

Without waiting for the buggy to stop, Grace rushed forward, calling for Lizzie by name.

"I have heard so much about you!" Grace cried out, skipping the outstretched hand and hugging Lizzie instead. "I feel as though I know you already."

Lizzie glanced at Frederick. "I hardly know how to respond to that!"

After proper introductions were made to the other guests, Grace walked arm in arm between Charlotte and Lizzie, chattering away about her summer with Elinor, her dearest friend and cousin on her *maem*'s side. With Frederick dispatched to Pennsylvania to help Charles, she had been sent away to be cared for by Elinor's family, she stated. However, Lizzie wondered if the situation with George had anything to do with the young woman's trip.

"I think I'm planning on joining the church in the spring," she confided to Lizzie.

"That's a big decision," Lizzie replied, but with an approving smile. "And in the spring, *ja*? We usually have our baptisms in October."

Grace nodded. "We have baptisms twice a year. I know most places only have them in autumn, but we have a large number of youths in our district." There was a moment of silence before Grace leaned forward. "You must have a large district too," she whispered. "With such large families."

"We have twenty-two families in our *g'may*, but most of the youths are older, it seems," she admitted.

"You have four siblings, *ja*? What's that like?"

Lizzie laughed. "I suppose I cannot answer that, just like you probably couldn't tell me what it's like to *not* have four siblings. Although you do have Frederick…"

Grace glanced at him, a look of adoration in her eyes. "*Ja*, he's a right *gut bruder* to me. Yet he's so much older. Sometimes I feel that he's more like a *daed*." She returned her attention to Lizzie. "Nothing like having a sister, I'm sure."

Lizzie noted the wishful longing in the girl's voice and realized that, had she accepted Frederick's proposal and become his *fraa*, Grace would have gotten her wish: a sister. And Lizzie knew that being an older sister to Grace would be a much more rewarding job than being an older sister to Mary, Catherine, and Lydia.

For the next half an hour everyone sat and talked in the small sunroom where the resting sofa and rocking chairs were located. Frederick had gone into a closet to fetch some folding chairs, setting them in a circular fashion so that everyone could visit in comfort. Most of the discussion centered on the summer crops and how bountiful they had been. There was also discussion about some of the recent visitors who had stopped by to pay their respects to Christiana, at least four families in the last week alone!

At the mention of visitors Christiana interrupted herself

and abruptly turned to her niece. "Anna, fetch that letter that arrived here yesterday," Christiana demanded, pointing to the desk on the far side of the room. As Anna obediently obliged, slowly standing to begin crossing the room without one word, Christiana turned to look at Lizzie. "It's a letter meant for you, Elizabeth, delivered here by mistake. I meant to have someone run it up to the Kaufman's, but I knew that you would be here today and whatever news was in the letter could probably wait."

A letter? Whoever would have written to her while she was in Ohio? Curiosity got the best of her and Lizzie turned to watch as Anna began shuffling papers and opening drawers, her shoulders hunched over and the glasses on her nose slipping so that she had to push them back in order to search the desk. When she found the letter, she carried it to Lizzie and politely handed it to her.

"*Danke*," Lizzie managed to say, her heart breaking for the frail woman before her that had expectations of marriage to a man who Lizzie knew had feelings for another. Yet, despite that knowledge, Lizzie knew that a second offer of marriage would not be forthcoming. Her heart sank as she glanced around the room, too aware that everyone was watching her. "It's from my sister Jane."

"Well, read it, child!" Christiana insisted with an impatient wave of her hand. "We won't mind if you do."

Reluctantly and with a minor feeling of irritation at being told what to do by a woman she barely knew, Lizzie opened the envelope and began to read the words. She felt the color drain from her cheeks as her eyes stared at each sentence, so carefully placed on the page. She knew from the silence in the room that everyone was watching her, and she tried to maintain her composure. Yet she could not help the tears that came to her eyes as she read the terrible news from the hand of her sister Jane: Lydia had run off with George Wickey.

"I...I must return to the house," she whispered, standing

quickly and hurrying to the door. She heard chairs scraping against the floor and knew that Charlotte was starting to follow her. But she simply could not share the news with Christiana Bechler or the Detweilers.

Without glancing back, Lizzie ran down the lane and cut through the pasture to retreat to the safety of the Kaufman home. Once inside she ran to her room and threw herself on the bed, the letter still clutched in her hand. The tears flowed freely now for the awful truth that Jane's words had contained. She could only imagine how distraught *Maem* must feel at Lydia's betrayal of the entire family. And with someone like George Wickey!

"Lizzie!"

She knew that she had to tell Charlotte but dreaded leaving the room. It was as though the secret was not real as long as no one else knew it. Yet she also knew that she had no choice but to share it with her friend. Wiping the tears from her eyes, she opened the door and, to her surprise, saw Frederick standing beside Charlotte.

"What has happened?" Charlotte asked.

"It's Lydia," Lizzie managed to say. She glanced at Frederick but could not maintain eye contact. "She's run off." A sob escaped from her lips, and she quickly covered her mouth with her hand. "With George Wickey!"

"What?"

Frederick inhaled sharply and narrowed his eyes.

Upon seeing his reaction, she felt the tears start to flow from her eyes. What must he think, she wondered, horrified that he was there to hear such awful news. "She's ruined, Charlotte! They were discovered missing after the singing last week, and someone saw them at the Beachey farm...alone!"

"Oh, help!" Charlotte whispered.

"But that's not the worst of it! She disappeared with him a few days later...to Philadelphia!"

Charlotte collapsed onto a chair, her eyes staring at the floor. There were no words to describe how they felt, for they knew that Lydia's choice had most likely ruined her chances of finding a proper suitor now that speculation would run through the Amish grapevine about her time alone with George.

"Where are they now?" Frederick asked, his voice calm and even.

Lizzie managed to look at him. "I don't know. This letter was dated three days ago."

"You leave tomorrow?"

She nodded.

"Would you like for me to find a driver to leave immediately? To take you back at once?"

She hesitated. Who would drive on a Sunday? If only that could be arranged, she knew that she would feel better. But to make such an imposition was not worth it, she told herself. "*Nee*," she said, fighting the tears that welled in the corner of her eyes. "What is another day at this point?"

He studied her for a moment then nodded his head.

Lizzie wondered why no one had called her, why she had heard this news from a letter. Wilmer had a phone in the barn with an answering machine. She decided that they had not wanted to tell her while she was away, and they were waiting for her return so as not to upset her. Yet Jane had been wise enough to mail a short letter so that Lizzie would know what to expect when she returned.

"Ruined at sixteen," she mumbled and noticed Frederick grimace. She knew that he was thinking of his own sister and how close Grace had come to falling into the same trap. At one time Grace had thought herself in love with George. Clearly Lydia must have felt the same way, for certainly her youngest sister, while foolish and immature, would not do such a thing on a mere whim!

❧ *Chapter Twenty* ❧

THE HOUSE WAS morbidly quiet when she entered early Monday afternoon. The kitchen was a mess, dishes piled high in the sink. Unfolded clothing and sheets were piled onto the table. The floor looked as though no one had swept it in a week. Lizzie set her lone suitcase down on the floor and looked around, disgusted with the chaos that greeted her.

She heard a noise come from her parents' bedroom, and she ventured toward the closed door. Weeping. She knocked once, twice, then opened the door, surprised to see Jane, Mary, and Catherine seated on the bed, offering comfort to their *maem*.

"What on earth?"

Catherine jumped up and ran toward her older sister. "Oh, Lizzie, it's just so awful!"

Jane caught Lizzie's eye and shook her head, indicating that no one dare know about her letter.

"Lydia has run off with George Wickey!"

With a quick look around the room Lizzie tried to assess everyone's reaction to Catherine's proclamation. *Maem* wept even harder, the pile of tissues that surrounded her on the bed deep enough to tell Lizzie that she had not moved much from that spot since the news was uncovered. Mary seemed pale and forlorn, with nothing in particular to say.

"What is this about?" Lizzie demanded impatiently. "Could someone please explain?"

The story quickly unfolded in more detail than Jane's letter had described. It was clear that a mild flirtation had been occurring between George Wickey and Lydia for far longer than anyone realized. After Charles returned to Ohio, George had disguised his favor toward Lydia by appearing to call on Lizzie. With Lizzie gone visiting to Ohio, George had convinced Lydia to go riding with him in his buggy late at night, after the family was asleep.

Daed suspected something was going on when he heard pebbles being thrown at a window. He hadn't thought much of it until the morning. But he noticed buggy marks in the dirt at the end of the driveway along with grass that was pressed down, indicating that a horse had been standing there. However, he never suspected Lydia. It was normal for young men to come calling under the cover of night, and he suspected it was for one of the older girls.

Lydia's birthday had given her more of a free rein. At sixteen she could now attend singings and be courted. George had not waited more than one single day after her birthday to escort her home from the singing. Only he did not bring her home. Instead he took her to his farmhouse, and another Amish man had spotted them leaving the house late that evening.

It hadn't taken long for the Amish grapevine to begin circulating the story of their unsupervised time alone. With the house in an uproar over Lydia's newly compromised reputation, something that *Maem* lamented morning, noon, and night, it had been easy for George to convince Lydia to run off with him several nights later. A driver reported that he had taken them to the train station, and that was the last anyone had heard of them. Thursday morning, as soon as *Daed* discovered Lydia missing, he immediately went to the Beachey farm to find Lydia and confront George. What he found, instead, was a herd of cows in agony from not having been milked or fed.

That had been when Jane had written to Lizzie.

Since then, *Daed* had taken care of both farms, demanding that Mary and Catherine assist him while Jane tended to their *maem* and to the house. He hadn't asked for help from the community, for he was too embarrassed that his daughter had shamed the family. *Maem* had barely left the bedroom, spending her days weeping and crying over the humiliation of Lydia's actions.

"This is ridiculous!" Lizzie announced. "Lydia isn't even a baptized member of the church!"

Maem wailed louder.

"She has shamed no one but herself! And with someone as unworthy as that George Wickey!"

Jane gasped at Lizzie's uncharitable words.

Lizzie shook her head. "I fail to see why that is so disturbing to anyone! Look what he has done! If that is whom Lydia wishes to be aligned with, so be it! To lie around and cry, why...I can't think of anything worse to do!"

Without another word Lizzie left the room and immediately began to tackle the chore of cleaning the kitchen. She let her anger guide her response to her youngest sister's horrible decision to do something so rash and disreputable. And it bothered her even more that such an action by a young, wild girl could reflect on the rest of the family.

She stopped washing the dishes and caught her breath.

Wasn't that exactly what Frederick had said back in Ohio when they had been discussing the issue about young Amish girls hanging out of the buggy? Hadn't she been the one to say that it reflected on the family while Frederick had stated that it was the fault of the youth alone? Yet now that her own family was disgraced, Lizzie found herself agreeing with him that a family should not be judged because of the actions of one member. But if that were so, then why had he discouraged Charles from pursuing Jane? Jane, who was the soul of discretion, even if her *maem* wasn't?

"Oh," she whispered, suddenly realizing how Grace's actions must have affected Frederick. He had already experienced the

Sarah Price

pain—and the shame—of family disgrace. Perhaps he had been hoping to save Charles from a similar fate. Knowing the conflicting emotions that coursed through her at this moment, she couldn't really blame Frederick for his abundance of caution.

The following morning *Daed* discovered a phone call on the answering machine: a message from the bishop. Apparently— the bishop had reported—Lydia and George had returned to Leola and were back in residence at the Beachey farm. *Daed* explained this to the rest of the family, a dazed look on his face.

"And, what's more," he continued with a complete lack of expression in his voice, "they are married."

"Married?" *Maem* repeated in disbelief.

Daed nodded his head. "It appears that they eloped, then they came back and went begging to the bishop to be baptized in October in order to become members of the Amish church."

Immediately, *Maem*'s demeanor changed. Any tears that had been in her eyes dried practically instantly as she, once again, repeated the word: "Married!" She took a deep breath and almost smiled. "Why, that's *wunderbaar gut* news indeed!"

Lizzie watched the conversation between her parents as if she were watching a volleyball game. Her mind whirled as she tried to make sense of what she had just heard. If it was *wunderbaar gut* news, that was yet to be seen. However, by eloping and returning to the bishop—something that Lizzie had never heard of occurring before in her lifetime—Lydia was not disgraced. Not fully.

Yet, deep down, she knew that George Wickey was not an honorable man. Wasn't this the same course of action that George had adopted in Ohio? Hadn't Frederick told her that George had preyed on Grace Detweiler when she too had turned sixteen? And for what? A parcel of land? What was it that George wanted this time? He already had charge of the Beachey farm and had abandoned it, leaving it untended for almost a week! Thankfully her *daed* had been able to care for

204

the dairy herd. And, after such a disgraceful elopement, there was hardly any chance that *Daed* would permit them to live on *his* farm.

"I want to go see them," *Maem* announced.

Lizzie got into the conversation when she heard that. "I don't think that's a good idea," she said slowly. "Receive her here in a few days or even weeks, *Maem*, but don't go there."

"Why ever not?"

"I think this should simmer down a bit," Lizzie tried to explain. She could only imagine how Lydia would behave, and based on her own emotions in dealing with the stress and anguish that had befallen the family, Lizzie knew that she wanted nothing to do with either one of them. "After all she has put us through, I think you should wait a spell." She glanced at her *maem*. "For the benefit of us all."

Maem started to argue, but *Daed* quickly held up his hand and stopped her midsentence. Immediately *Daed* agreed with Lizzie, recognizing the wisdom of his daughter's statement. However, it was decided that he would stop by the Beachey farm to confront his youngest *dochder* and new husband alone and find out exactly what had occurred. He also wanted to make certain that George was taking care of the animals properly.

Lizzie suspected that there was more to *Daed*'s intended visit. Knowing her *daed* as well as she did, she figured that he wanted to have a private word or two with both his youngest *dochder* and this irresponsible man who had, unexpectedly, become his first son-in-law.

❧ Chapter Twenty-One ❧

IT WAS ALMOST a week after Lizzie returned from Ohio when she first saw Lydia.

Lizzie had arrived at church with her family early in order to greet people. They had decided to go together and face their fellow church members on what was the first worship service since Lydia had run off with George Wickey. Despite the news of their youngest *dochder*'s wedding, both *Maem* and *Daed* were still smarting from the humiliation caused by the actions of their daughter. Lizzie and Jane had whispered about how to deal with the situation and provide the best possible support to their parents. They decided that attending the service together, as a family, so that they could stand by their parents and surround their *maem* with love and support was, indeed, the best way.

However, upon their arrival, *Maem* soon found herself flocked by her friends, who demanded the latest information and updates about Lydia's unexpected behavior and ensuing marriage. While Lizzie was certain that many people speculated about a possible underlying reason for the hasty marriage, she could hear her *maem* immediately putting that gossip to rest by happily telling everyone that George was a *wunderbaar* and most welcomed addition to the family. A family, she added, whose growth she genuinely looked forward to, as she was eager to become the happy *grossmammi* of many *boppli* to bless the union at some point in the *far* distant future.

Only time would quell *that* rumor, Lizzie thought wryly.

Despite all of *Maem*'s proclamations of family bliss, she was hard pressed to maintain her composure when Lydia walked into the building with George following two steps behind her. In fact, a general hush filled the room and every eye was trained on the newly married couple.

For many members of the *g'may*, this was the first time they had seen George Wickey, for this was certainly the first worship service he had attended. He looked stiff and uncomfortable in his Sunday suit, avoiding eye contact with the Blank family and retreating to the side of the room where the younger men were gathered. A few of them, the unmarried ones who had not taken their kneeling vow as of yet, seemed to have already made George's acquaintance, a fact that made perfect sense to Lizzie now. Those nights after the storm, when he had disappeared and not returned until the early morning hours, he most likely had been with a group of friends on a wild *rumschpringe*, two of whom were standing with him now. Lizzie easily recognized them as having developed a rather questionable reputation as of late.

In complete contrast, if Lydia was embarrassed or self-conscious about her recent actions, she gave no such indication. She smiled from ear to ear as she greeted the line of women, shaking their hands and kissing their lips, sparing a few words in response to those who were able to overcome their surprise at her unexpected appearance to congratulate her on her recent nuptials.

Lizzie took a deep breath, dreading the idea of having to greet her *schwester*. She felt deeply uncomfortable and a little bit angry at how carelessly happy Lydia appeared, oblivious to the pain that she had caused so many.

When Lydia had finished with the greeting line, she looked around until her eyes rested on her four *schwesters* standing off to the side. Rather than acknowledge that they were clearly avoiding her, Lydia smiled and immediately pranced up to her sisters, her fingers reaching to adjust her white prayer *kapp* upon her head, a sharp contrast with the black *kapps* that her four unmarried sisters wore.

"I can't believe not one of you has come to visit me in my new home," Lydia pouted playfully, moving her head from one sister to the next in such a fashion that the untied white ribbons of her *kapp* flipped through the air. "I would think you'd want to offer some congratulations!"

Lizzie took a deep breath and shook her head. "This is neither the right time nor the proper place, Lydia."

Her youngest sister laughed and waved her hand at Lizzie. "Oh, Lizzie," she said cheerfully. "You don't have to always be so serious. I was just teasing you." She glanced around the room and waved to one of her friends. "I know you must have been shocked by my marriage. I must admit that I was too." She looked back at her sisters as she sighed. "But when you have someone as wonderful as George Wickey…" She let the sentence trail off, and Lizzie could hardly imagine what Lydia might have meant by that. There were a half dozen ways that Lizzie could have completed the sentence, but none of which, she figured, that Lydia had possibly considered.

"*Vell*, as long as you are happy…," Jane quickly offered with a forced smile, trying to sound genuinely happy for Lydia.

"Oh, *danke*, sister Jane!"

Mary and Catherine mumbled their own congratulations. Lizzie remained silent on the point.

"*Ja, vell*," Lydia said in an uppity tone. "I best go stand with the other married women since we are to be seated soon." She giggled at the statement as if overly delighted to no longer be forced to sit on the benches reserved for the unmarried women in their church district.

After the three-hour service Lizzie found herself standing beside Leah Lantz, as the men began to set the benches into the wooden brackets that transformed them into tables for the fellowship meal.

"How are you doing, Lizzie?" Leah asked softly so that no one else but her daughter's friend could hear.

Lizzie smiled her appreciation at her best friend's *maem.* "Only as well as could be expected," she replied halfheartedly. She hadn't seen Leah or William since the driver had returned them to Leola, and understandably so, as too much had been happening at the Blank farm. "I'm so terribly grateful for your support on the trip home and can only apologize again for the way we left the Dutch Valley."

"Never you mind about that," Leah said. "It's not something you could have prevented, and it certainly wasn't something that *you* caused."

Still, Lizzie couldn't help but feel guilt over the entire trip. What should have been a fun and light visit had turned dark and soured more with each passing day, from running into Frederick at the Bechler farm, to his unexpected proposal, to Jane's letter that contained the most dreadful news about Lydia. Lizzie knew only too well that her visit with Charlotte had not been as it should have been.

"*Ja, vell,*" Lizzie said with a sigh. "At least they are married now."

"And how remarkable that their whereabouts were finally discovered by Frederick and that he was able to locate them," Leah added casually, her voice soft so that no one else could hear.

Her words almost went unnoticed by Lizzie, but at the mention of Frederick's name, she whirled around and stared at Charlotte's *maem.* "What do you mean that he located them?"

A shadow passed over Leah's eyes and she glanced around. Women were beginning to set the tables, so they still had a few moments before it would be time to sit. "I thought you knew," she began. "It was Charlotte who told me in a letter, just this past week."

"Knew what, Leah?" Lizzie urged.

"Well, it seems that Frederick left for Pennsylvania that Sunday, shortly after visiting with you. He hired a Mennonite driver and went straight through to Philadelphia. He found the two of them at a youth hostel known for hosting Amish youths in their *rumschpringe*, and he brought them back to Lancaster. I don't know how he did it, but somehow he was instrumental in finding a way for them to get legally married before returning them to the Beachey farm."

Stunned, Lizzie took a moment to comprehend what Charlotte's *maem* had just told her. *Certainly Leah is misinformed*, she thought, for the words Leah spoke seemed unreal and foreign to her. After all, the story that Lizzie had been privy to was that George and Lydia had simply reappeared of their own volition, after having eloped. She had never suspected that someone else had been involved in making the two disgraced youths marry and bringing them home. "I don't think I understand you properly," Lizzie whispered, still in disbelief. "How would Frederick have known where to find them?"

"Apparently George had made similar plans with another young lady just the year before," Leah said, not mentioning Grace Detweiler's name. "Since you certainly couldn't have known, I can only imagine that Frederick didn't want anyone to become aware of his involvement, so I won't be telling others, Lizzie. I reckon he'd tell the story himself if he wanted others to know. But I must confess that I am most impressed with that Frederick. He is one right *gut* and most godly man. Not only did he arrange for a proper marriage, I heard that he even spoke to the bishop and has arranged for both to take the October kneeling vow so that they can still join the Amish church!" Leah laid her hand on Lizzie's arms. "He saved your *schwester* from ruination, that's for sure and certain."

Indeed! Lizzie's head whirled, and she had to lean against the wall to regain the strength to keep standing. What could all of this mean? Lizzie was at a loss to imagine how he had possibly managed to beat them back to Pennsylvania and how he had been able to track down the wayward couple in a city as large as Philadelphia! It was almost impossible to comprehend.

Even more amazing was the fact that he had been in Leola and yet no one had known. In just one day he had arranged for a quiet marriage so that it appeared that the young couple had eloped, thus saving Lydia from certain disgrace. And he had met with the bishop and negotiated entrance for the newly married couple into the church, the only way to calm the Amish gossip line and ease the pain of the Blank family. Yet at no point had Frederick made his presence known, nor had he tried to take any credit for what he had achieved. If ever a man with less pride had walked the earth, Lizzie was hard pressed to think of one.

Still, one larger question loomed over her head: Why? Why would Frederick Detweiler spend the time and money to travel so far? Why would Frederick Detweiler take it upon himself to salvage the future of her ridiculously naïve sister and the less-than-honorable George Wickey? She couldn't begin to make heads-or-tails sense of the entire situation.

She stayed where she stood, in the back of the room, watching as the first seating of people situated themselves around the tables. Lydia had insured that she had secured a place to sit for herself, despite the table being crowded. Lizzie watched her sister as she chatted away, happily talking about her new husband, completely unaware that, once again, she was making a fool of herself.

With her appetite lost, Lizzie slipped through the door. She stood in the sunshine and shut her eyes for a long moment. For the life of her she could not imagine what all of this meant. Instead of pondering it, she decided to walk, knowing that an hour by herself in the cool air was her best chance of clearing her head of the dozens of questions that were swarming within it.

❧ Chapter Twenty-Two ❧

SEVERAL WEEKS PASSED, and mid-September brought with it cooler weather and shorter days. But the biggest change was the return of Charles Beachey and Frederick Detweiler to Leola. No one had heard any forewarning of their arrival. There was no gossip mentioning the men being back in town. Instead, the two of them merely showed up at church service as if they had never left.

When they walked into the church service, a deep silence fell over the gathering. Even the bishop looked up, a bit perplexed as to why the room had become so still. Jane felt her breath catch in her throat, and unknowingly she reached out to clutch Lizzie's hand.

Charles nodded his head and smiled as he quickly took his place among the men. Frederick merely glanced around the room once, catching the attention of the bishop, whom he acknowledged with a familiar nod, and followed his friend. At no point in time did Frederick's eyes seek Lizzie's, and she felt herself anxious for such a moment to occur.

She remained disappointed.

For the entire service Lizzie felt nervous and couldn't concentrate. *Whatever does this mean?* she wondered. She had never confided in Jane about what she had learned in the Dutch Valley, not wanting to reveal that the disgraceful behavior of their *maem* and sisters prevented Charles from pursuing Jane. And now, without any warning, Charles had returned to Leola? Was there reason to hope?

For as anxious as Lizzie remained during the service,

fidgeting despite her best efforts to sit properly, Jane was the complete opposite. She stayed calm and composed, her eyes on the bishop or on her *Ausbund*.

During the final hymn Lizzie thought she saw Frederick glancing in her direction. She couldn't be certain, for someone had accidentally dropped their chunky black *Ausbund* book. The noise caused several people to turn and look in the direction of the noise, Frederick included. At that moment, while the congregation sang, she caught his eyes looking at her, for the briefest of seconds. And then he returned his attention to the hymn.

> Our Father in the kingdom of Heaven,
> Hallowed be Your name forever,
> Let us come to Your kingdom
> Through Jesus Christ Your beloved Son,
> Which He has taken in.
>
> He is the way and also the door
> Through which man shall come to You,
> Besides there is no other path.
> Whoever does not want to walk this way
> Will not be permitted in Your kingdom.
>
> Your will be done here on earth,
> The same be fulfilled in us
> As in the kingdom of Heaven.
> Praise and honor be prepared for You
> Always and eternally.
>
> We ask you, O Lord God,
> Give us the heavenly bread from above
> Now at this hour,
> Which is Your godly Word
> That flows from Your mouth.

With which You nourish our souls,
That we give You praise and glory
Now and forever.
Your name is marvelously great,
To whom alone belongs the honor.

It was a beautiful hymn, one of Lizzie's favorites. Besides loving to listen to the congregation sing it, one syllable at a time, she was also familiar with the story behind the hymn. By studying the *Ausbund* hymns and reading *Martyrs Mirror*, Lizzie had learned of how the Anabaptists had suffered persecution during the sixteenth and seventeenth centuries. She knew that this particular hymn was a special version of the Lord's Prayer that one of the early leaders of the Anabaptist movement wrote during his years in prison in the early 1500s.

When the hymn ended, Lizzie took a deep breath, feeling a sense of renewal. Truly, nothing that happened during her earthly life could compare to what awaited her in heaven. Despite the heavy feeling in her chest when she had watched Frederick walk into the worship room, Lizzie knew that she could not change what had happened or the words that had been exchanged. From the ruins of those experiences God would rebuild her, but only if she honored Him.

During the kneeling prayer, her face pressed firmly upon her folded hands, she said a prayer to God to heal her heart and redirect her soul. She praised God for His goodness and glory, knowing that she had not been as godly a person as she had thought. She prayed for His forgiveness and guidance to become the very godly woman she wished she could be. And she prayed that her *schwester* Jane would not be hurt by the reappearance of Charles Beachey into their community.

When she had ended her prayer, Lizzie stole a quick peek at her sister but, to her surprise, noticed that Jane looked natural and undisturbed by the unexpected arrival of the very man who had left with no warning and who had spared her any form of communication for more than two months. Not once had Jane complained, at least not out loud or to Lizzie. She had written only one letter to Charles's sister, Carol Ann, expressing her concerns for their *daed*. That letter had received only the briefest of responses, and the brevity of its nature had indicated that Carol Ann had no desire to continue communicating with Jane or anyone else from Leola.

Maem approached her *dochders* after the service, lifting up her chin and narrowing her eyes. Her distress was more than apparent, even before she spoke. "I think that it takes some nerve," she whispered sharply to Jane and Lizzie. "Just breezing into the service with no warning whatsoever!"

"It's a church service," Lizzie pointed out. "No one requires an invitation."

Her *maem* waved her hand at Lizzie. "That's not the point." She looked around the room, a look of disinterest on her face. "*Ach vell*, it is of no bother to us, I reckon. Doesn't concern us at all, does it now?"

Jane managed to smile, but Lizzie could not help but frown. She could see through her *maem*'s transparency and didn't like the way she sounded. Pride, she thought. Always that pride getting in the way of true godliness. "I reckon it concerns us as much as it did before," she replied sharply. "They are neighbors of ours, and therefore we should extend ourselves to them as much as we would to any other!"

With that, Lizzie turned on her heel and marched straight to the two men who were standing at the back of the room, waiting for the second seating of food since the gathering room was smaller than usual. She knew that people were watching her every move, and she decided that she didn't care. It was proper to greet newcomers and guests to the service, and she was going to do just that.

"Charles Beachey," she enounced politely, extending her hand to shake his. "It's nice to see that you have returned to Leola!"

He shook her hand, a broad smile on his face. "It was a rather quickly made decision," he said, his eyes darting over her shoulder as if anticipating that Jane would have joined her. When he realized that Lizzie acted alone, he seemed disappointed. "And your family is well?"

"Quite," she responded. Turning to Frederick, she noticed that he avoided meeting her eyes. "And it is nice to see you too, Frederick Detweiler." She extended her hand and noticed that he paused before reaching out to shake it. "It's a nice time of year to travel," she remarked. "With quite lovely weather, wouldn't you agree?" she added, paraphrasing the same remark Frederick had made to her during his first surprise visit with her back at Wilmer and Charlotte's home.

He lifted an eyebrow at her question, and she thought she saw something spark in his eye. She wondered whether or not he had picked up on her teasing and decided that he had, a thought that brought joy to her heart. "Indeed," he said politely, taking her hand and shaking it. If he held it for a moment too long, no one else appeared to notice.

"And your *daed*, Charles?" Lizzie asked, returning her attention to the other man after she withdrew her hand from Frederick's. "I hear he is much better. We all prayed for his recovery."

"Oh *ja*, right as rain but taking it easy on the farm these days," Charles admitted. "*Danke* for your prayers."

"Are you visiting or planning on staying?" she ventured to ask.

"I...I am not rightly certain," he mumbled, his eyes once again roaming around the room. "I have some unfinished business to settle that will determine the outcome."

This news delighted Lizzie, for she could only suspect one type of business that would have drawn Charles back to Leola.

217

Still, she kept her enthusiasm to herself and smiled at both men. "*Ja, vell*, I will not keep you further from visiting with others," she managed to say. "It was right nice seeing you both again."

Later that afternoon Charles and Frederick reappeared, this time at the Blank farm. *Maem* was resting on the sofa, a glass of lemonade in her hand while Mary sat on the ladder-back chair, playing her harmonica despite having being asked twice to stop by her seemingly annoyed *maem*. Catherine, having quieted down since her younger sister's marriage to George Wickey, was busy writing a letter to Lydia. Jane and Lizzie were playing a game of Scrabble while their *daed* was enjoying a nap in the bedroom, punctuated by occasional bouts of snoring that the entire family could hear.

It was Catherine who first heard the carriage pull down the driveway. She stood up instantly and hurried to the window, glancing outside as she waited to see who had arrived. And then, with a gasp, she spun around and cried out, "Jane! *Maem*! It's Charles! He's come calling!"

At this announcement the room suddenly became a flurry of activity as everyone quickly tried to put things away and remove unwashed dishes from the counter. The Scrabble game was forgotten, and with one arm Lizzie brushed the remaining tiles into the box so that Jane could put it away. Pillows were fluffed and the counter wiped. It was the best they could do for not having expected visitors on a sleepy Sunday afternoon.

When the knock was heard on the door, *Maem* nodded to Catherine to answer it. Jane and Lizzie were seated on the sofa, their hands folded on their laps as if they had just been casually sitting there in conversation. *Maem* had taken her place in the rocking chair, a worn leather copy of the family's *Martyrs Mirror* on her lap. It was the perfect vision of serenity when not one, but two gentlemen, entered the room.

Lizzie felt her heart skip a beat as she realized that Frederick stood behind Charles, both men holding their hats in their hands. They were still wearing their Sunday suits and looked rather handsome for the effort.

"Why, Charles Beachey," *Maem* finally said. "And Frederick Detweiler. What a surprise it was to see you both today at worship!"

Charles looked nervous and fidgety, his eyes meeting *Maem's* but always glancing back at Jane. *"Ja,* it was nice to be back," he replied politely.

"What brings you back to Leola, then?" she asked, her voice a pitch too high to sound natural.

"The farm," he responded politely. "It needs tending, of course."

"I see," *Maem* replied, a hint of disappointment in her voice. "Well, the dairy must be well tended, with George and my Lydia living there."

Lizzie wanted to roll her eyes at the mention of George and Lydia. It had been a miracle that the Beachey family had not thrown the two of them onto the streets after the terrible stunt they had pulled. If anything, the dairy cows were probably under-milked and ill cleaned. Lizzie was certain that Charles and Frederick had returned to find the farm and the house in disarray. Lydia had always been one to procrastinate and wait for others to do the worst of the chores, pretending to busy herself with something mundane. Lizzie could scarcely see her youngest *schwester* being willing to do laundry, forget about cleaning the house or knowing how to cook a decent meal.

"That's just the thing," he said slowly. "They will be moving, and that would leave the farm unattended once again."

At this statement *Maem's* mouth dropped, and she stared at him, speechless. The room remained silent as his announcement was repeated silently in their heads. No one could speak. While the family had seen Lydia and George at the worship service that morning, they had not talked with them at any length. Nor had anyone in the Blank family visited them at home, with *Daed* and the two older sisters still disappointed in and recovering from their sudden disappearance and their unexpected nuptials.

Finally, breaking the silence, Lizzie managed to speak up. "Moving? We have heard nothing about this."

She noticed Frederick taking a deep breath, but he did not reply. Instead it was Charles who spoke up. "They have acquired a farm just south of Strasburg."

Maem's eyes opened wide. "In Strasburg?"

Lizzie felt the same sense of shock as her mother. A farm in Strasburg meant a new beginning for the couple, away from gossip and ruined reputations. A farm in Strasburg meant that they were far away enough to start over while being close enough to visit. A farm in Strasburg meant that they would be on their own to succeed or fail without the help of family to come to their aid or rescue them from financial excess. They would be forced to grow up and face the reality of their situation, at last.

"How on earth could they afford their own farm?" Lizzie gasped.

"Farms are rather pricey in that area, ain't so?" *Maem* added with more than a hint of curiosity in her voice.

"It's only forty acres or so, and some of that wooded," Charles said, acknowledging both Lizzie's and *Maem*'s questions. "Quite manageable for just the two of them."

The way that he stated it caused Lizzie to turn and stare at Frederick. He avoided her eyes, but she still could read his expression. Without being told, she knew exactly what had happened. The family had come together to salvage both George Wickey and Lydia Blank; they had bought him a farm, thus giving him a chance to begin again. Yet, since she knew that this was not the first time the family had come forward to save George, she could scarcely find a reason why they would have done something like this a second time.

Maem tried to regain her composure as she digested this information. "She hasn't even told us," she said incredulously.

"It just happened this past week," Charles admitted. "Until everything was settled, it was thought best not to mention it." He glanced at Jane, almost apologetic. "Dashed hopes and all."

"Oh, help," *Maem* said, pressing her hand against her chest. "My Lydia! To have her own farm!" As the realization sunk in, she looked pleased, and her expression changed from shock to elation. "I always knew that she'd make something of herself."

"*Maem*!" Lizzie hissed.

Her *maem* looked up, suddenly aware that she had spoken out loud but not seemingly bothered by it. "Where are my manners? Please come sit and visit. Mayhaps stay for a light supper?"

Charles took a deep breath and shook his head. "*Nee*, but *danke*," he said politely. "I would like, if possible, a word alone with Jane."

The room fell silent.

Everyone stared at Jane. Even *Maem* seemed stunned by this very non-private request, but she nodded before retreating to the bedroom where *Daed* still lay napping. Quietly, Lizzie stood up and gestured to Catherine to follow her. They stepped out the back door where Mary was sitting, her harmonica in her hand and pressed against her lips, quietly practicing a popular Amish song. Lizzie nudged her and whispered for her to stop playing and join her and Catherine for a walk. The three women walked toward the front of the house and over toward the barn, where the spring kittens lounged in the fading sunlight, their now gangly bodies seeming too big and awkward, like those of adolescents.

Lizzie noticed that Frederick had retreated to the front porch. With his hat on his head and his hands behind his back, he stared off into the distance. If she wanted to go to him, to speak to him, she knew better than to do so. Being bold with a man was not something that any Amish woman would dare to do. However, she couldn't help but wish that, once again, as he had done in the past, he would take a few quick steps to catch up with her.

He didn't.

Charles did not stay alone with Jane for very long: five minutes at the most. When he departed from the house, he smiled nervously at Frederick, and the two men quickly took their leave of the property. Lizzie held back her two younger sisters, waiting until the buggy pulled away from their house and turned onto the main road before they hurried back into the house.

Jane remained seated in the same place, her cheeks flushed and her eyes bright. She stared up at Lizzie and quickly glanced away, but not before her sister caught the look of happiness on her face.

Upon hearing the other women reenter the room, the bedroom door opened and *Maem* bustled out, her dress making a whooshing sound around her bare ankles. "Well, tell us all!" she demanded impatiently.

Jane looked up at her *maem* and laughed at the so-familiar look of eagerness upon her face. "There's nothing to tell, *Maem*. He begged my forgiveness for disappearing and not writing."

"Oh, help," *Maem* mumbled, sinking back into her recliner. "Is that all, then?"

"*Nee*," Jane said, a sly look on her face. "He asked if I was going to the singing this evening and if he could pick me up and accompany me."

At this news *Maem* seemed rejuvenated. "Pick you up? *Before* the singing?"

Jane tried to hide her delight. "*Ja*, before the singing."

"Oh, my Jane!" *Maem* clapped her hands together. It was a rarity for a young man to take a woman *to* the singing. That was usually saved for couples who had already announced their plans to be wed. It was highly unusual for such a request to be made unless marriage was the final intention. "It's all but settled then!"

"*Maem!*" Lizzie exclaimed disapprovingly for the second time in less than an hour. "Mayhaps that's how they do it in Ohio." The last thing Lizzie wanted was to see her sister hurt once again. It would do no good for *Maem* to begin planning a wedding just because Charles had come calling. Deep down, however, Lizzie hoped his intentions were, indeed, to correct his wrong. "Besides, it's best not to raise up one's hopes only to see them dashed!" she added, referencing Charles's own comments from earlier in the visit.

At this statement Jane laughed and waved her hand at Lizzie. "My hopes are not up again, Lizzie. I'm just pleased that we can be friends."

Lizzie tilted her head and stared at her sister, giving her a look of disbelief. "Friends?" She paused, waiting for Jane to nod her answer. "Friends? I think *I* was friendly with Charles Beachey. And I certainly did not see him asking for *my* forgiveness or asking to take *me* to the singing. Friends, indeed!"

Jane smiled and blushed.

Lizzie tried to look reproachfully at her sister, but the mirth in Jane's eyes could not be contained. It was clear that there was something else that Jane was not sharing with them, and whatever this news was, it made her most happy. Lizzie frowned, realizing that there was more to this visit than met the eye, and for that she was grateful.

❧ *Chapter Twenty-Three* ❧

LIZZIE WAS SEATED on the bench by the table, husking the last of the summer corn along with Jane and Catherine. The Blank women had been canning food all week: peaches, apples, beets, beans, meat, and now corn. The pantry was already chock-full with rows and rows of different-sized glass jars with colorful food that would be used throughout the upcoming season until the family garden grew again in the spring. All week long the house had contained wonderful smells of freshly baked bread mixed with whatever fruits or vegetables they were canning on that particular day. If spring was Lizzie's favorite season, autumn was a close second.

She loved the shorter days and crisp morning air that came along with them. Every day upon awaking, while it was still dark outside, Lizzie would wrap a black shawl around her shoulders and hurry out to the dairy to help *Daed* with the morning milking. The sun would be just starting to rise in the sky when they finished. It seemed like such a peaceful time of year, despite the frenzy to prepare the food for the approaching winter months! At least with canning there was a routine to the day, affording plenty of time to quietly reflect within oneself.

During the canning season Lizzie's favorite activity was the canning of meatballs. While it was always a sad day when a cow had to be taken to the butcher, she knew that the animals were there to serve them and that their family had to eat. When her *daed* would bring back home the boxes of ground meat, Lizzie was always the first to begin overseeing the canning process: a touch of salt, a little pepper, meat rolled into balls after mixing

225

with some more spices and herbs, then stored in the glass jars. Mary and Catherine would wipe the lids and set them into the canning pans in order to seal the containers.

But today it was corn. Her *maem* liked to freeze some of the sweet kernels as well as make enough corn relish for the pantry to last the family the entire winter. If there was one thing Lizzie did not like, it was shucking the corn. She disliked the mess of the shells on the table and the strands of silk that would stick in between the rows of yellow corn. With great determination she would pull at the little silk threads, trying her best to rid each ear of every one of them. Usually that was a job she would have delegated to Lydia, but this year Lydia would have to can her own food for her own pantry with George.

It gave Lizzie a mild sense of satisfaction to know that Lydia was now on her own and forced to tend to her own kitchen without the help of her *maem* or siblings. For all of Lydia's gayness and rash behavior, certainly she had not thought through what she was doing when she ran off with George Wickey. No amount of sweet words and dreamy looks could have prepared Lydia for being a farmer's wife, that was for sure and certain.

"Oh, hurry with that corn, Lizzie," *Maem* snapped. "And be certain to sweep the floor proper when you are finished!"

Lizzie rolled her eyes but did not retort.

From outside the faint noise of a harmonica announced that Mary was coming. She had been in the barn, helping her *daed* with chores while Lizzie worked in the kitchen. The harmonica stopped and the screen door opened, a squeak of the hinges announcing that someone was entering.

"There's a phone call for you," Mary said, walking into the house.

Everyone looked up at the same time, wondering to whom she had addressed this. When they realized that Mary was looking at Lizzie, Jane and Catherine turned to stare at each other then at her.

She felt her cheeks color at the attention. "For me?" The two words came out in a strange voice, one that she did not recognize. Lizzie could scarcely believe that Mary had directed the statement to her.

Mary looked equally as surprised as she nodded her head. "*Daed* answered it and he told me to fetch you. Some woman wants to speak to you."

"Did you take her number then?"

Shaking her head, Mary gestured toward the barn. "She insisted that she'd wait on the line until we found you."

This was odd indeed. No one ever called Lizzie. There was no reason for it. The phone was kept in the barn for work purposes and, on rare occasions, for making phone calls to arrange for a driver or confirm a visit with friends. Those calls were almost always made by *Maem* or *Daed*, that was for certain. Never had Lizzie received a call with the exception of a few times from Charlotte when she had lived in Leola.

Lizzie hurried out the door, not bothering to put on a pair of shoes or grab a sweater. It was cool outside as the weather was beginning to change, but it was not cold enough to bother Lizzie. She ran across the grass and toward the barn where, in the back room, the phone was hanging by its cord.

"Hello?" she asked hesitantly into the receiver as she picked it up.

"Elizabeth Blank?"

The voice sounded familiar, but Lizzie couldn't quite place it. "*Ja*," she confirmed, still trying to place the voice on the other end of the phone line. "And you...?"

A pause. "Christiana Bechler, as if you didn't already know!" came the sharp and piercing reply.

Immediately Lizzie panicked. Why on earth would Christiana Bechler from the Dutch Valley in Ohio be calling her? Her first thought was that something had happened to Charlotte, but the moment she thought this, she realized that Wilmer would have called her or Charlotte's parents. She couldn't begin to imagine why this woman would have contacted her. "Is everything all right?"

"Of course it is *not* all right! Don't trifle with me, Elizabeth Blank. You know exactly why I am calling!"

Lizzie almost laughed. If she never received any phone calls, why on earth would she know why this woman, whom she had only briefly met on her trip to Ohio, would be contacting her? "I can assure you that I do not."

There was a momentary silence on the other end. Lizzie had the distinct feeling that Christiana was trying to collect her thoughts before speaking any further. Yet it was obvious that something was on her mind; she was clearly upset and had something important to say. It dawned on Lizzie that the woman would have most likely received the phone number from Charlotte or Wilmer. She wondered why neither one would have alerted her that Christiana Bechler had requested her private information.

And then Christiana spoke. "The most disturbing news has reached my ears, and I would have come to see you in person if the distance wasn't so great!"

Lizzie made a face and stared at the phone. She was astonished at what Christiana had said. Disturbing news? Visit in person? Clearly something was amiss, especially if it was so troubling to the elderly woman. Not trusting herself to speak, Lizzie waited for Christiana to explain.

"I am a very frank and forthright woman, Elizabeth, and thus I will not listen to gossip," the woman went on, the condescending tone of her voice not lost on Lizzie. "I have heard the most impossible news that you have designs to marry my nephew, Frederick Detweiler, and I am calling you to inquire as to whether this news is indeed true!"

A gasp escaped from Lizzie's mouth, and she quickly turned her back to the door in case anyone was nearby. She didn't want anyone to see her reaction or to hear her words. She tried to catch her bearings and figure out the best way to respond to the angry charges put forth to her.

"Well?" Christiana demanded. "It can't possibly be true now, can it?"

"You have said so yourself," Lizzie quipped, feeling pushed into a corner and not liking the feeling.

"Answer the question!"

"If the news is so impossible," Lizzie said slowly, enunciating each word, "I still cannot imagine why you would have contacted me!"

"Do not be insolent with me, Elizabeth Blank. Have you heard this rumor then?"

"I have not." It wasn't a lie. As far as Lizzie knew, only two people had known about the proposal: her and Frederick. Since she had confided in no one, it was apparent that Frederick had. However, she realized that, being such a private man, it was highly unlikely. So the source of such a rumor created a problem that Lizzie could not solve.

Christiana was not about to be satisfied with Lizzie's simple reply. "Are you saying that there is no truth to this story then?"

Lizzie felt her cheeks grow hot with anger. Who was this woman to contact her and ask such personal questions? "I do not have the same qualities as you do, I fear," she snapped. "I am not comfortable being as frank or forthright with you, a woman whom I do not know beyond a brief meeting, just weeks ago! I am not about to answer questions of such a personal and private nature."

"Elizabeth!" The shrill voice on the other end of the phone was growing increasingly irritated. "Do you deny that my nephew has proposed marriage to you?" she demanded.

Lizzie clutched the phone, her blood coursing through her

veins as she tried to control her temper. "It was you who just said it was impossible, ain't so?"

"Insolent girl!" Christiana snapped. "I will get to the bottom of this. My nephew might be swayed by momentary charms, but he will not forget his obligations to this family and to my husband's niece! And what for, anyway? Marrying into a disgraced family from Pennsylvania?" The way the word *Pennsylvania* rolled off of her tongue made it sound as if it were poison. "And you, with your flashing eyes and quick tongue, will not interfere with a marriage that has been discussed for years! What do you say to that?"

A dozen responses went through Lizzie's head, not one of them fit for vocalizing. She knew that she would have to pray for forgiveness later for having even thought such terrible things. Instead she clenched her fist and pressed her lips together, forcing out her words. "I dare say that your nephew is a grown man and is welcome to propose to whomever he likes, Christiana. If he chooses to marry your niece, I wish him the best. However, if he chooses to seek a life companion elsewhere, it is not *your* place to interfere nor mine to presume to tell *you* before *him* what I would or would not say!"

Without another moment's hesitation Lizzie said a quick good-bye and hung up the phone. She stood there for a few minutes, her hands shaking and her heart beating rapidly inside of her chest. She couldn't begin to understand what the meaning of that phone call and Christiana's accusations were. How could Christiana have come to learn of Frederick's proposal? Certainly he would not have told his *aendi*, not *that* particular *aendi* anyway. With her unwanted opinions and mannerism in expressing them, Lizzie was more than certain Christiana would have been the last person to have heard of his previous intentions from Frederick directly.

Besides, Lizzie had turned down his offer of marriage. She did not want to admit that to Christiana, for it was surely none of her business. And she knew that there was little hope of such an offer being repeated, especially now with Lydia's disgraceful disappearance and her hush-hush marriage to George Wickey. Why on earth would Christiana be interested in pursuing this conversation when the proposal had been asked, rejected, and both parties had moved on with their lives?

Lizzie leaned against the wall and shut her eyes. Despite learning so much about Frederick and growing in her respect for him, she knew that Frederick would never renew his offer, lest he be forever linked to George Wickey as a brother-in-law.

❧ Chapter Twenty-Four ❧

"OH, BOTHER!" *MAEM* said, her voice exasperated and weary, as she stared out the kitchen window. "Here comes Charles Beachey again, and with that disagreeable Frederick Detweiler!" She tossed her hand towel into the sink and turned around, addressing the four pairs of eyes that stared back at her. "Why must a pleasant visit be ruined with that man's overbearing and miserable presence?"

Lizzie caught her breath, surprised that Frederick had once again accompanied Charles to their home.

The previous Sunday Charles had picked up Jane before the singing. Despite his invitation to take her too, Lizzie had merely waved her hand at him and smiled at Jane. Three was a crowd, and Lizzie had no intentions of tagging along.

When Jane had finally returned home, Lizzie had been waiting up for her, eager to hear the details of their exchanges during the evening. In the quiet of their room Jane had shared with Lizzie about how they had talked the entire way to the singing and on the way back. It almost felt as if he had never left, Jane had said. Yet there was something wistful in the way that she said it, and Lizzie knew that Jane still had her doubts.

"Oh, fiddle-faddle!" Lizzie had exclaimed. "He may have left, Jane, but he did come back. And I can assure you that he is even more in love with you than ever!"

Jane had tried to smile at her sister's reassuring words, but without fully understanding Charles's reasons, reasons that he had chosen not to share with her during their time alone in the buggy, she could not be comforted. "If only I knew why," she had replied before dropping the subject.

Today, however, was Saturday, and he had not stopped at the farm during the entire week. *Daed* had confided in Lizzie that the Beachey farm had suffered under George's lax supervision that summer. Thankfully no crops had been ruined, and the herd of cows had been tended to when George and Lydia ran off, a fact for which Charles had expressed his profuse gratitude to *Daed* on more than one occasion. However, since George's return and marriage to Lydia, it was clear that the young couple was in way over their heads, and the farm, which had been pristine and well maintained prior to Charles's departure during the summer, was now in complete disorder.

Daed continued telling *Maem* how Charles had made plans to return to Leola to check on the farm when he had heard that George married Lydia. He had, unfortunately, been totally unaware that his young cousin had left town in the first place.

"I wonder why they thought it wise to leave the farm to George's care to begin with!" *Daed* had said, his words short and spoken with no emotion. "They certainly have their hands full, picking up where our son-in-law let go." The word *son-in-law* was uttered with heavy sarcasm. Lizzie knew that her *daed* had yet to forgive Lydia for what she had done and the emotional trauma that had befallen the Blank household. Indeed, George had yet to be invited to visit the Blank farm. It was clear that his presence was unwelcomed, at least for the time being.

Now, Lizzie hurried to the side window to watch the two men. They had not driven a buggy but apparently had preferred to walk. It was late September, and the weather was still nice for walking, especially in the late morning hours. Her eyes trailed Frederick, her heart beating inside of her chest. Charles seemed nervous and paced a bit as he walked, stopping as if he were about to backtrack, then returning to Frederick's side.

As usual, Frederick remained calm as he slowed his pace and seemed to patiently wait for Charles.

Without a doubt Lizzie knew why Charles was there. She felt tears of joy in her eyes, which she blinked rapidly in order to avoid shedding them. "Jane, you should change your apron," Lizzie said without turning around. She could hear Mary and Catherine scurrying around the kitchen, quickly straightening up as much as they could. They had been making cheese all morning, using fresh milk from the cows to set until the big, chunky curds could be drained and pressed. In the side room three cheese presses were already at work with large plastic containers filled with sand holding down the arm of the press in order to apply as much pressure as was needed on the plastic molds filled with curds and covered in cheesecloth. The result would be beautiful wheels of homemade cheese: Colby, cheddar, and even Monterey Jack.

When the footsteps were finally heard on the front porch, the kitchen was straightened up and only a dried spot of milk lingering on the linoleum floor gave any indication that they had been working all morning. *Maem* answered the door, politely greeting both men, although Lizzie thought she heard an edge to her voice when she specifically greeted Frederick. It pained her to think that her *maem* was so prejudiced against the very man who had saved Lydia and the family from complete disgrace. Yet she knew it was not her place to share this information with her parents based on Leah's comments alone. Besides, from what little she had learned of Frederick, he preferred his good deeds to remain secret.

"*Gut mariye*," Charles said politely, nodding at the women in the room. His eyes lingered on Jane and he paused, a smile on his lips wavering from nervousness.

"What a pleasure to have you stop in," *Maem* said, a little too enthusiastically for Lizzie's taste, especially after her prior comments regarding Frederick. "Would you like to sit for a spell this time?"

Charles almost trembled as his eyes left Jane's, and he glanced at her *maem*. "*Nee, nee*," he quickly replied, his nervousness more than apparent. "But I would like to speak with Jane outside for a moment if that is fine with her and I am not interrupting something of greater importance."

Maem caught her breath and looked over at her oldest *dochder*. The color drained from *Maem*'s face. If there was ever a doubt, this was not the time. With wide eyes and pale cheeks, *Maem* nodded to Jane. "Go on, Jane," she whispered, gesturing toward the door with her head. "We have everything under control here in the kitchen."

Lizzie remained at the counter, watching as Jane stood up and walked across the kitchen floor. She was pleased to see that Jane had quickly replaced her soiled work apron with a fresh, clean one that covered the bottom half of her purple dress. As Jane passed Charles on her way outside, he quickly followed, leaving his friend Frederick standing in the doorway.

As she watched Frederick for a moment, the harsh words from Christiana rang in Lizzie's ears and she bit her lip, wondering if he too had heard those rumors. Since she couldn't imagine that he had started them, surely he would have thought she had told others about having turned down his proposal. That very thought had been bothering her since she had spoken with his *aendi*. The last thing she wanted was for Frederick to think she was mocking him behind his back and telling people she had rejected his offer of marriage.

And then there was the issue about Lydia. As Lizzie stared at him, her eyes glazing over and her mind wandering, she found herself wishing she could have had the opportunity to thank him for what he had done for Lydia and her entire family. Yet, with so much going on and the stoic nature with which he stood there, she neither wished to make him uncomfortable nor speak of her gratitude in front of the others.

Still, the silence was weighing too heavily on her, and she felt that something should be said to welcome Frederick into the house. After all, he more than deserved to be treated as a valuable guest of the family; a benevolent friend would even be an understatement, she reckoned. "Would you care for some meadow tea? It might be the last fresh batch until spring," she said lightly.

He looked at her and then quickly averted his eyes. "*Nee*, but *danke*," he replied.

"I was surprised to learn that you had returned," she managed to say, wishing that Mary, Catherine, and her *maem* would leave the room. "I trust your family is well in Ohio?"

"Quite well," he replied, his eyes meeting hers once again. She was relieved to see that there was no malice in his look.

"And Grace?"

He smiled, a soft and thoughtful smile. "She is fine, Elizabeth, and sends her best regards to you."

"It's a shame you could not bring her with you," Lizzie observed lightly but immediately regretted her words. The color flooded to her cheeks, knowing that her attempt at small talk had backfired. She didn't want him to think that she was insensitive to Grace's emotions in regard to George Wickey. After all, it had only been a year ago that Frederick had interfered with George's plans to elope with his then sixteen-year-old sister. "Oh, help. I didn't mean..."

He nodded his head and lifted his hand as if to calm her, the gesture reassuring Lizzie that he knew she meant no harm by her carelessly worded statement. "I understand. The change of scenery would have pleased her, *ja*, but she is better at home with *Aendi*." He paused. "Plus, I prefer to not leave *Aendi* alone for long periods of time, if it can be avoided."

To her relief Mary and Catherine busied themselves in the

sunroom while *Maem* excused herself to tidy up her bedroom. Lizzie took the opportunity of this unexpected privacy that presented a chance to speak more directly to Frederick about what was really on her mind.

"I understand you have had another change of scenery recently too," she began, her voice low enough so that she could not be overheard. "It seems that you keep returning to Pennsylvania."

He lifted an eyebrow in feigned ignorance.

"When Leah told me that you were the one who found Lydia and George and, subsequently, arranged for the marriage," she continued, "I...I was speechless, Frederick. My entire family owes you so much gratitude for your kindness and willingness to be so unselfish in helping them. I cannot thank you enough for what you did."

She thought she saw something soften in his expression, the darkness lifting from his eyes. Hesitantly he took a step into the room so that he stood closer to her. His eyes drifted to where Mary and Catherine had positioned themselves. Convinced that they were busy talking to each other and not listening, Frederick responded. "I had hoped no one would find out. But I see that this has not happened." There was remorse in his voice when he said that, and Lizzie knew that he was sincerely disturbed that his actions had been shared with her. "For that, I'm sorry. However, it was not for your family's sake that I did it, Elizabeth," he said. "It was only for you...only you."

His words took her breath away, and she stared at him directly, their eyes meeting for too long a moment to not cause her cheeks to flush once again. *Only you*, he had said. Whatever could that mean? She started to open her mouth to speak, but nothing would come out. She was finally able to whisper, "I...I don't know how to respond to that."

"Speechless again?" he quipped, a light teasing tone to his voice, one that she had only heard once before, back in Ohio at his farm.

There was no further time for conversation as the door opened and Jane walked in, her eyes glowing and her cheeks flushed despite being streaked with tears. She took one look at Lizzie and burst into more tears, despite the smile on her face. With a sigh of relief Lizzie hurried to take her oldest sister into her arms and hug her. There was no need for words or explanation as Charles walked in behind her, a broad grin on his face as he nodded toward his friend.

"Looks like I'll be settling in Pennsylvania after all," Charles announced, looking at Frederick, who managed to smile his approval. "Jane has delighted me with the honor of agreeing to accept my offer of marriage."

The door to their parents' bedroom burst open and *Maem* bustled out, her arms open and her mouth in as big a smile as Charles's. She hurried to Jane and held her, laughing and crying at the same time as she announced that she had known it all along. "I couldn't have wished for a happier arrangement," she gushed. She reached her hand out to take Charles's. "What a *wunderbaar gut* couple you shall make!"

For a few moments there was quite a commotion in the kitchen. Charles beamed at the joy with which the family had received his proposal. Catherine crowded around Jane, begging to help with the wedding while also lobbying to be seated across from a very specific list of young men in the *g'may*. Mary seemed happy but greeted the news with a quiet smile, not quite sure of how to respond to issues dealing with love.

As for Lizzie, her eyes caught sight of Frederick, and when he looked at her, she found herself fighting tears. At that moment she knew all that had occurred behind the scenes, all of the kind and generous deeds that Frederick had done to correct the alleged wrongs that she had so mistakenly accused him of. Yet she knew that it was too late for any chance to correct the wrongs that she had done to him.

There was a bittersweet joy in that moment. Lizzie listened

as *Maem* began prattling off a list of people who simply had to be invited to the wedding while Jane laughed nervously at the attention from Catherine. It was a joyous setting; yet as Lizzie held Frederick's gaze, she longed to thank him personally for so much more than just having salvaged Lydia's reputation.

It was almost an hour after Charles had finally left that Lizzie had a chance to speak privately with her sister. Jane could scarcely contain her happiness and her tears of joy at having been asked to marry Charles Beachey. Despite her claim of being at peace with his departure, it was clear to Lizzie that what she had suspected all along was true: Jane had truly loved him and her heart had been broken.

"What on earth did he say to you?" Lizzie asked, holding Jane's hands as they sat on the edge of the bed the sisters shared upstairs.

Jane laughed and covered her mouth as if to hold back the sweet sound of her bliss. "Oh, Lizzie, I cannot begin to believe how the pain of the past few months has been ever so worth it, now that I know he truly loves me and that we are to be together forever!"

"Tell me everything!" Lizzie pressed eagerly.

Jane glanced down at the floor, trying to remember exactly what had occurred. "*Vell*," she began, "he apologized for having left so quickly and never sending a letter to me. Originally it had been his intention to return to Leola, but someone convinced him that I did not truly care," Jane said, a brief frown on her forehead. "He was as heartbroken as I was. Can you imagine?"

Indeed Lizzie could.

"Then the Lydia and George situation happened," she said, a deep frown creasing her brow. "And when he heard that the farm was in such a state of disarray, he considered selling it. He said the thought of coming back here to stay was simply too painful for him."

Lizzie was seated on the edge of the mattress, waiting to hear what had happened next. "But he came back!"

"*Ja*, he did! And he knew when he saw me at church that he had been wrong. He never should have listened to whoever told him I didn't care. And then Frederick urged him to come calling. Of all people!" She clapped her hands in delight and laughed. "To think that there may be a heart in that proud man after all!"

If Lizzie wanted to correct her sister, she did not. Oh, she could have shared everything that she had learned about pride and how they had all been so wrong when they had misjudged Frederick. There were many lessons that they all could learn from her secrets. However, she didn't want to tarnish the day. Instead she wanted Jane to enjoy this blessed moment without getting into the details of who Frederick Detweiler truly was. Besides, she told herself, if she did start telling Jane the story, she would have to admit that she too had experienced a broken heart. The only difference was that she feared she had missed the opportunity to mend it long before it had actually been broken.

"He wants to announce the wedding right away and have the ceremony as soon as possible," Jane continued. "Frederick will stand by him, and since he must return to Ohio, it's better to have the wedding sooner than wait for the wedding season."

It made sense, and Lizzie knew that many more established couples were not waiting for the traditional time when weddings took place in late October and November. Despite the autumn harvest, they would have an early October wedding, even if that meant fewer people could attend the ceremony and fellowship afterward. From the look on Jane's face, it was clear that she didn't care. All that mattered to her sister was that she had, at last, gained the right to be called Charles's Jane, and that would be how she would be known for the rest of her life.

The bittersweet feelings that Lizzie felt didn't matter. All that mattered was her sister's happiness, and that, blessedly, was clearly in abundance.

❧ Chapter Twenty-Five ❧

W**ITH THE WEDDING** fast approaching, *Maem* was a flurry of activity, trying to finish the canning for winter while preparing for a marriage service at their house. Jane had already made her light blue wedding dress, and it hung from a hanger on the back of their bedroom door. It was her wedding dress and would one day be the same dress in which she would be buried. In between those years she would have *bopplis* and gardens, harvests and worship service, laughter and even tears. Her life would now be centered on tending to the Beachey farm and taking care of Charles and her family.

Lizzie took to walking in the early morning, right after the breakfast meal. She found herself constantly deep in thought, replaying the events of the past few months in her head. She knew that change was inevitable and that all of these new experiences were life events that had been destined to occur. Yet she couldn't help but wonder about so many things happening within such a short period of time.

She found herself drawn to one of her favorite verses in the Bible: "'For I know the plans I have for you,' declares the LORD, 'plans to prosper you and not to harm you, plans to give you hope and a future.'" Lizzie was well aware that God's hand was behind everything that had happened: from the storm that forced Jane to stay at the Beachey farm until the roads were cleared, to Jacob Beachey's illness that called Charles home, to Charlotte marrying Wilmer and Lizzie's subsequent visit to Ohio. There was even a reason behind Lydia's hasty marriage to George, which was what ultimately caused Charles to return to Leola, resulting in his upcoming nuptials with Jane.

For I know the plans I have for you...

It astounded Lizzie to realize that God had planned this marriage. He had sanctioned it long before Charles had even met Jane, perhaps even before they had been born. Indeed, He wanted them to prosper in love and life. He also already knew their future and the future of their *kinner*.

She felt a wave of warmth flood through her body, and she crossed her arms as she walked. What plans did God have for her? she wondered. In what ways was she meant to prosper? If at one time she had only wanted to live at home in order to help her *daed* during the day and read her books during the night, she could hardly imagine anymore what His plans were for her. Her original idea for her future now seemed dreary and unfulfilling. There had to be something more.

She only hoped that her one opportunity for true happiness had not already come and gone. Her pulse quickened as she asked herself if, indeed, her own unconscious prejudices had blinded her to what God intended. Is that even possible? she wondered with a worried feeling in her heart. Could her own prejudices and sins really stand in the way of God's will being fulfilled?

For another half hour Lizzie tried to grasp the magnitude of what had occurred, trying to dissect it and understand the unknown. Finally she had to give up and hand it over to God. Instead of second-guessing everything, she paused and said a silent prayer of gratitude to Him for having allowed Jane to reunite with her beloved Charles. She knew that it had been His plan all along to arrange this marriage. What Lizzie couldn't understand was why it had been such a long and arduous emotional journey, involving so many people. If God intended for Jane and Charles to be together, why had so many other things occurred?

Still, she knew better than to question God: *For I know the plans I have for you.* God had been in control the entire time. Only He knew the reasons for the other situations that had occurred in the meantime. Lessons learned, experiences endured, life lived.

"Was your walk refreshing or taxing?" Jane asked her when Lizzie returned. She had been sitting at the table, dishing cookie dough onto four baking sheets. However, when Lizzie walked in, Jane quickly set down the spoon and stood up.

"Both, I reckon," Lizzie sighed.

When Lizzie looked at her, Jane studied her face. "You look far away. Is everything all right?"

"Oh, *ja, ja,*" Lizzie said quickly. The last thing she wanted to do was worry her sister before her big day. And given the fact that she was uncertain as to what was at the heart of her emotional turmoil, how could she have even begun to explain it? She forced a smile, hoping that it might compel her heart to stop hurting. "I can't believe that in just a few short days you will be married!"

Jane laughed and reached her arms out to hug her sister in a rare physical display of sisterly affection.

"You will be Charles's Jane from that day forward!" Lizzie added, enjoying the moment of closeness with her sister.

"If only every woman could experience a fraction of the happiness that I feel," Jane said enthusiastically. The glow in her blue eyes showed how deeply she meant her words. "I wouldn't change a thing for the world!"

"I'm so happy for you, Jane," Lizzie laughed, her heavy mood slowly lifting. After the emotional turmoil that had occurred with the elopement of her youngest sister, it was uplifting to have a *wunderbaar* marriage to celebrate with her special sister.

"Now, I do have something serious to ask you," Jane said, unexpectedly sobering from the giddiness of the previous moment. She took a deep breath and laid her hand on Lizzie's arm. "You know that I would like you to be my *newehocker*," she said. "To sit with me and help me. The day would not be perfect if my special sister were not beside me. You have always been such a dear friend as well a right *gut schwester*. I would have no one else but you be there with me."

While Lizzie had always presumed that she would be Jane's attendant, she hadn't been prepared to be asked quite so formally. "I...I would be honored, Jane," she managed to say.

Delighted with Lizzie's acceptance, Jane turned around and hurried to the other room, only to return with a new dress that hung from a hanger. It was of navy blue fabric and perfectly sewn. "I knew you'd agree, so I took the liberty of making your dress for you!" With great finesse she displayed the dress, waiting for Lizzie's reaction.

"When did you have time to make it?" Lizzie laughed, astonished at Jane's gift. She took the dress from her sister and held it against her body. "And such a pretty fabric!" She looked up at Jane. "It's quite different, ain't so? Wherever did you find the fabric to make it?"

Jane clapped her hands in delight. "Oh, Charles and I went out for a buggy ride to that dry good store past Intercourse. I wanted something special, not just from Smucker's store. When I saw this fabric, I just knew you'd look perfect in it."

"Why, that was only a few days ago!" Lizzie exclaimed, amazed that her sister had been able to create something so beautiful in such a short period of time. "I never saw you work on this once!"

"You've been walking so much lately that I took that time to cut the pattern and sew it. I wanted it finished before I asked you," Jane explained, her eyes sparkling with delight at the secret she had managed to keep from her own sister. "The other thing you should know is that Charles has asked Frederick to be his *newehocker*. That means you will be seated with him."

If Jane's news was meant to disturb Lizzie, it did anything

but that. Instead she found herself anticipating the wedding for an entirely new reason: she'd be seated next to Frederick and could, perhaps, express her gratitude for any part that he had in talking with Charles about Jane's true feelings for him. Somehow she knew that he was behind this joyful match having come to fruition. "I think I can suffer through that," Lizzie said, her tone serious but the expression on her face teasing. "Even if only for an hour."

They both laughed at her joke, despite the fact that Lizzie's heart was racing as she counted down the number of days left until she would have time to speak with Frederick at last.

❧ *Chapter Twenty-Six* ❧

THE SUN SHONE on the Tuesday of Jane's wedding to Charles. It was cool outside, as was typical for early autumn, and the leaves were just beginning to change colors. The backdrop of color against the crisp blue sky made for a beautiful day. With more than seventy gray-topped buggies parked in the yard and driveway of the Blank farm, there was no need to announce that a celebration was underway at the house.

Now that the marriage ceremony was completed, Jane and Charles sat at the *Eck* table, smiling as they greeted the people who approached them with well wishes. Lizzie stood by the door, watching with a bittersweet smile on her own face. The mix of people in the large gathering room and kitchen brought a smile to her face. Their friends and family from Lancaster moved about the room in sharp contrast to the Amish who had journeyed from Ohio to witness the wedding ceremony and participate in fellowship. While the former outnumbered the latter, due to the distance and time inherent to the journey, it was clear that everyone was happy for Jane and Charles. Even Carol Ann had appeared to be genuinely pleased when she approached the table to extend her warm wishes and blessing for a happy marriage.

Indeed, Lizzie was terribly happy for her sister and felt relief that they would not move back to Ohio. Yet there was a longing in her heart for her own happiness.

She slipped out the door and wandered behind the house. What she needed, even if for just a moment, was to be alone, some time to think about everything that had happened in just the past few months. So much had changed, both around her and within her. She stood by the fence and hugged herself in her familiar way, watching the cows graze so peacefully on the far side of the pasture.

Jane would be living at the Beachey farm immediately. Most Amish women remained in their family home for the winter, since it took time for many Amish men to become established and acquire a house or a farm. Charles, however, already had both, and there was no reason for Jane not to join him.

She would miss having Jane around the house. She knew that they would visit often, but Lizzie was also aware that Jane would need some time on her own to get familiar with life at the Beachey farm.

"Elizabeth."

She turned at the sound of her name. A familiar voice. Yes, it was Frederick, walking toward her, a serene look on his face as he approached. She felt her heart jump into her throat. "I...I just needed some fresh air," she heard herself say in a rather apologetic tone of voice. "It gets so hot in there, with all those people, *ja*?"

He stood before her and tilted his head, studying her expression. There was a softness to his eyes, and she found herself caught in them. "I shall be leaving for Ohio in a few days," he announced.

"Oh?"

"I have no further business here in Pennsylvania," he offered as an explanation.

The news startled her, and she felt her pulse quicken. If he left for Ohio, she knew that she would never see him again. She looked away, praying that he could not read her thoughts. "I see," she whispered.

"But," he continued, pausing after the word, "it is my intention to attend the Sunday service one last time."

"I cannot thank you enough for all that you have done, Frederick," she said, forcing herself to look at him. "I...I..." She wanted to say more, but the words would not come to her lips. "You have proven me quite wrong, Frederick Detweiler, and I have learned a valuable lesson about pride."

He smiled, a wistful smile that said much more than his silence.

"I...I wish you well on your journey home," she forced herself to continue, hating each word as soon as it came out of her mouth but knowing it was the proper thing to say. The six-hour drive back to Ohio meant good-bye, and that was something she did not want to face.

He cleared his throat and for just a moment stared over her shoulders, his eyes drinking in the scenery: the cows, the pastures, and the sun beginning to sink toward the horizon. And then he returned his eyes to meet hers. "I am standing before you, Elizabeth Blank, for a different reason," he said calmly. "You see, a few months back, when you were in the Dutch Valley, I asked you a question and you responded, citing two reasons for denying me that which I wished for so desperately."

Lizzie held her breath.

"I am standing here to ask you another question, a different question, and one that I hope will be answered in a much more satisfactory manner," he went on. "I understand that my *aendi* had a conversation with you, one that has given me a renewed hope that if I were to repeat that question, the one that you found so distasteful when I asked it in Ohio, mayhaps the answer would be different?"

"Is that your question, Frederick?" she asked softly when he paused, her heart pounding inside of her chest. "For I don't rightly understand what you are asking."

He cleared his throat and seemed to reach deep within himself for courage to proceed. It was an unusual side of Frederick, one that she had not experienced before but that she found quite charming as it contrasted sharply with his typical stoic and controlled manner of approaching situations. "The question is whether or not your feelings for me have changed. You see, my own feelings for you have not changed, Elizabeth. But one word from you, just one single word, and I will return to Ohio, never to bother you any longer." He paused, taking a moment to compose himself before he dared to reach out and brush a stray hair that had fallen from beneath her prayer *kapp*. "Yet, if *your* feelings have changed, I would like to know it so that, mayhaps, we could announce our intentions at the church service this Sunday, and I would delay my journey back to Ohio until I could travel with a companion...a wife."

Lizzie took a deep breath, exhaling slowly. Her heart pounded inside of her chest, and she could scarce remove her eyes from his gaze. "I...I hardly know what to say, Frederick." When she saw a light flicker in his eyes, she immediately continued. "I had no hope of your feelings staying the same, Frederick, especially after I so unfairly abashed you, and despite the fact that mine have, indeed, changed so far to your favor, I am speechless and finding it difficult to answer your question."

For a moment he did not respond. He seemed to be reflecting on her words as if gauging their true meaning to ensure that he had heard her properly. When he realized what she had said, he seemed to relax, just a touch, and his eyes softened once again.

"Then I shall speak to the bishop, *ja*?"

Lizzie bit her lower lip and nodded, feeling shy around this man whom she had just promised to marry, a man whom only a few short months earlier she had vowed would be the last man on earth she could ever consider spending the rest of her life with. Only now she could not imagine spending one more day apart from him.

With a hint of trepidation he reached for her hand. His thumb caressed her skin, and he smiled. His smile was soft and gentle, showing a mixture of relief and tenderness. "Frederick's Lizzie," he whispered.

She gave a small laugh, more from nervousness, and he pulled her into his arms. He laughed with her, holding her tight against his chest, not caring if anyone saw. She pressed her cheek against his shoulder, shutting her eyes and enjoying the feeling of finally being held by this man.

"I had all but given up hope," he said softly, his lips near her ear. "Yet I could not leave Leola without seeking you once again. I feel like a moth drawn to a candle!"

At this comparison she laughed again. "I shall never burn you, Frederick, nor singe your wings!"

"I wouldn't care if you did," he retorted, pulling back just enough to stare down into her face. "But I would much prefer that you'd kiss me."

She glanced over his shoulder, careful to insure that no one was around or watching. Then she stood on her toes and lifted her face, just slightly, with her eyes fixed on his. "A good *fraa* always obeys her husband," she whispered as she let her lips brush lightly against his.

As she pulled back, still staring into his eyes, she felt him shiver. For a moment, she wondered if he was cold, but before she could ask the question, he had pulled her back into his arms and was pressing his lips against hers, kissing her with months of pent-up passion and love that she knew he had feared in vain. She shut her eyes and returned his kiss, knowing that she too had feared his love had been lost forever.

"I want to speak to the bishop right away," he murmured, pressing his forehead against hers. "I want our engagement announced this very next Sunday and the wedding to be held as soon as possible. I can't bear the thought of one more day passing without you by my side."

"Or I, you," she replied softly, her eyes shut and her lips still tingling from his kiss.

They returned to the house, a new ease to their gait as they walked side by side. He glanced at her frequently, as if to reassure himself that she was still beside him and had, indeed, accepted his proposal. Lizzie, on the other hand, was holding her breath, feeling as if she were floating above herself, unable to fully believe that she was engaged to Frederick Detweiler and would return to Ohio as his *fraa*.

"There you are!" Jane said when Lizzie approached the *Eck* table where the bride and groom sat, waiting to greet their friends and family. She glanced at Frederick, who followed close behind. "I have been hoping you would stop by! I have missed your company!"

Charles laughed and nudged his wife. "Have I become so dull already?"

A blush covered Jane's cheeks.

"Congratulations," Lizzie said, reaching out to shake both Charles's and Jane's hands. "I am so happy for the both of you. I need not wish you well, that's for certain, for two happier people could not have found each other."

Frederick lifted an eyebrow but said nothing.

"Unless, of course, that would be us," she added softly, a feeling of warmth crossing her cheeks.

Without a moment's hesitation Charles jumped to his feet and extended his hand toward Frederick. "Is this true? I can hardly believe it!"

Jane tilted her head, a quizzical expression on her face as she was not comprehending what her sister had just said. "Lizzie, are you...?"

With a nervous smile Lizzie nodded her head. "*Ja*," she said. "I will be Frederick's Lizzie from this day forward."

"Oh..." Jane seemed stunned, her eyes glowing as she looked first at Lizzie then at Frederick. "I...I can scarcely believe it! This is such *wunderbaar gut* news!"

Frederick maintained his composure, but the look on his

face spoke volumes about what he was truly feeling. "Best go speak to the bishop now," he said, excusing himself from the group, leaving Jane to gush over Lizzie's announcement.

Jane reached for Lizzie's hand, leaning forward so that no one could overhear. "Is this for real? Are you sure?"

"I'm ever so sure," Lizzie said, the color rising to her cheeks. The reality was hitting her, and she felt overwhelmed with emotion. "I was so wrong, Jane, so terribly wrong about him!" She felt tears well into her eyes, and with a shaking hand, she pushed them away and tried to smile. "We misjudged him. And I can only thank God for helping me see the truth."

"I'm stunned," Jane said, her eyes searching Lizzie's and clutching her hand. "But I'm happy at this news. I always knew it would take a special man to capture your heart."

Lizzie laughed through her tears. "Oh, *ja*, special indeed! Frederick Detweiler is definitely that and so much more!"

Later in the evening Frederick approached Lizzie, his cheeks flushed and a glow in his eyes. He leaned over her shoulder and whispered into her ear, "I have spoken to the bishop and to your *daed* as well."

Lizzie seemed taken aback and stared at him. "My *daed*?" She only hoped that *Daed* did not share the news with her *maem* at Jane's wedding, knowing only too well that *Maem*'s reaction would be one that needed containment.

Frederick seemed relaxed, more relaxed than she had ever seen him, and she found that she felt comforted and protected in his presence. "Your *daed* seemed most surprised, Elizabeth," he said, trying not to smile at her. "I suspect that he would like a word with you."

"I suspect so too," she retorted playfully. She could only imagine her *daed*'s reaction that she, Elizabeth Blank, was not only to marry Frederick Detweiler, the most disagreeable of men, but also to move to Ohio. "And the bishop?" she asked.

"He will announce it on Sunday, and the wedding shall be in one week."

One week. The two words sent a conflict of emotions through her. Joy and fear. Excitement and apprehension. She felt a shiver run the course of her spine as she stood before this man, standing closer than was proper for mere friends. Indeed, his stance by her side was a clear indication that she was, forevermore, spoken for. When she thought back to their kiss, that remarkable kiss, a blush flooded to her cheeks and she saw him smile.

"And you blush because...?"

She lowered her eyes and hid her own smile, refusing to give him the pleasure of a response to his question. "I think it's best if I find my *daed* now," she whispered before quickly moving away from him and in the direction she had last seen her *daed*.

He was standing alone, his eyes glazed over when she approached him. It took him a moment to escape his thoughts and return to the present. Setting down his empty cup on a table, he indicated that she should follow him as they escaped the crowds in the house and retreated outdoors. Slowly they walked away from the house and any ears that might overhear.

"Is this true, Lizzie? That you have agreed to marry Frederick Detweiler?"

She nodded her head, not trusting her voice to speak without revealing too much emotion.

"But you despise the man!"

At this announcement she laughed, which triggered the tears of joy to fill her eyes. "Oh, *Daed*, I was so wrong about him," she blurted out. "So very, very wrong."

"I should hope so," *Daed* quipped. "Otherwise I would think you have lost your senses, *dochder*! I have heard nothing else about him from you besides all of his flaws. And now I hear that you are to marry him and move to Ohio! Are you sure about this?"

"I'm as sure about this as anything, *Daed*," she said happily, wiping hastily at the tears in her eyes. "If you only knew what he has done..."

"Mayhaps you best tell me, so that I can understand this shift in your feelings," he replied. "I would feel so much better knowing what has caused this very unexpected announcement!"

They walked down the lane and behind the barn while Lizzie shared what she had learned. She spoke rapidly and with an excitement that bordered on giddiness, laughing at times when she recalled her own sharp opinions of Frederick that happened to be so mistaken and incorrect. When she told her *daed* about Lydia and all that Frederick had done to save her from disgrace, she heard *Daed* catch his breath as he stopped walking.

"My word, *dochder*," he said softly. "Is all of this true?"

"*Ja*," she nodded empathically. "As true as true can be."

"I had no idea," he replied, his eyes distant and his mind wandering. "I'd say he is a right *gut* man, Elizabeth, and one that might actually keep you in line. I never thought it possible, and secretly, I had hoped to keep you with us. But how could I possibly deny such a man to care for the best son I never had!"

Lizzie laughed at her *daed*'s statement and, without hesitating, gave him a hug, something that she hadn't done since she was a small child. To her surprise he hugged her back and laughed with her, apparently as delighted with this news as any man could be upon hearing that his favorite child was to leave the nest for the right person and for the right reasons.

❧ *Epilogue* ❧

S PRING CAME EARLY in Dutch Valley, Ohio. Lizzie stood by the fence, watching as Frederick crossed the back paddock, his straw hat tipped back on his head and a smile on his face as he approached her. In the distance a truck could be heard rumbling down the road, a sound she rarely heard at the farm in the Dutch Valley, unlike back in Leola. The noise broke the silence, but thankfully it quickly faded.

Her husband had already plowed and planted the back fields, but he liked to walk through them each day, checking that things were growing and that there were no signs of problems. Oftentimes he rode his favorite Standardbred stallion, Larkin, to cover more of the ground in less time and better survey his land. Today, however, that was not the case, for he had instructed the young single men who worked on his farm to plow a plot of land for Lizzie's garden, and he had made a point to personally partake in the task. Lizzie hadn't wanted to compete with his *aendi*'s garden and had decided to grow flowers instead of vegetables. Frederick had smiled to himself when she originally mentioned her concerns, but he supported her decision.

Sunflowers, she had decided. Rows upon rows of beautiful sunflowers. Those, indeed, were her favorite flowers, because they always seemed to face the sun and grow from the warmth of the golden rays.

Lizzie had shared her plan with Frederick: she would sell the sunflowers to the *Englischers* who frequented the neighbors' farm stands and make sunflower seeds from those that did not sell. When Frederick heard her idea, he initially laughed, his eyes glowing as he reached for her hand and pulled her into his arms.

"That's very entrepreneurial of you, Elizabeth!"

She rested her hand on his shoulder, staring into his face. "I learned this and much more from you, my husband," she replied, a response that pleased him, for he gifted her with a soft kiss when he heard her words.

She had come upon the idea when she realized that she too was like a sunflower. After all, it had not been that long ago, in her time of anguish and un-granted pride, when she had ultimately faced the light of the Lord and taken comfort and spiritual growth from His benevolence.

How peculiar, she realized, was the fact that she now lived a happy life in Ohio, far away from her childhood home, as the *fraa* of an Amish gentleman farmer! Pride, she pondered. It can, all too often, lead to such prejudice! Had she been guilty of letting her pride dictate her actions? Was it the result of her upbringing? Was it because she had been one of five daughters while striving to become "the best son her *daed* never had"? Was it because of *Maem*, whose sole purpose in life lately was to marry off her *dochders*? Did these facts engender resentment, pride, or, as with sister Lydia, a strong propensity for noncon-formism and emancipation?

These were all good questions, questions whose answers would come in due time, she realized. But learning from them could be even more important than getting the answers, for life had a way of constantly changing. Still, there were moments when everything appeared to return to its rightful place, like the scattered pieces of a puzzle coming together to form a beautiful picture.

After all, Jane and Charles had found the love of their lives within each other. Lydia and George, despite their precipitated nuptials, would ultimately stumble upon the right path, God willing; even Charlotte, her childhood friend, had found her rightful purpose in life with her union to Wilmer.

With three of their *dochders* now married and out of the house, *Maem* and *Daed* would surely join forces and find that elusive son-in-law who, in times yet to come, would first help *Daed* with his tasks then ultimately take over the farm. For this, indeed, was the way of the Amish.

Lizzie's new life in Ohio had soon fallen into a wonderful routine. She had spent her winter days working on a wedding quilt with many of the women from the *g'may* as well as with Charlotte, who was now with child, and *Aendi*. By the time the last snow fell, the quilt was stretched across the bed that she shared with Frederick. It had taken her some time to get used to living in Ohio and not being near her family, but the friendship of Charlotte, the company of Grace, and the help of *Aendi* had lightened her heart and prevented homesickness. Still, she missed Jane and wrote to her every week. Jane was only too eager to respond.

To Charles's delight Jane had proven herself quite the homemaker as well as his true partner and new best friend. He was as much in love with her as Jane was with him, and they were making plans to grace the Beachey farm with a new arrival. Plenty of new arrivals. From what Lizzie could glean from the letters, both from Jane and from *Maem*, not a happier couple resided in Leola, that was for sure and certain.

Now, with the spring season in full bloom, Frederick's days were spent working around the farm. He awoke early each morning, slipping quietly from beneath the sheets so as not to awaken Lizzie. Some mornings she would stir and open her eyes to see him watching her as he dressed in his work clothes. He would smile and sit on the edge of the bed, running his hand along her shoulder and down her arm before leaning over to kiss her forehead and gently instruct her to go back to sleep.

But sleeping in late was not something that Lizzie was

capable of doing. Instead, she would quickly arise and get dressed, eager to face the morning. She had tried to help Frederick in the dairy but he always chased her away, frowning when she came outside with the intention of milking the cows. So her mornings were spent inside, baking bread and cleaning the house. With just four people living there, the house rarely needed much in the way of cleaning, but Lizzie liked a pristine home and knew that both Frederick and his *aendi* appreciated her efforts.

After evening chores Frederick would change his clothes and join Lizzie downstairs. He never sat around the house in his work clothes, always wearing properly cleaned pants and shirts with shiny boots. At first Lizzie had wondered about that until she realized that, in his own way, he was still courting her. Work clothes were for planting and milking, not for spending time with his *fraa*.

He would read the paper while she worked on her crocheting. As the weather became nicer and the days grew longer, they took to walking during the sunset, side by side down the road. Some nights they walked in silence, just enjoying each other's company. Other nights they talked, sharing stories about their day or news about friends and family.

Today, however, he greeted her with a smile as he approached her from his walk across the field. "*Wie gehts?*" he asked as he stood opposite her at the fence.

"Feeling restless," she replied.

He smiled at her and removed his hat, wiping at the sweat that glistened on his forehead. He glanced down and gestured toward her expanded stomach. "Is the baby jumping a lot, then?"

Lizzie flushed. "*Ja*, he sure is."

"We still have a few months," he said, reaching out a hand to stroke the front of her dress. Then, in a moment of curiosity, Frederick looked back at her and repeated her word. "He?"

"Oh, *ja!*" she said, nodding her head. "I reckon that only a boy could move about as much as this *boppli!*"

He laughed and, glancing around to make certain no one was watching, leaned forward to tenderly kiss her lips. "A boy is *gut,*" he said softly. "The more hands to work the farm, *ja?*"

She smiled and lowered her eyes, changing the subject. "The garden plot looks right *gut,*" she said. "*Danke* for having the men plow it for me."

Dipping his head in a single nod, he acknowledged her gratitude. Then he stepped onto the bottom board of the fence and, in a fluid motion, jumped over the top rail so that he stood beside her. "Come, Elizabeth," he said as he extended his hand to take hers in his. "Let's walk for a spell. We can admire the pastures and watch the cows, giving thanks to the Lord for His abundance in providing us with so much and being able to provide others with the opportunity to learn and improve."

She tilted her head and sighed, a happy sound. "I reckon the most important thing He has done is bring us together, Frederick, and for that I thank Him every morning and every night as well as every second in between."

He responded by simply nodding his head. Together they walked down a path behind one of the fences surrounding the pasture. She could tell that he was touched by her words, but in typical Frederick fashion, he did his best to maintain complete control of his emotions. She didn't care, for she was used to his mannerisms.

Together, walking hand in hand, they disappeared down the path, the very path where Lizzie had encountered Frederick so long ago when she had gone for a walk to clear her head and try to make sense of what she had learned about this man. The irony was not lost on her that, when they reached the point of their encounter the previous summer, he paused and glanced down at her, hesitating before lifting her hand to his lips and kissing the soft skin on the back of it.

Two small robins landed on a branch of a nearby tree. The birds perched near each other and began to sing, chirping back and forth as if a planned hymn to nature. Indeed, their song was one of sweetness and innocence, a proclamation of the birth of spring and the glory of God. It was a song that echoed in the silence and followed the young couple as they disappeared down the path, oblivious to the beauty that surrounded them as they focused, instead, on each other and the abundance of love that God had granted them.

Indeed, despite their initial pride and prejudices—the very two traits that had ultimately united them—God had yet worked out His greater plan, a plan that only He had known and one that not only brought prosperity and happiness to all, but also taught them both a great lesson in life and faith.

Coming in 2015 from Sarah Price, The Matchmaker

❧ Chapter One ❧

L
EANING OVER THE back of the kitchen chair, a very
busy Emma Weaver struck an unknowingly pretty picture as she bent forward to rearrange the yellow and
purple flowers in the glass jar. The late summer blooms had
been plucked from her flower garden only an hour before, and
their sweet scent wafted through the room as she moved them
around for the third or fourth time in less than ten minutes.
Satisfied at last, she stood upright, nodded her self-approval
toward the bouquet, then quickly assessed the room with her
cornflower-blue eyes.

The table was set with plain white linen and her *maem*'s best
china, a gift from her *daed* when they had just been married.
It was something that Emma loved to use when guests came
for supper, especially on Sunday evenings. The sitting area was
freshly cleaned just the day prior, for it was forbidden to clean
on Sunday, regardless of whether or not it was a church Sunday
or a visiting Sunday. The blue sofa and two rocking chairs with
blue and white quilted cushions looked welcoming for their
soon-to-arrive guests.

"Ah, Emma!" a deep voice sounded out from the staircase.

She looked up in time to see her *daed* shuffling down the
stairs, taking each step one at a time as his weathered hand
held the railing. With his long white beard and his thinning
hair he looked older than his sixty-five years, a fact that worried Emma on a regular basis. "I thought you were resting,
Daed," she said as she hurried to meet him at the bottom of
the stairs. Taking his arm, she helped lead him to his favorite

chair: a blue recliner that was covered with a pretty crocheted blanket she had made for him last winter.

"Such a quiet house nowadays," he mumbled as he sat down and raised the foot of the chair so he could rest his legs. "How sad for you that Anna went off to get married!" He clucked his tongue a few times and shut his eyes as he rested his head on the back of the chair. "Poor Anna, indeed! Why ever would she want to do such a thing anyway?"

Emma laughed, the sound light and airy. "*Nee, Daed*," she quickly retorted. "We must be happy for Anna! Old Widower Wagler seemed right pleased last Tuesday, and I dare say that Anna was radiant in her blue wedding dress!"

"Radiant indeed!" her *daed* scoffed. "Left us alone is what she did. Who shall entertain you now, my dear Emma?"

"Now, *Daed*!" she reprimanded him gently. "I don't need anyone to entertain me, and you know that. We have quite enough to keep us busy, and I'm happy for Anna to finally have a home of her own."

Without giving him a chance to retort, Emma turned and hurried back into the main part of the kitchen. Everything was set up for their soon-to-be arriving guests. The bread she had baked just the day before was sliced and on a plate, covered with plastic wrap so that the flies wouldn't land upon it. The bowls of chow-chow, beets, and pickled cabbage were likewise covered and set upon the counter. Only the cold cuts and fruit spreads remained in the refrigerator.

For a few long, drawn-out moments Emma fussed at the table, wanting everything to be absolutely perfect for their dear soon-to-arrive guests.

"Careful there, Emma," her *daed* said, lifting his hand to point in her direction. "That's a sharp knife there on the edge of the table!"

Laughing, Emma put her hands on her hips and frowned at him, a playful twinkle in her eyes. "*Ach, Daed*! I'm not a child anymore! I *see* the knife!" As if to make a point, she picked it up and wiggled it in the air. "No danger here."

"Emma Weaver!" A disapproving voice came out from behind her. Startled, she dropped the knife and jumped backward as it clanked on the linoleum floor.

"Gideon King!" she cried at the sight of the man standing in the doorframe. "You scared me!" she cried at the sight of the man standing in the doorframe. Annoyed, she quickly bent down to pick up the knife. Wiping it on her apron, she set it back on the table before hurrying over to greet their first guest.

"And *you* were teasing your *daed*!" he said, a stern look upon his face. "Good thing I walked in when I did! You could have cut yourself!"

"I almost did cut myself!" she retorted, making a playful face at him. "No thanks to you for scaring me so!" Despite her words, it was clear that the presence of the newcomer pleased her.

"That's no way to greet our guest, Emma," her *daed* chided. "Come, Gideon! Greet this old man!"

The tall Amish man with thick black hair and broad shoulders crossed the room in three easy strides. He shook the older man's outstretched hand. Emma watched with a smile on her lips, knowing that it had been a long week for her *daed* without Gideon stopping in to visit him. With no sons of his own, her *daed* had come to look upon Gideon as a son of sorts. Since Gideon's younger *bruder* had married Irene, her older and only sister, Gideon was as good as family. And by the way he constantly reprimanded Emma, his voice more oft full of criticism than pleasure, she often felt as if she had, indeed, acquired an older *bruder*.

"It's *gut* to see you, Henry," Gideon said. "Looking well, as always."

Henry gestured toward the sofa, indicating that Gideon should sit down. "Have you just returned, then?" He didn't wait for the man to answer before he continued. "Tell us about your trip."

Without waiting for an invitation, Emma joined the two men, plopping herself on the sofa next to the new visitor. "*Ja*, Gideon. Do tell us about Ohio. We missed you at Anna's wedding last week!"

Stretching out his legs, Gideon smiled at the young woman next to him. "I wouldn't have missed it if I hadn't needed to attend to some business in the Dutch Valley," he said. "And I rode out with a couple who were going to visit their *dochder* who recently married a widowed bishop out there. They were traveling with a young woman from around here."

"From around here?" Emma's mouth fell open. "Do I know her, then?"

"Elizabeth Blank," was the simple response.

"Why! I wonder that she must be related to Widow Blank and Hetty!" She looked from Gideon to her *daed*. "Have we met this woman, *Daed*?"

Henry seemed to ponder the name for a moment, his brows knitted together and his eyes squinting as he did so. "I'm not so sure of our being acquainted with an Elizabeth Blank," came the answer.

Emma, observing Gideon brushing some dirt from his pants, smiled to herself at how fastidious he always was about his appearance, especially on Sundays. He glanced up at her and sighed, the hint of a smile on his face. "You can't know everyone, Emma. I know how hard you try, but it would be quite impossible, it seems."

"Gideon! You tease me so!"

He laughed. "I am all but a *bruder* to you, Emma. Isn't that what *bruders* are supposed to do?" He changed the subject back to his trip. "It was a nice visit, and she is a lovely young woman. A shame you *didn't* know her, Emma. Her wit would have amused you immensely!" With a pause, he turned his gaze to her *daed*. "Ohio was sure nice, especially at this time of the year. The rolling hills and winding roads make for a lovely backdrop for the long drive there!"

"Such a romantic!" Emma teased, which prompted Gideon to frown at her. Still, the fierce look on his face could not hide his pleasure at being reunited with his good friends after being away for so long.

"Speaking of romantics," he replied, a mischievous gleam in his dark brown eyes, "who shed the most tears at Anna's wedding, I wonder?"

Henry laughed and pointed at Emma. "You know her so well, Gideon. Surely you are aware that Emma wept through the entire service and the singing afterward."

"Oh, *Daed*!"

But it was true, indeed. She *had* wept, mostly out of elation for dear sweet Anna, who, after so many years living with them, had finally found happiness and married good ole Widower Wagler.

Only two months prior, Emma knew very little about Samuel Wagler except that he had recently moved into a ranch house within their *g'may*. Prior to that, he had lived with his older *bruder* and family in a neighboring church district, residing in the *grossdawdihaus* until it was needed by his *bruder* for his oldest son, now married and with an infant on the way. That was when Samuel had moved into their *g'may*.

Emma had noticed the way his dark eyes seemed drawn to Anna during his first church service in his new district. It had only taken Emma a few minutes to formulate a plan and invite Samuel to share supper with them. And from that moment on she had been delighted to watch the commencement of Samuel's courtship of Anna. Delighted, that is, until she realized that by marrying Samuel, Anna would be moving away to live in that ranch house with her new husband.

That realization had saddened Emma and had been the other cause for tears during the wedding day.

After all, Anna had been like a mother to Emma and Irene. After their *maem* passed away when Emma was not even in school yet, their *daed* had vowed to raise his two *dochders* on his own. He had married later in life and his *fraa*, while younger than he, had great difficulty in carrying her pregnancies to full term, making the two children who did survive all the more precious. Henry doted on his two *dochders*, a fact that contributed to his decision to remain single. So, while other widowers tended to marry within a year or two, Henry Weaver refused to consider that option. Instead, he had readily agreed when his older *bruder* volunteered Anna, his eldest and still unmarried *dochder*, to move to the Weaver residence and care for the children. What had been offered as a temporary solution soon became permanent for Anna. She had enjoyed tending to the needs of her two young cousins, and with the full appreciation and support of her *onkel* Henry Weaver, she found that she had no reason to leave.

That was until, fifteen years later, Emma had introduced the now forty-five-year-old Anna to Old Widower Wagler.

"*Ja vell*," she said dismissively, trying to downplay the memory of her emotions at the wedding service. "Anna sure did look right *gut* standing next to Samuel, and any emotion I felt was from sheer joy at her marriage! A strong marriage is a *wunderbaar gut* thing, ain't so?"

Both men cleared their throats and shifted in their seats in response to her statement. After all, with neither being married, how did she expect them to respond?

She looked pleased with their silence.

"And you may have forgotten that it was I who helped arrange the match between the two," she added, her pride of having a hand in the match more than apparent. "And this, after so many had speculated that Old Widower Wagler would never marry again."

The two men looked at each other, a brief glance that said more than words could communicate. While Gideon merely shook his head, it was her *daed* who commented. "Emma, it's not for you to play matchmaker. Promise me you will do no such thing."

"*Nee, Daed*," she retorted. "Not for myself, of course. But it gives me such joy to see others happy! Just think...after so many years Samuel has a new wife and, as such, a new life! Perhaps now his son shall return and live with him once again. Why! We haven't seen him since his *maem* passed away. When was that, *Daed*? Almost fifteen years ago?"

"Just before your own *maem* passed, I believe," Henry added, a solemn look upon his face.

"Think of how happy that would make Samuel!" She practically hugged herself in delight, the thought of Samuel being reunited with his son bringing her a great deal of joy. "I must acknowledge my success in having made such a match for both Samuel and Anna. And, with that in mind, how could I possibly not strive to do the same for others?"

At her words Gideon leaned forward and stared at her. "Success? If you noticed the interest that Samuel had in Anna, you merely accommodated it with an invitation to supper. Nothing more, Emma. I wouldn't call that a 'success' as if you had a hand in making a 'match.' It was bound to happen with or without your interference, something that is more likely to do more harm to yourself than good should you persist in trying to arrange such matches."

Clearly his words did not suit Emma, and she scowled. Still, despite Gideon's reprimand, she refused to let her mood be altered. "I have one more match to make," she announced. "Why, our very own bishop's son seemed to hang on every word of their wedding service. I'm certain he is longing to settle down himself." She looked at her *daed*. "And rightfully so! He's almost an old bachelor like someone else we know so dearly!"

"Emma!" Henry coughed at her statement and glanced apologetically at Gideon. Being sixteen years Emma's senior, Gideon more closely shared Henry's concerns and mind-set than Emma's. "Marriage is not for everyone."

The members in the *g'may* had stopped speculating long ago about when Gideon King, a well-established and prosperous Amish businessman in his own right, would settle down and start his own family. He seemed more than happy to relish in simple things such as weekly visits with friends. Still, Emma's statement had caused a degree of discomfort in the room, at least for Henry.

"I so agree!" Clapping her hands together, she quickly changed the direction of the conversation. "I understand that Gladys is bringing a young woman with her today to visit and share the supper meal."

Last Sunday after worship service Emma had invited *Maedel* Blank and her *maem* as well as Gladys Getz to join them for supper the following week. While the Blanks were regular guests at the Weaver's Sunday gatherings, this was only the second time that Emma had extended the invitation to Gladys, who had never married but had taught school for years.

When Anna had lived with the Weavers, both she and Emma had always enjoyed inviting people to their home for Sunday meals, selecting those who might not have other family in the area with which to share fellowship. Henry certainly never seemed to mind, enjoying the time spent with new and interesting people. Emma's eclectic mixture of guests always seemed to bring a lively energy to the *haus*.

Today, however, promised to be especially entertaining, for Gladys had mentioned that she would be bringing a guest with her, a young woman from New York who had recently moved in with her. She had referred to the woman, Hannah Souder, as her niece, but last Thursday during her weekly visit to the Blanks Emma had learned from Hetty that the only relation between the two was of the heart, not the physical body.

Now, Emma turned her head to look at Gideon. "Have you met her yet, then?"

Gideon shook his head, his dark curls falling over his forehead. "*Nee*," he responded. "I have not." Leaning forward, he stared directly at Emma. "She arrived at Gladys's just the other day, I heard. Apparently she was staying with another family south of Strasburg beforehand, but I do believe that she is originally from a community in New York. She lived with Gladys's *schwester* if I recall properly."

"New York?" Emma said, lifting her eyebrows. She had forgotten that Gladys had family in New York. "Whatever is she doing here, then?"

"Visiting." The answer was direct and simple as if it explained everything. But it was clear that Emma's curiosity was piqued. "Knowing Gladys, this Hannah Souder is a lovely, God-fearing woman, even if so little is known of her family."

It was the sorrowful way he said those words that caused Emma to gasp. "Gideon! Pray tell!"

He took a deep breath and sighed as he sat back in his seat. "I should have said nothing. I'd prefer not to spread idle gossip, Emma. It's not fair to say." He hesitated, leveling his eyes at Emma. "Or to judge. After all, the Bible tells us 'to aspire to live quietly, and to mind your own affairs, and to work with your hands.' Mayhaps you might want to reflect on that. Gossip is surely the work of evil."

She looked visibly put out and made a face at him. "I should say so," she responded, although her expression hinted at some disappointment that Gideon was not going to explain his comment about this Hannah Souder's background. There was no time to further the discussion as they were interrupted by the sound of a buggy pulling into the driveway. Glancing over her shoulder, she sought the view out the window. "It appears our guests have arrived!"

Her *daed* quickly put the recliner into an upright position and looked around the room. "I hope it's not too warm in here for them." A look of worry crossed his face. He looked first at Emma and then at Gideon. "Mayhaps we should visit outside in the breezeway. You know that when the air is so still it's not good for the lungs."

Emma shook her head as if dismissing his concern, even though she hurried over to a closed window and lifted its lower pane. "Is that better, then?" She didn't wait for an answer as she hurried to the door to greet the Widow Blank and her *dochder*, Hetty.

"Our dear Emma," Hetty gushed as she led her aging mother by the hand through the door. Both women were rather petite, although the elder Blank walked with great difficulty, hunched over and shuffling her feet. Hetty, however, was bright and alert, with round glasses that often slipped down to the edge of her nose. "How right *gut* of you to invite us to supper! I was just talking to my *maem* about how kind and thoughtful you are!" She turned and peered at her mother. "Didn't I say that, *Maem*? About Emma being so kind and thoughtful?" She didn't wait for an answer as she turned back to Emma. "And such a lovely home it is! I don't think we've been here before when it hasn't always looked just perfectly maintained!"

Emma smiled but did not respond.

Hetty hurried by Emma and greeted the two men that were in the sitting room. "Henry! Gideon! So nice to spend some time indoors with you both! You have a most thoughtful and kind *dochder*, Henry. Reminds me so much of my niece, Jane!" She glanced over her shoulder at Emma. "I received a letter from her just yesterday! Shall I read it? She always has such *wunderbaar gut* stories!" She started to reach into the simple black cloth bag that hung from her wrist.

"*Nee*, Hetty," Emma was a little too quick to reply, but she kept a pleasant smile on her face. The last thing Emma wanted was to encourage the dreaded reading of Jane's weekly letters to her *aendi* and *grossmammi*, especially with other company on the way. While the reading was inevitable, trying to limit it to a single iteration was most likely the best that Emma could hope for. Besides, she didn't want to remind Hetty that she had already been subjected to the reading of Jane's letter just three days ago. "I hear another buggy pulling into the driveway, and it would be most disagreeable to have to stop in the midst of the letter when they walk inside. You'd only have to start all over again, and I would think that would be rather tiring on such a warm day, *ja*?" Emma didn't wait for her guest to answer but politely excused herself as she started back to the door, more to escape the constant chatter of Hetty Blank than out of curiosity as to who had just arrived.

Pushing open the door, Emma was pleased to notice that it didn't squeak as it normally did. Her *daed* must have fixed it during the latter part of the week, she thought. *Such a gut man*, she pondered, then turned, just briefly, to gaze at him. He was hovering near Hetty and her *maem*, wringing his hands as he inquired whether the two women thought it was too warm inside for visiting or if they were comfortable enough. Shaking her head to herself, Emma stepped outside and waited to greet the newly arrived visitors.

Gladys exited the buggy first, her prayer *kapp* slightly askew on her graying head, and waved at Emma before she slipped the halter over the horse's head. She moved the reins safely back and constrained them so that they would not slip over the horse's croup and spook it while it was hitched to the side of the barn. Emma waited patiently for Gladys's guest to emerge, and when she did, Emma was immediately intrigued.

Hannah Souder was not exactly a pretty young woman, but the wisps of ginger hair that stuck out from beneath her prayer *kapp* and her bright, big eyes immediately spoke of an eagerness to please and learn. Her beauty seemed to radiate from the inside. Her steps conveyed the impression that she was bouncing behind Gladys with such eagerness that Emma found herself smiling, already liking this new addition to their Sunday supper gathering, even if her prayer *kapp* was not heart-shaped like the Lancaster Amish. Instead, it hugged the back of Hannah's head, more rounded and stiffer like the rest of the Amish wore in her New York settlement. Even her dress, a pale pink in color, which Emma thought did not particularly flatter her coloring, was slightly different in design.

"*Wilkum!*" Emma greeted Gladys with a warm handshake before turning to Hannah. "And you must be Hannah Souder! I have heard much about you and have been looking forward to meeting you!"

"*Danke.*" The response was simple and soft. She was shy. That was apparent from the way she couldn't quite meet Emma's eyes. As she made her way into the house, Emma observed her with curiosity. She noticed right away that Hannah barely exhibited any form of social grace as she was introduced to the Blanks, Henry, and Gideon. Despite the smile on her face, she stared at the floor shyly and made certain to stand behind Gladys, rather than next to her. She even hesitated to shake hands with Emma's *daed*. Still, there was a kindness about the young woman's face that made her immediately appealing to Emma.

"I have the Scrabble game set in the sunroom," Emma announced.

Hetty clapped her hands and glanced around the room. "Oh, how I love Scrabble! Such a fine way to spend time together. I'd love to play; wouldn't you, *Maem*?"

When her mother squinted and frowned, clearly not hearing what her *dochder* had said, Hetty repeated her question louder. "Scrabble, she said. Scrabble!"

Emma smiled as the two women hurried into the sunroom, joined by Gladys and Hannah, to play the game while she finished preparing the supper meal. She worked in the kitchen, preparing the platters of food while listening to the laughter and arguing in the other room over their selection of words. Her *daed* and Gideon sat on the sofa, talking about local news and occasionally interrupted to share their opinion about the validity of a word used in the board game. For Emma, it was the perfect Sunday afternoon, and her insides felt warm with the love that was permeating her home.

It was close to four when the gathering moved to the table for the light supper. With everything properly prepared earlier, there was little that Emma needed to do after setting the platters and bowls in the center of the table before calling the guests to come for fellowship. *Daed* took his place at the head of the table, and Emma was quick to sit beside him.

"There's an extra place setting," Gideon pointed out as he sat at the other end of the table. "Are you expecting another?"

There was no need to answer as the door opened and a young man walked through. "My deepest apologies, Emma," he said as he removed his hat and greeted the gathering. "My *daed* asked me to visit with the neighbors, and the time got away from me!" He smiled at the others who were already seated around the table, his eyes falling upon Hannah. "Why, I do believe that I know everyone here except for one! Do introduce me, Emma!"

With his freshly shaved face and bright blue eyes, Paul Esh brought a crisp liveliness to the gathering, and Emma was quick to introduce him to Hannah. When she lowered her eyes and blushed at his attention, a thought struck Emma in regard to the young woman's social inadequacies and apparent shyness.

I can help her, she thought, *the way Anna helped me.*

Her mind quickly worked, playing forward the different ways she could repay Anna's kindness and devotion toward her

Sarah Price

over the years. After all, Anna had taught her how to properly balance being a godly woman with her commitment to helping the community. *It is more blessed to give than receive*, had been the way that Emma was raised. After the fifteen years of sacrifice Anna had made, raising her *onkel*'s *kinner* rather than her own, Emma had taken great satisfaction in seeing her happily married at last.

Now, this newcomer to their community, obviously from a smaller and less cosmopolitan settlement of Amish, could benefit from Emma's friendship and guidance. Emma could help Hannah both adapt to the ways of the Lancaster County Amish as well as possibly finding her a suitable match…just as she had done with Anna!

With a new sense of purpose Emma leaned forward and paid extra attention to every word Hannah spoke and to her every interaction. She also observed how her guests interacted with the young woman, especially Paul Esh. The more Emma watched, the more convinced she was that her role in assimilating this newcomer into the community in order in insure that Hannah was properly acclimated and accepted, and possibly even married, was meant to be.

Now that Anna was happily settled into her new life with Samuel, it was time for Emma to guide another young woman to a long life of wedded bliss. And, by the end of the evening, she was convinced that Hannah was the one that God intended for her to guide.

❦ *Glossary* ❦

ach vell—an expression similar to "Oh, well"

aendi—aunt

Ausbund—Amish hymnal

boppli—baby

bruder—brother

buwe—boy, young male

daed—father

danke—thank you

dochder—daughter

Eck table—a corner table for the bride and groom to sit at their wedding feast

Englische—non-Amish people

Englischer—a non-Amish person

ferhoodled—confused

fraa—wife

g'may—church district

gown shanner—you're welcome

grossdawdi—grandfather

grossdawdihaus—small house attached to the main dwelling

grossmammi—grandmother

gut—good

gut mariye—good morning

ja—yes

kapp—prayer covering or cap

kinner—children

leddich—unmarried

Loblieb—a special hymn sung during church

281

maedel—an older, unmarried woman
maem—mother
nee—no
newehocker—attendant at a wedding
ole—old
onkel—uncle
Ordnung—unwritten rules that govern the *g'may*
rumschpringe—period of "fun" time for youths
schwester—sister
Wie gehts?—"What's going on?"
wunderbaar—wonderful

❧ *Other Books by Sarah Price* ❧

The Amish of Lancaster Series
#1: Fields of Corn
#2: Hills of Wheat
#3: Pastures of Faith
#4: Valley of Hope

The Amish of Ephrata Series
#1: The Tomato Patch
#2: The Quilting Bee
#3: The Hope Chest
#4: The Clothes Line

The Plain Fame Trilogy
Plain Fame
Plain Change
Plain Again

Other Amish Fiction Books
Amish Circle Letters
Amish Circle Letters II
The Divine Secrets of the Whoopie Pie Sisters (with Pam Jarrell)
Cry of Freedom: Gettysburg's Chosen Sons
A Gift of Faith: An Amish Christmas Story
An Amish Christmas Carol: Amish Christian Classic Series
A Christmas Gift for Rebecca: An Amish Christian Romance

The Adventures of a Family Dog Series
#1: A Small Dog Named Peek-a-Boo
#2: Peek-a-Boo Runs Away
#3: Peek-a-Boo's New Friends
#4: Peek-a-Boo and Daisy Doodle

Sarah Price

Other Books
Gypsy in Black
The Prayer Chain Series (with Ella Stewart)
Postcards From Abby (with Ella Stewart)
Meet Me in Heaven (with Ella Stewart)
Mark Miller's One: The Power of Faith

❧ *About Sarah Price* ❧

THE PREISS FAMILY emigrated from Europe in 1705, settling in Pennsylvania as the area's first wave of Mennonite families. Sarah Price has always respected and honored her ancestors through exploration and research about her family's history and their religion. At the age of nineteen she befriended an Amish family and lived on their farm throughout the years.

Twenty-five years later Sarah Price splits her time between her home outside of New York City and an Amish farm in Lancaster County, Pennsylvania, where she retreats to reflect, write, and reconnect with her Amish friends and Mennonite family.

Contact the author at sarahprice.author@gmail.com. Visit her weblog at http://sarahpriceauthor.com or on Facebook at www.facebook.com/fansofsarahprice.

FREE NEWSLETTERS
TO HELP EMPOWER YOUR LIFE

Why subscribe today?

❏ **DELIVERED DIRECTLY TO YOU.** All you have to do is open your inbox and read.

❏ **EXCLUSIVE CONTENT.** We cover the news overlooked by the mainstream press.

❏ **STAY CURRENT.** Find the latest court rulings, revivals, and cultural trends.

❏ **UPDATE OTHERS.** Easy to forward to friends and family with the click of your mouse.

CHOOSE THE E-NEWSLETTER THAT INTERESTS YOU MOST:

- Christian news
- Daily devotionals
- Spiritual empowerment
- And much, much more

SIGN UP AT: **http://freenewsletters.charismamag.com**

8178